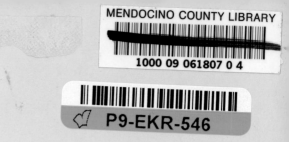
"M"   20.00

Van Gieson, Judith

Parrot Blues

PARROT
BLUES

ALSO BY JUDITH VAN GIESON

The Lies That Bind
The Wolf Path
The Other Side of Death
Raptor
North of the Border

PARROT BLUES

A NEIL HAMEL MYSTERY

JUDITH VAN GIESON

■ HarperCollins*Publishers*

HarperCollins books may be purchased for educational, business, or sales promotional use. For information please write: Special Markets Department, Harper-Collins Publishers, Inc., 10 East 53rd Street, New York, NY 10022.

FIRST EDITION

Designed by Caitlin Daniels

Library of Congress Cataloging-in-Publication Data

Van Gieson, Judith.
    [1st ed.]
    Parrot blues : a Neil Hamel mystery / Judith Van Gieson.
        p.   cm.
    ISBN 0-06-017706-3
    1. Hamel, Neil (Fictitious character)—Fiction.   I. Title.
PS3572.A42224P35   1995
813'.54—dc20   94-24233

95 96 97 98 99 ❖/HC 10 9 8 7 6 5 4 3 2 1

For Dora

PARROT
BLUES

I'm very grateful to the following for their help with my research: Bobbie Holaday; Terry Baker; Jeff Hobbs; Chip Owen; Janice Steinberg; Dr. Steven G. Tolber; Shirley and Jim Tanzola; Mona and Jim Tanzola; Irene Pepperberg and Alex; Gwen Campbell, Susan Stacey and Patti Ferris of the Avian Propagation Center at the San Diego Zoo; Warren Illig at the Phoenix Zoo; and Noel Snyder.

1

It began with the sound of high-heeled shoes. It ended with the sound of a hand shuffling money, but that was many miles away. The heels clipped the sidewalk to a staccato beat. They were stilettos, maybe, or spikes, heels that left their impression on the pavement. A key turned in a lock, a dead bolt snapped from its chamber, a door swung open. There was a gasp and then a woman's angry voice asked, "What are *you* doing in here?"

"What do you think?" a man answered. "You're coming with . . ." He left the sentence unfinished, slurring his words from laziness, possibly, or drink.

"No, I'm not."

"Yeah, you are."

"Stop it, you're hurting me." A slap was followed by a thud, then the sound of wings beating furiously. Someone or something screeched.

"You can't take Perigee. Terrance will be livid."

"Fuck Terrance. Ouch. Goddamn it. He bit me." The laziness left the man's voice once he got bit.

"What did you expect?" the woman asked.

There was another, lighter thud. More wings began to beat, the screeching escalated; the cry of one annoyed individual became the cacophony of a pissed-off flock. It was a whirlwind of sound, but words floated to the top like feathers riding the airwaves. "Hello-o?" queried the voice of a tentative woman. "Call my lawyer," demanded a deep-throated man. "I'll get you, my pretty, and your little dog too," cackled the wicked witch of the West. "Start me talkin', babe, tell you everythin' I know," growled a whiskey-soddened blues singer. "Pretty boy, pretty boy," a new voice croaked. The next word, "*malinche*," was a vindictive hiss.

"Move it," said the man.

"I'm coming," answered the woman. "Stop shoving me."

The cacophony stopped as suddenly as it had begun. The door slammed shut. Boot heels scuffed the pavement, mingling with the pointissimo of the high-heeled shoes, but the snap had gone out of that step. The cassette player whirred. I struck a match, lit a cigarette, blew out the match. My client, Terrance Lewellen, who was sitting on the other side of my desk, reached over and clicked off the cassette player. It was a sleek, black, expensive model that belonged to him. He took the cassette out and placed it on my desk.

"I made you a copy," he said.

"That sounded like it was taking place in the next room."

"I use a Marantz extended-play recorder; it's the best in the field."

What field was that? Electronic surveillance? Bugging? Whatever you call it, it's illegal without the consent of the people involved.

"Actually," my client continued, "the incident took place at the Psittacine Research Facility my wife runs at UNM."

"Your wife wears high-heeled shoes to work?"

"My wife wears high-heeled shoes everywhere; her arches shrunk, so she can't wear anything but. Her name is Deborah Dumaine. She works with Amazon parrots and has taught them to do things no one ever believed parrots were capable of. If you ask them how many blue blocks are on a tray, they'll tell you—when they feel like it. They're smart. They're also first-class mimics. You have to watch what you say around an Amazon; you're likely to hear it repeated . . . over and over and over again.

"Ha. Ha." Terrance Lewellen laughed a big man's double-barreled laugh. He wasn't a big man exactly—he was about five feet five inches tall, a few inches shorter than me, and I never wear high-heeled shoes. But he took up a lot of cubic space. His shoulders were broad, his belly big enough to hide his belt buckle. His hands had the thick, doughy shape of a bear claw pastry. His eyes were deep set and grayish green. They could twinkle when he laughed, glitter when he got mad, turn as opaque as one-way glass when he sat back and waited for a reaction. His shirt was undone a couple of buttons, revealing gray chest hair that didn't match his brown piece. It was a bad piece, but nobody ever sees a good one. It was the same hair that middle-aged actors and newscasters wear, not big hair, TV hair. If Terrance had gone natural, he might have looked distinguished. The piece made him look like a late-night infomercial salesman, which could have been exactly the effect he intended. Terrance was a successful businessman, a seasoned and wary corporate raider. He never revealed his hand if he didn't have to, and he didn't leave much to chance. He took out a cigar and lit up. I hate the smell of cigar smoke, but my own cigarette butt was burning in the ashtray, which limited my right to complain.

"Were those the Amazons screeching?" I asked.

"Yes. Deborah's grad students have let them get out of control. They're spoiled rotten."

"How many were talking?"

"It's hard to tell. One Amazon can do many voices, and many Amazons can do one voice. They sound just like people, they sound like dogs, they can sound like the dishwasher if they want to. That last parrot voice on the tape was Perigee, my male indigo macaw. The macaws are bigger and better looking, but they don't have the vocabulary of an Amazon and they're more likely to talk in their own voice than to imitate."

"That was the one that said '*malinche*'?"

"Yes."

"Do you know what that means?"

"No."

"Malinche was the Indian girl who became Cortes's mistress and interpreter in the new world. There are those who believe she betrayed her people, and *malinche* means traitor to them. She's still a figure in pueblo Indian ceremonials."

"How 'bout that?" Terrance Lewellen leaned back, stretched his legs and exposed a pair of scaly cowboy boots, expensive but ugly. Ostrich hide? I wondered. Snake? "The Amazons belong to Deborah's lab; the indigo macaws belong to me," he continued. "When I got to the lab, Perigee was gone. He's one tough hombre and he put up a hell of a fight. Feathers were all over the floor."

There was a sleek leather briefcase with a combination lock on Terrance's lap. He keyed in the combination and snapped the briefcase open, giving me a glimpse of his cellular phone. He took out a long, thin feather and handed it to me. I thought indigo was the color of jeans after they've been washed a few times, but the feather was a turquoise that was as deep and iridescent as the Sea of Cortez.

"It's a tail feather. Beautiful, isn't it?" asked Terrance.

"Yes," I replied.

"Keep it."

"Thanks." I stood the indigo plume in an empty glass on

my desk and it arced gracefully over the side, a hit of beauty whenever I needed a break from my sun-baked Albuquerque lawyer's life.

"The Latin name of the indigos is *Anodorhynchus leari*," Terrance said. "They are extremely rare in captivity, damn near extinct in the wild and very, very valuable."

Some people are collectors by nature, some are dispersers. My own personal motto is to never own anything you can't afford to lose; it's too much trouble. "Where did the indigos come from?" I asked Terrance.

"The Raso in Brazil." His eyes sparked. "I cannot believe that Deborah allowed Perigee to be taken." He smashed the fist of one large hand into the palm of the other.

"It didn't sound like she had a choice."

"She had the choice of not associating with Wes Brown, a worthless human being if ever there was one."

"The voice on the tape?"

"That's him. Those were his boot heels, too. He grew up in Southern California, but he thinks he's a cowboy."

Terrance, I knew, had grown up in West Texas, which gave him a license to wear boots. "Macaws have the bite of a snapping turtle," he continued. "I hope Perigee got a chunk out of Wes Brown's hide."

"What is Deborah's connection to him?" It wasn't quite the question I wanted to ask, but timing is of the essence in law and interrogation, and the time wasn't ripe for my question yet.

"He's a smuggler. He contacted us on occasion and tried to sell us smuggled parrots. We refused. Deborah hated his guts, but she encouraged him. She had a notion that she would learn something useful about his smuggling operation."

"Did she?"

"I doubt it."

"How did *you* get the indigos?" Parrots that were very

rare and very valuable were also likely to be very illegal, one explanation for why Terrance had come to me with his story and not the police or his corporate law firm.

"I used to be in oil exploration and was doing some exploratory drilling for Petrobras in the Raso in the late sixties and early seventies. I like to bring something back from all the places I drill. On my first trip there, one of the natives offered me the indigos, and I accepted. They were a hand-raised pair, too tame to survive in the wild. That was before Brazil signed an export ban, and it wasn't illegal to take indigos or any other parrots out of the country. Things have changed."

Considering the exchange rate between the third-world cruzeiro and the oil-world dollar, and the escalating pace of parrot extinction, the macaws had probably turned out to be a better investment than the oil.

"Deborah and I met in the Raso," Terrance said. "She's a linguist. She was studying the language of the indigenous people before they become extinct, too. While she was down there, she got interested in parrots. She tried teaching the macaws to speak, but that didn't work, so she turned to Amazons. Now that she's famous for her work, she's become the adrenaline queen. She never sleeps. She travels all the time. The birds don't like it." He peered into an ornate scroll of silver and turquoise on his wrist, found the time, snapped open his briefcase and brought out a small bottle with a long neck. He removed the plastic cap, squirted once into each nostril and sniffed. "Goddamn allergies," he said.

It was comparable to pulling out dental tape and flossing in public, satisfying to the person doing it, repulsive to anyone else. "Is that really necessary?" I wanted to ask, but I didn't because Terrance Lewellen was watching me with cat-at-the-mouse-hole eyes, waiting for a reaction. He exuded a vibe having to do with power, success or plain old testosterone that made him hard to ignore. He was the kind of short man who usually has a tall, good-looking woman on his arm (with the spike heels Deborah wore, she was bound to be taller), and the reason wasn't entirely money. He was coarse, but he was smart. He appreciated beauty, and beauty likes to be appreciated. I picked up the indigo feather and ran my fingers down the barbs, thinking that if Terrance Lewellen were a bird he'd be a bantam cock. "Let me get this straight," I said. "You have a *pair* of indigo macaws?"

Terrance stuck the cap on and put the bottle back in his briefcase. "Yes."

"But Wes Brown only took one?"

"Right."

"Were they both in the lab?"

"Yes. When I developed a parrot allergy I had to move the indigos out of the house and into the lab. Wes Brown knows parrots. He knows macaws mate for life and that Colloquy will be one sad parrot without Perigee. She's already moping and pulling her feathers out. Wes is going to use that knowledge to extort money from me. I got this in the mail today."

He opened his briefcase again, took out a stamped envelope and handed it to me. Inside was the Relationships section of the Sunday *Journal*. In the Male to Female Relationships column, between "no Democrats or psychos. Harley-Davidson a plus" and "Love the Lord," he'd marked this: "Lonely indigo desperately needs mate. #12441."

I looked at the postmark on the envelope. Tuesday. "When did you record the abduction?"

"Monday evening."

Today was Wednesday, the message had appeared in Sunday's paper. "That's pretty good timing," I said. "The ad appeared the day before the crime; it was mailed to you the day after."

"Time is of the essence in crime," Terrance said, watching me and appropriating one of those phrases that seem to float around a lawyer's office. Maybe he pulled it out of the air or maybe he read my mind, because it's what I was thinking but hadn't said. Terrance made a point of saying the things other people wouldn't. "I got the ad today," he continued. "If the abduction hadn't worked, I never would have seen it and who else would have known what it meant? I don't read those ads. Do you?"

"Nope."

"To answer, you call 1-900-622-9408 and listen to the person's recorded message. Go ahead. Call it; tell me what you think."

I dialed the number and got a generic female operator's voice asking me to push the number one if I had a Touch-Tone phone. I did as I was told, pushed all the required numbers and eventually heard, "I'm so lonely without my mate. Bring me home soon, please" in a voice of quivering emotion and ambiguous sexuality. It could have been a husky-voiced woman's or a high-pitched man's. It could have been an Amazon parrot or an indigo macaw. It wasn't Wes Brown's voice, although it did stretch out the *o*'s in "so" and "lonely."

"Was that Perigee?" I asked.

"No. It was Wes Brown."

"Except for the drawl, it doesn't sound like him."

"He used the Scrunch, a digital voice changer. It has eight positions, ranging from deep male to high female. It can make a man sound like a woman, a woman sound like a man and a human being sound like a parrot." In the world of high-tech gamesmanship, Terrance Lewellen knew all the equipment.

"He hasn't asked for money yet."

"He will."

"If he does, he's going to cross the line between abduction and kidnapping." Neither was a crime I'd likely ever see again in my world of real estate and divorce. I didn't have the typical corporate attorney's client list of businessmen, crooks and businessmen/crooks. This case was getting more interesting by the minute. The inclusion of an endangered species made it almost irresistible. Still, I gave Terrance Lewellen a cautious lawyer's advice even though caution has never been my style and wouldn't turn out to be his either. "After twenty-four hours the FBI can step in. You ought to take this to them."

"The Fan Belt Inspectors, the Fucking Big Idiots?" Terrance's gray-green eyes had a feral yellow gleam near the center. He flicked an ash in my ashtray. "They'll screw it up."

"They can find out who placed the ad a lot more effectively than you or I."

"I know who placed it—Wes Brown—and I know how to handle him." If he had other reasons for not wanting to involve law enforcement, he didn't reveal them.

"Who does your corporate business?" I asked.

"Buddy Baxter at Baxter, Johnson."

"Why didn't you go to him with this?"

"I heard you had experience with endangered species. Is that right?"

"Right."

"Baxter doesn't know an endangered species from a sparrow. I want Perigee back. Wes Brown knows what he's worth on the black market. I'll pay him that much, but not a penny more."

"And your wife?" I asked. "How much are you willing to pay for her?"

"Zip, nada," he said. "Not one skinny dime. Deborah and I are getting divorced. She moved out of the house, and she's not my responsibility anymore. Brown is going to be rip shit when he finds *that* out."

"Why were you taping Deborah anyway? You weren't trying to catch her in an affair, were you?"

"Deborah? Naah. She's going through the change. She

hasn't been interested in sex for years. All she cares about are parrots."

"Women don't just dry up and sit on the shelf once they hit the . . . change . . . you know."

"Oh, yeah, now they've got estrogen, right? Well, Deborah wouldn't take it; she said it wasn't natural. After the oil business cratered, I moved into corporate takeovers and venture capital. There's a little company in Texas that I'm backing. You heard about the nicotine patch?" He looked at the cigarette I was still smoking. "Maybe not. Well, this company makes a testosterone patch. Think what that's going to do for aging baby boomers. It's a great place to put your money. *The* investment for the nineties."

I didn't have any money, and if I did I wouldn't be putting it into testosterone. If you ask me, what the world needs is not more testosterone, but better distribution of what's already out there. That thought lead to my next question, the one I'd been wanting to ask, being of a suspicious mind when it comes to male/female relationships. "You're sure Deborah wasn't having an affair with Wes Brown?" There was a certain intensity in their exchange that could have been the result of sexual repulsion or its flip side—attraction.

"Positive. I've been taping her, remember, and I know Deborah wasn't having an affair with anybody. Besides, Wes Brown is dumber than dirt. The guy isn't even a successful smuggler. Deborah's far too smart for him. He'd bore the hell out of her."

"Then why *were* you taping her?"

"Because when you're getting a divorce you need the best hand you can get. I've been through this before—twice—and I know to cover my butt. Deborah signed a prenup, which entitled her to take out of the marriage exactly what she came into it with—nothing. Now she's trying to welsh out of it. I wanted to know what she was saying to her accountant and her lawyer. I wired her apartment, too. That was a voice-activated system, and she's never home anyway. I didn't get anything worthwhile there."

"You must have gotten a ton from the lab," I said, thinking of all the voices I'd heard in a couple of minutes of cassette.

"I did. I had one of my security men install a spike mike in the wall, hook it up to the Marantz. I got everything that went on; most of it was parrot talk. My security man sorted through it."

"You are aware that bugging is a federal crime." Along with kidnapping and dealing in endangered species. Smuggling, too.

"Right, and when was the last time you heard of anybody getting prosecuted for it? The FBI is more interested in tracking figure skaters than in harassing a man for listening to his wife. Leave a message on the Relationships machine, will you? Tell Brown you're my lawyer and offer him a hundred thousand."

The opaque eyes watched and waited. Cigar smoke drifted toward the ceiling. Just how badly did I want this case anyway? Badly enough to say, "No."

"Why not?"

"Brown hasn't revealed his hand yet. You're not even sure he wants money. If he does, and you let him speak first, you'll get a better deal." Don't show your cards is one of the first rules of negotiation. Terrance knew that better than I. He leaned back; his corporate raider's eyes sparked. If this had been a test of how well I'd represent *his* interests, I'd passed. But there were other interests involved. "Do you think Perigee and your wife are in danger?"

"Not yet. I'm sure Brown has them hidden away in Door."

"The ghost town near the border?"

"Right, that's where he lives. It's a tough place to get in and out of. Brown'll feel safe there. He knows how to take care of parrots, and he knows Perigee is worth more to me in good shape. When it comes to macaws, a pair is worth more than the sum of two individuals; they're picky about who they'll mate with. As for Deborah, she can take care of herself. All right, call Relationships back and leave a message. Tell Brown to return what he took. The next move is up to him." Having finished his instructions, he put his Marantz in his briefcase and stood up. "How'd you like to see an indigo macaw?"

How'd I like to see a Mexican gray wolf again or an Arctic gyrfalcon? "When?" I said.

"Tomorrow at ten. Meet me outside the lab."

As his cowboy boots clunked across my waiting room floor, I thought that an oil man's ostrich didn't sound any different than a cowboy's cowhide. "Adios," I heard Terrance say to my secretary, Anna.

"See ya," she replied.

Through the security bars on my window I watched Terrance climb into the sleek black Jaguar he'd parked in our driveway and throw his briefcase onto the passenger's seat. "Jag," his vanity plates read. He pulled out of the driveway, and I dialed the Relationships number. I listened again to the ambisexuous, digitally altered, miserable voice and then I recorded it on my microcassette recorder, figuring that a voice that is already on tape doesn't need permission to be retaped. "I'm so lonely without my mate," the voice cried. "Bring me home soon, please."

"This is Neil Hamel, Terrance Lewellen's lawyer," I replied in a crisp female attorney's voice. "Return everything you've taken immediately." I left my phone number, although I didn't expect to be called back; a phone call was too traceable. The Relationships line was where these negotiations were going to be conducted.

Since Relationships was already in my hand, I made a quick survey of what was hot in today's market and glimpsed a microcosm of Albuquerque society: bikers, cowboys, Christians, newcomers; whites, blacks, Native Americans, Spanish; heterosexual, homosexual, bi. I wandered out into my reception area with the Relationships section still in my hand. A red rose was sitting in a vase on Anna's desk. She was fluffing her mane and reading today's *Tribune.*

"You looking for a new guy?" she asked when she saw what I'd been reading.

"Not me. Someone abducted Terrance Lewellen's wife and is communicating with him through the Relationships ads."

"Let me see." She read the ad. "His wife's name is Indigo?"

"No. That's a parrot that got taken too, an indigo macaw. It means more to him than his wife."

She began skimming the Males to Females section. "Look at this one. 'Motorhead, racer for loud engines and wild rides.' Sounds like my type."

"You already have a boyfriend." Known to me as Stevie, the stereo king.

"A boyfriend," Anna replied, "not a husband. Should I call motorhead?" Without waiting for my answer, she punched in all the numbers, listened for a few minutes and then hung up. "Dumb," she said. "Macho."

"What did you expect from a motorhead?"

"Okay, how about *this* one? 'SWM. Caring, liberal, kind, likes fine dining and travel. Looking for intelligent, romantic woman to share life with.'"

"I don't know about the fine dining part," I said. Anna's idea of fine food was a Lotta Burger with green chile.

"Let's call him." She listened briefly and turned the phone over to me. "I'm a sensitive, romantic guy," he said between long pauses. "It's hard for me to talk on these machines. Maybe it's hard for you too. If you want to just leave your number, that's okay. I'll call you back. I promise."

"Yuck. Too sensitive," said Anna and kept on looking. "How about this? 'SWM. Mountain man. Likes rock climbing, caving, animals, camping, outdoors. ISO . . .' what does that mean?"

"International sex object?"

"I'm seeking only?"

"In search of," said my partner Brink, who had wandered out of his office and was leaning over Anna's shoulder, reading. He'd obviously had more experience with newspaper Relationships (but less of the other kind) than Anna or I. When Anna wanted to meet men, she parked her car in the breakdown lane and put up the hood.

"'In search of,'" Anna continued, "'an independent woman to explore New Mexico with.' Sounds like your type," she said to me.

"I'm not looking," I replied, but she dialed the number anyway and handed the phone over to me even faster than she had the last time.

"You're not gonna believe this," she said.

"I hate these machines, don't you?" I heard. "If you want to just leave your number, that's okay. I'll call you back. I'm a sensitive, romantic guy who likes the outdoors." It was a hesitant male voice, the same hesitant male voice.

"Covering all the bases," I said.

"What a jerk," said Anna, who had begun looking through the Females to Males for Brink. "'Rubenesk.' What does that mean?"

"Fat," I said.

"Plump," said Brink, who was on the Rubenesque side himself.

"Look at this," Anna continued. "'SWF ISO single European or Latin American male, handsome, athletic body, cute face, who plays soccer.'"

"I've already got him," I said.

"I'll say," said Anna. She clapped her hands together. "I've found one for you, Brink. 'Do you like homemade chocolate chip cookies?'"

Brink liked any kind of cookies.

"'Blond, semi-full-figured DWF.' She's divorced. That's good. You need someone with experience. 'ISO a good heart, not good looks,' and—get this—'no country dancing, like lawyers, corny jokes.' Perfect!"

"Let me see." Brink snatched the Relationships section out of Anna's hand.

"Be careful with that; it's evidence," I said.

"Make me a copy, will you?" Brink asked Anna.

"You got it," she said.

Brink took the copy, went back into his office and shut the door, and not because he intended to do any work. "Do you think he's gonna call her?" Anna asked me.

"I know it," I replied, watching the button for his extension lighting up.

2

At 10:10 the following day, Terrance was waiting for me near the Psittacine Research Facility, not outside the door but at the end of the walk. He leaned against the corner of the building reading the *Wall Street Journal*. His briefcase was set beside him on the sidewalk. He looked at me, he looked at his watch. I don't wear a watch, but that wasn't why I was late. Unlike Terrance, who had pulled his Jaguar up onto the curb, I'd been looking for a place to park.

"Sorry I'm late," I said. "I couldn't find a parking place." In most cities the first thing people discuss when they get together is parking, but it isn't considered a fit subject for conversation in Albuquerque—unless you're meeting at UNM.

"Did you leave the message for Brown?"

"Yes."

"Call back the Relationships number this afternoon; there'll be an answer."

"Can he change the message on the Relationships tapes?"

"If you have a little sniffer, you can change the message on any tape."

"I suppose you can listen to the messages on any tape, too." Deborah wouldn't have had any privacy on her answering machine either.

"Yup."

"Where do you get all this electronic surveillance stuff anyway?"

"I get mine through a catalog. I don't know where Wes Brown gets his. There are places right here in Albuquerque where you can buy it if you want to."

"Is it expensive?"

"The Marantz cost me, but you can pick up a little sniffer for a hundred and fifty bucks. You can buy a Punch KRM-2 for as little as nine dollars."

"What's that?"

"Red pepper spray. It'll immobilize any aggressor—two-legged or four-legged—for thirty minutes. Every woman ought to carry one. If Deborah had, we wouldn't be standing here right now." He snapped open his briefcase and took out a red spray can about six inches long and another smaller one with a holster for attaching it to a key ring. "Here," he said. "They're on me."

"Thanks," I replied. My attitude has always been nobody's going to protect me if I can help it, but I took the Punch anyway and put it in my purse. It had to be less noxious than some forms of self-protection I've used.

Terrance folded up his *Journal* and put it in the briefcase. "Well," he growled, "let's get on with it. Now I'm not going to reveal any more than I have to to Deborah's students. I don't want them trying to be heroes, looking for Wes Brown and screwing things up."

He knew I wouldn't be revealing anything about this case

to anybody. There was, as always, the matter of client confidentiality.

"If my allergies start acting up—and they probably will—I'll have to leave the lab," Terrance said. "I want you to be another set of eyes, look around, talk to the students, see if they're concealing anything. All right?"

"All right."

We were walking down the same sidewalk Deborah had, but to our own beat. Terrance clunked along in his boot heels. I followed as silent as a scout in my running shoes. Running shoes are the preferred footgear for some crimes: stalking crimes, silent crimes. In daylight, this was an ordinary cement sidewalk, but high-heeled shoes heard walking alone on a sidewalk at night have a resonance. The faster the footsteps, the deeper the resonance.

When we reached the door with the sign that read PSITTACINE RESEARCH FACILITY, Terrance stopped and said, "You've got to take off your shoes the minute we get inside so you're not bringing in any germs. You'll see a pile of plastic booties to put on."

We went inside. I followed his instructions, slipped out of my running shoes, put on the plastic booties and took a look around while he struggled to get his cowboy boots off. "Goddamn," he said, "I wish they'd bring in a bootjack or a chair to sit on."

The Psittacine Research Facility was as noisy and hyper as a day care center. Next to the door we'd entered was an office with a window that faced onto the lab. Two students sat at a table in the middle of the lab talking to a parrot. The parrot was about a foot tall, bright green with a yellow head and red epaulets on its wings.

"Key," said one student, holding up that object and speaking slowly and distinctly, as if to a two-year-old.

"Awrk," said the parrot.

"Key," the other student said. "Key."

A female student stood at a counter feeding a baby parrot with a large dropper. The parrot was pink-skinned and speckled with gray feathers. It had a huge beak and feet. It was so ugly it was almost appealing. The student was tall and lovely. She wore washed-out jeans and a pale T-shirt, but even in that casual uniform her body attracted attention. She was slender, but voluptuous and strong. Her hair hung down her back, long, blond and silky.

"Alice Ashburn," Terrance sighed her name with that longing in his voice middle-aged men reserve for beautiful young women.

A male student, who was balancing a green and yellow parrot on his shoulder, hovered around Alice inhaling her pheromones. He was as tall as she was but as awkward as the baby parrot. The parrot was all beak and feet; he was all elbows. He wore wire-rimmed glasses and had the overeager manner of the first student to raise his hand in class, the last one to get a date. His hair was light brown and pulled back in a long, limp, sixties-style ponytail. He wore jeans and a T-shirt like Alice's, but he looked scrawny in his. If Alice had noticed that he was enamored of her, she wasn't letting on. She continued squeezing food into the baby parrot's beak.

"That's Rick Olney," Terrance said. "Ph.D. He's Deborah's assistant."

"What does he have his Ph.D. in?" I asked.

"Ornithology. He'll never let you forget it, either."

There are three ways to have power: body, brains and bucks. Alice had the body, Rick had the brains, Terrance had the bucks. I was segueing from body to brains myself, knowing full well I'd never have the bucks.

Rick noticed our presence, adjusted his glasses and did not seem at all pleased to see that Terrance Lewellen had entered the lab. He tucked in his elbows and walked our way, balancing the parrot on his shoulder. Dispensing with any preliminaries, he said in a tight voice, "Have you heard anything at all from Deborah?"

"Not a word, and you?" Terrance responded, telling the truth the way he saw it.

"Nothing. Deborah would not go off without telling us, and she would not take Perigee and leave Colloquy alone. Something is very, very wrong."

The pupils of the parrot's eyes dilated and contracted. Standing on Rick's shoulder put it high above the rest of us, and it seemed to like being there. "Hello-o," it called.

"Hi," I replied.

"Be quiet, Maxamilian," Rick said.

"That's Max," Terrance said to me. "He's a double-yellow-headed Amazon, and Deborah's prize pupil. He has a vocabulary of over two thousand words."

"Twenty-five hundred," Rick corrected him.

"Right," Terrance replied. "This is Neil Hamel, my lawyer."

"Call my lawyer," Max cackled.

"Your lawyer?" asked Rick in the deep-freeze voice people reserve for members of my profession and the IRS.

"My lawyer," said Terrance with no further explanation. In his world a lawyer (and probably a woman, too) was as necessary a part of the baggage as the briefcase he held in his hand. "How's Colloquy doing?"

"Not well; she misses her mate," Rick replied. "I don't like this, Terrance. Deborah's been gone two days now. It's time to call the police."

"Call the police," screamed Max, flapping his wings and doing a quick two-step on Rick's shoulder to keep his balance.

"No police," Terrance said.

"Deborah and Perigee could be in danger," Rick replied.

"They'll be in more danger if you call the police."

"I disagree."

Rick was towering over Terrance, who didn't get any taller but seemed to expand circumferentially as he went into intimidation mode, wielding the briefcase like a battering ram and moving right up under Rick's nose. "You're not getting paid to agree or disagree," he barked. "You call the police, I cut off the lab's funding. It's as simple as that."

Money talks, power shouts. Rick's eyes blazed behind the granny glasses, but he didn't say a word.

"Now I have to make a phone call," my client said, taking his briefcase into the office that had to be Deborah's. He was not behaving well, but people who do don't need lawyers. "Why don't you show Neil around the lab?" he asked Rick.

It wasn't a question, it was a command. Rick put Max down on the office desk, turned his back to me and Terrance and stomped across the lab floor as rapidly as his plastic footgear would allow. Terrance opened his briefcase, took out his phone and started talking about buying and selling stock in cell voice. One of nature's laws is, the more inconsequential the conversation, the more advanced the equipment, the louder the voice.

My options were to follow Rick or to expose, embarrass and possibly lose my client. Rick squared his shoulders and straightened his ponytail as he walked across the lab. He stopped at the table where the other grad students were talking to their Amazon, more emphatically even than they'd been before. There was a beat-up paperback copy of Ayn Rand's *The Fountainhead* lying on the table. On the far side of the lab I could see into another room, and it was very easy to be diverted from the tension by a spectacular blue bird sitting on a manzanita perch in a metal cage.

"Is that Colloquy?" I asked Rick.

"Yes."

"Can I take a look?" I asked him.

"It's Terrance's bird." He shrugged.

Colloquy was big and beautiful, a collector's item, a work of art. The place on the adjacent perch was conspicuously empty. Her tail feathers were a long and elegant train the same deep turquoise color as the feather that sat on my desk. Her feathers turned lighter and greener as they approached her neck, and there were bright yellow ovals around her eyes and beside her large beak. Her upper beak hooked over the lower with the deep curve of a scimitar that could snap off a finger. The indigo's size and color made her magnificent, her beak made her intimidating, but she had the goofy expression of a trickster or a clown.

"Hi, Colloquy," I said, walking up to the cage holding out my empty palm, a reflex action, the way a child learns to approach a strange dog. Maybe the bird would have preferred a full hand. The floor of her cage was littered with feathers, but she still had plenty left and they fluffed out as she lifted her long wings, squawked and flapped furiously at me like a big-haired woman having a bad hair day. "It takes more than that to scare me," I said, but when Colloquy began to screech in a voice that was loud and piercing enough to crack a piñon, I backed off. She had a sound to match her size. "Okay, okay," I said, dropping my hand.

Terrance had finished his business and slapped across the lab floor in his plastic booties. "She doesn't like strangers," he said to me. "Hey, Colloquy baby," he cooed to the indigo. "Come to Daddy. Your daddy's here." He reached into his pocket and took out a plastic bag, then he opened the door to the cage and stood next to the opening. Colloquy swung from her perch and climbed onto his shoulder. "Even I don't put my arm into the cage," he said. Colloquy settled her ruffled feathers, accepted the contents of the bag and gave me a look just like her master's when he'd provoked the reaction he wanted. She got a lot of expression out of one beak and two eyes.

"What's in the bag?" I asked him.

"Granola," he said. "My birds don't get monkey chow."

Colloquy swallowed her granola, snuggled up to Terrance and nibbled on his earlobe. One quick bite and the ear would be history.

"Baby, baby." Terrance stroked the indigo's brilliant feathers. "It's my allergy that's been keeping me away. You're still my girl."

Colloquy nibbled. Terrance sneezed, and his ear came close to extinction. "Goddamn this allergy," he said. "I'm gonna have to put you back already."

He took her back to the cage and sneezed again. The indigo settled onto her perch and hung her head in a exaggerated display until Terrance poured some granola in her dish. "I have to get out of here," he said to me. "You stick around, make yourself at home. Rick'll show you the lab." Rick had come into the room and had been observing the events from a distance with his arms crossed. Colloquy drooped as she watched Terrance go.

"She seems to like him," I said.

"She likes granola," Rick replied. "Her diet in the wild was licuri palm nuts, here it's parrot feed. Granola is a treat. People forget that the vast majority of parrots are—at most— only two generations away from the wild. Colloquy is first generation, but she must have been taken from the nest early and hand raised. Only a hand-raised bird will cuddle the way she does." He pulled out a drawer at the bottom of the cage and picked up the loose feathers.

"Who named them Perigee and Colloquy?" It didn't sound like Terrance's lingo.

"Deborah."

Suddenly a couple of voices floated above the lab's cacophony in the way that, even in a chorus, the voices of certain singers reach to the theater's last row. "Goddamn allergies." I heard Terrance sniff, and then the loud voice of Deborah Dumaine scream, "Terrance, you are *such* an asshole."

The feathers fell through Rick's fingers. Colloquy squawked and turned her head. I jerked around like a puppet on a string. Terrance, who was bent over at the door trying to squeeze his foot into a boot, dropped it, stood up and snapped, "Shut up, you red-headed bitch."

Max, who was perched in the window of Deborah's office, watched us, bobbed his large yellow head and laughed, for all I knew. Deborah Dumaine was nowhere in sight.

"Damn you, Max," Terrance said, pulling on his boot, picking up his briefcase and heading out the door.

"That was Max?" I asked Rick.

"Yeah."

"What made him do that?"

"Seeing Terrance keyed it. Parrots talk in reference," he said.

"It's amazing how much he sounded like Deborah. Even Terrance was fooled."

"People mistake parrots for their mates all the time. Parrots learn very quickly how to imitate humans if they want to. They pick up on sounds with emotional content, and they love the blues." Rick picked up the feathers he'd dropped. "They're social animals. In the wild they identify each other by their voices. Flocking and interacting are their only defense." His enthusiasm for his subject had let him forget for the moment that he was talking to Terrance Lewellen's lawyer. He smoothed the feathers. "Macaws mate for life. Colloquy's so unhappy without Perigee. They've been together twenty-five years or more, and they're still lovebirds." He sighed.

"How long do they live?"

"Thirty to forty-five years in the wild. They have a human life span in captivity when they're treated well."

"What do you do with the feathers?" I asked. Something that beautiful had to be valuable.

"Give them to the Hopis for their ceremonials."

"Does Colloquy ever talk?"

"Rarely, but Deborah taught Perigee a few words."

Alice poked her head in the door and smiled at Rick with a smile as bright and perfect as the rest of her. "The man from the DNA lab is here," she said.

"Excuse me," Rick said, remembering he had manners now that Terrance was gone. He went into the lab with the feathers still in his hand, and began talking to the DNA man.

While he did, I wandered into Deborah's office, following Terrance's instructions to observe what I could and my own need to observe whatever he'd done in there. The office was full of photographs, and Deborah was in most of them. On the desk was a framed clipping from *Time* magazine of Deborah with Max perched on her shoulder. She smiled for the camera. She was too mature and too confident to be a trophy wife, but she was good-looking, no "still" about it. You wouldn't expect Terrance to have married a little brown bird. Deborah had large features, a prominent nose, a dazzling smile and a mane of scarlet hair that was probably as false in color as Terrance's was in substance. She wore a tight-fitting purple dress with forties movie star shoulder pads and waterfalls of beaded Indian earrings. I could see her wearing high-heeled shoes with that outfit, *red* high-heeled shoes. I could see the flash that had brought her and Terrance together and could imagine the conflicts of will that had driven them apart. Max, who, within the limits of his clipped wings, had the run of the place, perched in the window. A parrot kachina sat on a shelf with real feathers sticking out of its head. Thumbtacked to a bulletin board was a quote from Frank Water's *Book of the Hopi:* "The Fourth World, the present one, is the full expression of man's ruthless materialism and imperialistic will. . . . With this turn man rises upward, bringing into predominant function each of the higher centers. The door at the crown of the head then opens, and he merges into the wholeness of all creation, whence he sprang. It is a Road of Life he has traveled by his own free will, exhausting every capacity for good or evil, that he may know himself at last as a finite part of infinity." Beneath that, someone had written, "God is in the details."

Rick had escorted the DNA man to the door and come into the office while I was reading the quotes. If he noticed anything out of order, he didn't say so. He opened a desk drawer and dropped the feathers in. "The Hopi word for parrot is *Kyaro*. The parrot clan is one of the highest-ranking Hopi clans," he said. "They emigrated from the south and probably brought parrots with them. They traded macaws along the ancient Indian trade routes, and the feathers were used in all the important ceremonies. Fourteen scarlet macaw skeletons were found in a room at Chaco Canyon."

"I didn't know that," I said. He didn't comment; he hadn't expected me to know. He was the scientist, I was the lawyer. But he was a scientist—like so many in New Mexico—who had an artist's passion for his work. His eyes ignited when he talked about it.

"Among the pueblo Indians it was said that only those households in which people of good character lived harmoniously could successfully breed macaws," he said.

"Have Perigee and Colloquy ever been bred?"

"Not since Terrance got them. He had them surgically sexed, so we know they are male and female."

"Surgically sexed?" I asked.

"There are only two ways to tell the sex of a parrot: to look inside or by DNA testing. DNA testing is becoming more popular. It's less obtrusive to the birds, it's infallible and it can be done with a drop of the bird's blood."

"How does it work?"

"Chains of DNA wind around their complement, and a torn-apart DNA fragment will seek its mate. The sex chromosome gene is radioactively labeled, separated into its two strands, which then search for each other. The bands on the DNA show the sex of the bird."

The phone on the desk rang. Someone in the lab answered an extension, but Max had already been prompted to go into phone display. He looked at the phone, looked at us, balanced on one foot and stretched out a wing. "Brrng," he called, perfectly imitating the sound of the ring. It was hard to believe the sound was emanating from twelve inches of green, yellow and red feathers and not a black receiver. "Hello-o?" Max answered the phone in the same tentative woman's voice I'd heard on the tape. He paused, then, "But, sweetie, I love you so much," he said, oozing sentiment. "Okay, 'bye." He completed the cycle by hanging up the phone and cocking his head at Rick for approval or a nut. Rick gave him the nut.

I gave him the approval. "That was a great performance, Max," I said.

"Grrrrrreat performance, Max," he repeated in the husky voice of a woman who has a lot of self-confidence or who smokes too much.

"You have to be careful what you say around these guys," Rick told me. "They're like computers. Garbage in, garbage out."

"Um," I said. "Does Max miss Deborah?"

"She's been traveling so much, he's gotten used to her being away, and he considers the rest of us his flock. See how happy he is in this picture?" He pointed to the *Time* photo. "That's because Deborah has her hair down. When he saw it up, he knew she was going away and he got huffy. He wouldn't talk if Deborah's hair was up." He picked up a pen and began poking at the desk. "I'm going to discover what happened to her, you know, with or without Terrance's help. He's hiding something, and I'll find out what it is. This work is Deborah's life. She would not go off and leave it, or us."

We were venturing into the confidentiality zone here, so I changed the subject. "Why do Max's pupils contract and expand like that?"

"It's a sign of excitement."

"What is it he's trained to do?"

"Lots of things. For example, he can identify a number of objects." He showed Max the pen. "What's this, Max?"

"Nut," Max squawked in a voice I hadn't heard before, maybe even his own voice.

"You know better, Maxamilian. What's this?"

"Pen," Max said, and then, "nut."

"Good boy," Rick said and gave him the nut.

"Max a million," said the bird.

Terrance, hugging his briefcase and his *Wall Street Journal,* waited for me outside. "You learn anything?" he asked.

"I learned that Max has a sense of humor, that he can imitate a phone call and that he likes nuts. I learned that college students still read *The Fountainhead.*"

"What's that?"

"Never mind," I said. "I learned that the Pueblo Indians thought macaws would only breed in a harmonious home."

"Anything else?"

"I learned about parrots; I didn't learn much about Deborah except that she's very attractive."

"Shoulda seen her when she was thirty-five."

"What about you?" I asked. He stared back at me with his opaque eyes. "What did you learn?" The cell phone call had struck me as a flimsy excuse to take his briefcase into Deborah's office. I couldn't have called him on it then without making a scene, but I could now.

"That she kept her file somewhere else, but I'll be damned if I know where. My security men have already searched here and her apartment, and they haven't found it yet."

The next question was why the information in that file was so valuable that he was willing to break federal and state laws and use me as a diversion to get it. I didn't expect the full answer, so I didn't ask, but it wasn't my MO to keep my mouth shut. "Listen, Terrance," I said, "as your lawyer I advise you not to do anything illegal and, if you want me to remain your lawyer, I'm telling you to never involve me in your fishing expeditions ever again."

"Okay, okay," he parroted, hiding behind his one-way eyes. "Never again."

3

My single, Latin American male who liked to play soccer and had no reason to read the Relationships section of the *Journal* moved his auto repair business to the North Valley and then computerized it when his partner, Manny, went back to Mexico. Computers are the way to go in the auto repair business. Cars have gotten computerized, and mechanics who can work on them are scarce. The ones who can do it make as much money as some lawyers.

The North Valley was, until recently, one of New Mexico's best-kept secrets, a rural village at the edge of the state's largest city, one part of Albuquerque that doesn't look like L.A. on the Rio Grande. The Spanish land grants once extended from the peaks of the Sandias to the river. They were divided among the grantees' descendants into long, narrow strips with access to the irrigation ditches. They're too narrow to do much but graze horses and trailers, which has helped to keep the North Valley rural.

A lot of the Valley is still zoned A-1 for agricultural, but that is being changed to R-1 for residential. These days that means two-hundred-thousand-dollar town homes and gated communities with a sentry at the gate. It costs to keep an area's rural character, but the crumbling adobes, the junk shops, the trailer ranches, the horses and the irrigation ditches still give the Valley a funky charm.

I went to the Kid's shop more often now that he'd moved north and Manny had gone south, Manny having never understood my presence in his partner's life. I stopped there on my way home from work. The shop was on Fourth Street in a cinderblock building that masqueraded as adobe but not well enough to fool anyone. The Kid had brought his flying red horse sign with him, and it marked the spot. Behind the building a long and hard-to-develop field backed onto an irrigation ditch. There was no access to the field but Fourth Street and the ditch, which was not a legal access, but that never stopped anybody from using it. Ancient cottonwoods with huge trunks and wandering limbs grew along the ditch. In the summer they provide shade, in the fall resting arms for migrating birds, and in the winter intrigue, when the exposed branches, twisting and turning like country roads, are silhouetted against the fiery evening sky. The yard behind the Kid's shop was, in the tradition of the rural west, a pile of junked cars and parts, but if you looked beyond the junk, you could see five thousand feet of the Sandia Mountains from the base to the peak. Even on no-burn days, when you're not allowed to burn wood in your fireplace and our sky is most polluted, the entire mountain is visible. Our worst days are the equivalent of California's best days. On their worst days their mountains aren't visible at all except as disembodied white stuff floating like whipped cream on the smog. That's one reason why so many Californians are coming here, and why the North Valley is changing from A-1 to R-1.

The Sandias have many moods, and from the Kid's shop

you can see them all. They can be dusky mauve against a deep
blue sky, watermelon pink in the glow of the setting sun, a
black cutout backlit by the rising moon, gray hulks with
hunks of rock shaped like gorillas' buns. Cumulonimbi get
snagged by the peaks, falcon-winged cirri hover over, snow
clouds slide down the face of the mountain and wash it clean.
There is one view from Albuquerque's Valley and another
from the Heights. Some people like to look out, and some like
looking up. I was becoming a Valley person myself.

"The Indians believe that's where the goddess of the wind
lives," the Kid told me, pointing toward the Sandias' peak.

"You coming for dinner?" I replied. "I have an interesting
case I want to tell you about."

"Okay," he said. "I'll bring the food."

He met me later at my place in La Vista Luxury Apartment Complex with a Lotta Burger bag—two double burgers
with green chile and a mound of fries. The green chile was a
little bland for my taste, but blandness was a novelty for him.
We cleaned up, as usual, by throwing the papers away. Most
evenings I don't talk about what I did at work; it's too boring,
but the Kid is always interested in animals and in birds.

"The case involves wildlife," I said. The Kid nodded. He
has thick black curls and is sometimes known as *El Greñas,* the
mophead. When I got to the parrot part of my story, his hair,
already electric, took on an extra buzz.

"My client is a bit of a blowhard," I said. "I don't know
whether or not to believe him."

"What is a blowhard?"

"Someone who likes himself too much and who talks too
much. His wife and a very rare parrot have disappeared. They
appear to have been kidnapped."

"What kind of a parrot is it?"

"An indigo macaw."

"I never heard of it. Where is it from?"

"Brazil."

"How does he treat the bird?" the Kid asked.

"Good. He feeds her treats. He lets her nibble on his ear."

"Does she like him?"

"She's crazy about him."

"The Indians say a man who is good to animals has a good heart."

"Anglos say that about a man who is good to his mother."

"*Claro,*" said the Kid. When he quoted the Indians, I figured he was really talking about himself. In this part of the world, Indian myths are so pervasive and powerful it's hard to tell where you leave off and they begin. It's easy to believe that there was once a better and more harmonious life in New Mexico, but you never know how much of the myth is true, how much of it you believe because you want to believe. Often there is nothing to go on but relics, artifacts and skeletons like the fourteen macaws found in the ruins at Chaco Canyon. Did the macaws reproduce because they'd found a harmonious home? Were the Indians breeding them for their feathers? Or their meat? Did the anthropologists and archaeologists put their own spin on the parrots' bones? Who knows? The facts are usually vague enough that you can leave your own imprint.

"If you could have been an Indian in the old days before the conquest, what kind of Indian would you have been?" I asked the Kid.

"In Mexico, an Aztec. Here, an Apache," he said, mentioning two warrior tribes. He'd have made a good Apache. His long legs and strong thighs could have covered the Chiricahua Mountains as well as a soccer field. He could look wild and romantic with a scarf tied around his head, and he wouldn't look bad in a blue coat and white pants either, the Apache scout uniform after the pale eyes arrived.

"Me too," I said, although I was grinding out a cigarette in my plate, and my legs hadn't been running anywhere lately.

"And I know *who* I'd be," the Kid said.

"Who?" Not Geronimo, I hoped; he'd already been over-emulated.

"Mangas Coloradas. He was a leader. He was six feet six inches tall and lived to be seventy years old. That was a long life for an Apache. When he was fifty he was shot by the soldiers and his men put him on a . . . how you say it? . . . a *litera*."

"A litter."

"And they ran him all the way to the doctor in Mexico."

"I'd like to have been Dextrous Horse Thief Woman," I said. "She could ride, shoot and steal horses as well as any man." Mythmaking for sure. The truth was, I hate riding, and I don't like horses. But I do like doing things as well as a man. "Did the Apaches have parrots?" I asked the Kid. "The Indians at Chaco Canyon did. Chaco isn't that far from Apache country."

"I don't know. There were parrots in that part of New Mexico then, but they only live in old Mexico now. I saw them sometimes coming across the border. The *lorobandistas* color their heads yellow so they will look like *Amazonas*. When the feathers grow, the roots show. *Amazonas* are more valuable because they can talk."

"I met a parrot named Max at UNM who imitated my voice perfectly. What do *you* hear in my voice?" I asked him.

"I hear . . . " the Kid imitated a certain sound, not perfectly, but close enough. I wouldn't want a parrot to get hold of *that* and repeat it to death.

"Is that all?" I asked him.

"I hear a lawyer sometimes. Sometimes somebody else."

"Like who?"

"I don't know. Dextrous Horse Thief Woman." He laughed.

"Um," I said.

There are voice analyzers that can tell whether or not a person is lying. Terrance Lewellen would know where to get one and how much it cost. But there isn't any equipment, as far as I know, for analyzing where you've been. I heard New York State and New Mexico in my voice, but the Kid hadn't mentioned that. Maybe the differences in states were too subtle for a non-native English speaker to notice. The differences in countries are more obvious, and in his Spanish I hear Argentina and Mexico and even the U.S.A. In his English I hear the outlaws, the solitaries, the artists, all the people who come here alone to get away from someplace else. New Mexico is a place that values roots, tradition, family, history. People come here because they are attracted to those things, but they have to sever their own ties to do it. There is the code of the communal and the code of the individual in New Mexico. Sometimes they coexist in harmony, sometimes not.

Telling the Kid about Max the parrot jump-started one of his stories, which are never very long but are always fairly complicated. I lit a cigarette, adding another layer of gravel to my voice, moving another step away from being Dextrous Horse Thief Woman. "When I was a boy in Argentina," he began, "we hear parrots on my street. They knew the children's names, and they call the names when we go by the house on the way to school and when we go home again. *Que cacofonia.*"

"What did they call you?" I asked.

"*El Pibe.*" That means kid in Argentine Spanish. "Every time I go by the house I hear *El Pibe, El Pibe,*" he squawked in a good imitation of a parrot. "That is what my brother, Sebastian, called me. Now everybody calls me that. We always hear the parrots, *pero* the curtains are always closed and we never see them."

Pero means "but," and it's the last word a native Spanish speaker gives up.

"My brother and I wanted to know what the parrots looked like, and what color they were. We knew about parrots because my uncle had them, and we gave them their food when he was away. My brother said the parrots were *Africanas.* I said they were blue-fronted *Amazonas,* a bird that lives in Argentina. Their voices are different from *Africanas.* One day we tricked them. My brother walked in front of the house and I went along the side very quiet. 'Sebastian,' the parrot said to my brother when he walked by. '*Hola,* Sebastian.' There was a space," he separated his hands a few inches, "and I looked in the window."

"What did you see?"

"An old lady," he said. He hunched up in his chair like a woman who hadn't been taking her calcium. "There were no parrots in the house, only an old lady who lived alone and sat in the window and talked to the children. She knew all our names. She was all alone and she had nothing to do."

"Why was she pretending to be a parrot?"

He shrugged. "Maybe she thought a parrot would be more interesting to children."

"Did she ever find out that you knew?"

"Never," he said.

Even though I got up early the next morning, the Kid had already left for work. It's a good idea to greet the wind goddess in the morning and bow down to her before going to bed. From my window at La Vista all you can see over the rooftops and telephone poles is the tip of the mountain, not how widely or firmly it is rooted. Still, I paid my respects.

When I got to the office, Anna stood in front of the mirror spritzing her hair with a spray bottle and scrunching it up. Anna has enough hair for three people without adding frizz, but the increase in volume did emphasize the compactness of her body. Her hair was a twenty; her body a six. She was wearing high-heeled shoes with ankle straps over black ankle socks. It was one of those fashions that can only be worn by the very desperate or very young, a style that had its time and place. The place was East Central. The time was after midnight. But what did it matter what she wore as long as she did her work?

"Could you cover the phones for a minute?" she asked me. "I have to go to the bank."

"You're spritzing your hair to go to the bank?"

"Hey. Any place you go now you're on camera."

"You're not planning to stick up the bank, are you?" And look her best on the most-wanted poster?

"No. I'm gonna use the ATM, but there's a camera there too. I don't want some guys sitting around watching the surveillance tapes and saying I'm a mess."

"Could you wait a minute?" I asked. "There's a phone call I have to make." Actually, it was a phone call I *wanted* to make, the reason, in fact, I'd come in early.

"You got it," Anna said.

I went to my office, dialed the Relationships hot line and sat through the operator's instructions, as impatient as a SWF hot on the trail of a SWM. Terrance was right again; the message had been changed. The plaintive ambisexuous voice now said, "Max a million. I am *verrry* valuable," rolling the r in the "very." The words were perfectly clear, but what the hell did they mean?

The phone rang. "For you," Anna called.

It was Terrance. "You hear the message yet?"

"Yeah."

"What do you think it means?" he asked in his gruff, hard-driving, corporate raiding voice.

"I don't know," I had to admit.

"Well, I know," he said. "Brown thinks he's gonna get a million dollars out of me. No bird's *that* valuable. You be around this afternoon?"

"Yeah."

"I'll be by," he said.

"I'll be here," I replied and hung up.

"Now I'm going to the ATM. Okay?" Anna asked me.

"Okay," I said. I listened to her walk down the sidewalk toward her car, which she'd parked in the lot tucked behind the Hamel and Harrison building, and I couldn't help comparing the sound of her footsteps to the sound of Deborah's. Deborah had been crisp and commanding in her high-heeled shoes, at least before the abduction. Anna was tentative and teetering in hers, which she never was in life. Maybe she had a loose ankle strap. Her walk had the fluttering uncertainty of prey; I'd have to warn her to be careful where she stepped in those hooker's shoes.

Terrance had said, "*I'll* be by," but he didn't show up at my office, *they* did. That's the kind of guy who calls to tell you about the vacation he just took, never mentioning that he took a woman with him. When that kind does show up with a woman, he doesn't tell you who she is. Some men like to make introductions about as much as they like to ask directions.

"This is Sara," Terrance said, sitting down in a client chair and plunking his briefcase on the floor. Sara sat next to him and dropped her beaded and fringed suede purse into her lap. He'd made an introduction of sorts, but it didn't tell me anything *I* wanted to know, like Sara who? So I began my own discovery, a combination of interrogation and observation.

"I'm Neil Hamel, Terrance's lawyer," I said.

"I know," Sara replied. "Terry told me about you." She smiled at Terrance, who didn't seem like a Terry to me. He didn't correct her, he didn't smile back. Sara was definitely a bottle blond, possibly a trophy blond. Her hair was pulled up on top of her head with wispy tendrils hanging down around her face. Her eyes were the color of a Texas bluebonnet. I'd say she was a good twenty years younger than Terrance, which didn't make her young. It made her close to forty, in fact, an age I know well, the age at which a lot of women come to New Mexico to find themselves. If they end up in Santa Fe (and I was already convinced that Sara was a Santa Fe woman), the first step is to throw out all the old clothes and buy into Santa Fe style. Sara had done that with a vengeance. The next step is usually to find a guru or a mission. No problem; there are plenty of those around. Then comes finding an affordable place to live, a job and a man, and that's where the trouble starts. There aren't many of any of the above, and there's a ton of competition (some of it rich and beautiful) for the few there are, and this at an age when a woman doesn't need competition. Santa Fe breeds female insecurity like Yuma, Arizona, breeds killer bees. Sometimes women find the life they're seeking in the city different, sometimes not. The chic life isn't always an easy life.

The upper part of Sara's outfit was a short white jacket that copied the navy blue ones the U.S. cavalry wore. The Apaches called them blue coats, but the Apaches who put them on to track down their own were considered turncoats. Indian women took the jackets from the bodies of dead soldiers, hung fringe from the epaulets and sewed bone hairpipes slanted like ribs across the chest. The decoration of the uniforms had a significance for the Indian women, but what it meant to Sara I couldn't say. I'm one of those who believes it's unwise to purchase or wear what you don't understand. In my experience Indians don't reveal themselves readily to non-Indians, and why should they? Dressing like one isn't going to make you one. When it comes to clothes, I follow the Albuquerque KISS principle: keep it simple, stupid.

With the jacket Sara wore a choker made of beads and feathers, a white broomstick-pleated skirt and tan cowboy boots. She was tall and willowy enough to carry the costume off, but her eyes were bluebonnets in the wind. They danced away from contact, and the fine lines beside her mouth were as jittery as an aspen.

"How long have you been in Santa Fe?" I asked to prove to myself that I'd been right.

"Three years," she replied. Three years is the turning point there. Either you decide it's not working and get out of town, or you stay forever. "I came out here to visit Terry and Deborah, and I stayed." She reached over to pat Terrance's bear claw hand. "Deborah's my sister," she said.

"Your *sister*?" And I'd been assuming she'd come here as an appendage to Terrance. I'd been on target about the place, but way wide of the connection.

"Her half-sister," Terrance corrected, sliding his hand out from under Sara's and reaching for his briefcase and a cigar.

"We have the same father. Deborah got his brains."

Was she implying that she got his looks? The trouble with looks is that they eventually go out the window. Brains are more dependable. I would have said that Deborah got some looks too, but she hadn't made a career out of them. Deborah had to be ten years older than Sara, which could have made her the child of the father's first marriage, and Sara the child of the second, or the third or . . .

"I'm *so* worried about Deborah." Sara picked at her fringe. "She's been getting so much attention since that *Time* article came out. Any crazy could have seen that and abducted her."

"It wasn't *any* crazy. It was Wes Brown crazy," Terrance said.

I thought I'd detected a flicker of jealousy under the pyre of sisterly admiration, and I couldn't resist fanning the flame. My motto has always been, never envy a woman until you've walked a mile in her shoes or slept a night in her bed, but I don't have a sister. "What do *you* do in Santa Fe?" I asked Sara. There weren't any university labs to run there, I knew, but there were a lot of tables to wait on.

"I'm an art consultant." She took a card from her purse and handed it to me. Sara Dumaine, it said, Zia Gallery, Art Consultant. That could mean she sold art on commission. Whether it was good art or crap art or wearable art or T-shirt art, I couldn't say. Maybe she was making a living at it, maybe not. "I think Deborah's success was hard for her to deal with; there were so many demands," Sara continued. "She was having a problem with success management?" She ended that sentence with the raised inflection of up talk, the tentative way some women have of expressing (or hiding) themselves.

Terrance pulled out his lighter and lit the cigar. "Success management, my ass," he butted in, punctuating his remark with the smoldering cigar, his version of down talk. Up talk leaves room to continue. Down talk does not. "Deborah didn't have any problem with success management. She was a bitch long before she got into *Time* magazine, and she was a bitch after. Deborah, in fact, was a habitual bitch." A man who disses the woman who proceeds you will sooner or later end up dissing you. It's a useful guide for a woman to follow through the minefield of male/female relationships, but for some other woman, not me. I wasn't looking, and if I was I'd know better than to look twice at Terrance Lewellen even if he was richer than God, especially if he was richer than God. Rich enough, anyhow, to be asked to pay a million-dollar ransom and to afford a substantial legal fee.

"Can we put some effort into getting your wife and your bird back?" I asked, doing something to earn my fee.

"I'm not paying any million dollars, I'll tell you that. I'd have to sell most of what I own to raise that kind of money."

"The gallery could sell the Lochovers for you." Sara turned toward Terrance, and her serpentine tendrils curved like dollar signs around her face.

"Anybody could sell the Lochovers," Terrance said. "After

he died, the demand for him went ballistic. Offer Brown three hundred thousand dollars."

"Will he accept that?"

"Let him make a counteroffer if he doesn't like it."

"Your wife and your bird are at risk, and the negotiations are taking up precious time," I said.

"What time?" Terrance demanded. "You call the machine, he calls the machine, we call the machine." He stood up to go, stubbing out his cigar in my ashtray. "Place my offer. I'll check in with you later."

Sara's fringe bobbed as she stood up and slung her purse over her shoulder. "Nice meeting, you," she said with a tentative but orthodontically correct smile.

"Mucho gusto," I replied.

She was a willowy aspen, Terrance a barrel cactus, but in volume he had her beat. Maybe there was a heart under all his barbs, maybe hot air. As they went through the door, Sara made a motion to pat his shoulder, but she stopped herself as if she'd seen the prickers there.

The minute they were gone and the Jag was rolling down Lead, I called the Relationships hot line and listened again to "Max a million. I am verrry valuable."

"This is Neil Hamel, Terrance Lewellen's lawyer," I replied. "Our offer is three hundred thousand dollars."

Then I wandered into the outer office where Anna and Brink were killing the day. Brink was telling Anna about his first date with the semi-full-figured DWF now known as Nancy. "She's a great cook," he said.

"What did she make?" asked Anna.

"Roast chicken with squash, cranberry sauce, corn bread and apple pie for desert." It sounded to me like she'd been to Boston Chicken.

"Stop," said Anna. "You're making me hungry. Who was that with Terrance Lewellen?" she asked me.

"His half-sister-in-law," I said. Or his soon-to-be ex-half-sister-in-law, I thought.

"Cool jacket," Anna said.

"It looks like a dead soldier's jacket," said Brink.

"It is," I replied.

"I bet it cost more than my suit."

"You're right," I said.

I burned up the afternoon dialing and redialing the Relationships line, wishing I had a button to do it for me. It wasn't till after five that I heard the miserable, digitally engineered voice say, "Not enough. Double or nothing. Indigo *dying* without mate."

4

"Six hundred thousand!" said Terrance Lewellen. "No bird in the world is worth more than a hundred." It was Friday evening, but we were still in our respective offices talking on our respective-but-disparate phones. Mine doesn't have a visual image, but the thought occurred to me that Terrance's might, and it provoked an automatic reaction. Before I knew it, I was smoothing my hair and cranking up a smile.

"You asshole," I mumbled to myself, since only one of those would be vain and stupid enough to primp for Terrance Lewellen.

"What?" he asked.

"Nothing," I replied. "Didn't you tell me that a pair of macaws is worth more than the sum of two individuals? You're getting a pair when you get Perigee back, since Colloquy is so miserable, maybe even endangered, without her mate."

"Yeah, but even a pair, even the *only* pair, isn't worth six hundred thou."

"There *is* a woman's life at stake."

"Okay, okay. I'll offer Brown four hundred to get this business over with and to make Colloquy happy again, but it's my top offer. I won't pay him one penny more." I couldn't see him, but I knew what he was doing, stabbing the air with the butt of his cigar.

"I'll place the offer," I said.

"You do that," he replied. And then, since the weekend was upon us, we exchanged numbers where we could be reached.

Before I went home I called the R line and left my message. "This is Neil Hamel. Four hundred thousand is our final offer."

The weekend—and the wait—began. The Kid worked, so there was nobody to watch me punching numbers into my home phone like I'd gone on a Relationships bender. The R line had the addictive pull of popping bubbles in bubble wrap or culling a cigarette from the pack. The first thing I did when I got up on Saturday morning was dial in; the message remained the same: "Not enough. Double or nothing. Indigo *dying* without mate." I called while I was having a cup of Red Zinger tea after my shower. Same unhappy voice, same message. What the heck, I was doing my job, I rationalized, and fifteen minutes later I dialed again. The only way I know how to quit something is to do it to wretched excess. By midafternoon I'd reached the saturation point. I made one more call, got one more message, put on my running shoes, went up to Miranda Martinez Canyon and took a hike.

Miranda Martinez Canyon is a green *V* wedged deep into the rocky brown Sandias, a woman's canyon at the base of the wind woman's peak. At the parking lot the only vegetation you see are the skinny, porous arms of the cholla and an occasional juniper the size of a boulder. The farther you climb, the more piñones and scrub oaks appear. Bushes turn into trees, the vegetation gets greener and lusher, until the pine needles have the shimmering weight of fur. I never hike to the end of the canyon myself, only far enough to forget I'm in a city. I don't know much about Miranda Martinez or why a canyon was named after her, but my name on a canyon is a mark I'd like to leave behind. Since it was a weekend the trail was full of chattering hikers and barking dogs, but I can wander fifty feet off the trail and convince myself I'm in a wilderness, and that's what makes Albuquerque a livable city—go fifteen minutes in any direction and you're out of it. I climbed to a favorite hiding place and hid behind a rock. The gray sprawl of the city was visible through a notch in the boulders. I looked once at the shimmering river and the monoliths of the downtown buildings, turned my back and looked away. Two hang gliders circled the Sandia peaks, red on top, white-bellied as a hawk underneath. They caught the wind, turned and drifted in and out of vision. The wind goddess was up there lazily exhaling and puffing the hang gliders up, inhaling and dropping them down. She was in a relaxed mood today, but I've seen her when she was pissed. Who hasn't? Those are the days when she tosses boulders down the mountain, smashes tumbleweeds into your fender and trash in your fence, when she flaps open the chinks in your armor and her fury invades your soul. Some religions worship at the altar of the ornery goddess.

I watched the hang gliders rise and fall and wondered where the other players in the kidnapping drama were and what they were doing. Colloquy would be squawking, pulling out her feathers and taking a chunk out of any stranger who got too close. Perigee might well be doing the same. Terrance could be dialing the Relationships line obsessively or he could be as in control as he pretended to be and playing golf. Sara Dumaine might be selling some rich tourist some bad art. It was a Saturday in August, high season for the art market in

Santa Fe. What about Deborah Dumaine and Wes Brown? I wondered. Where were they? Maybe he had her locked in or tied up somewhere near the border in Door. Maybe she was a pissed-off wind goddess who'd had the wind knocked out of her. Maybe she was in serious danger. Maybe she was dead.

There's always the possibility that a kidnapper will get paranoid and kill the hostages, a danger that appeared to concern me more than it did Terrance Lewellen. It couldn't be in the hostages' best interests to drag out the negotiations. What's two hundred thousand if you've got it and lives are at risk? But I wasn't representing the hostages' best interests. I was representing my client's, and that's the trouble with being a lawyer. It puts you in the middle of the action, but not necessarily on the right side, if there is a right side. Representing my client while keeping the big picture in mind was a straddling act. Would Baxter, Johnson handle it any better? I asked myself. Probably not was my answer.

I don't wear a watch, but the piñones' shadows were spreading like a Navajo woman's skirts and telling me I'd stayed too long. Miranda Martinez closes at dark. While I'd been thinking about my case, everybody else had been going home. I was all alone as I walked down the trail. While being up there alone at dusk might be dangerous, it was also what made it interesting. As I walked I watched the lights of Albuquerque spread across the Valley and twinkle on one by one. The colors I saw were red, yellow and blue, the colors of stars in the blackest of skies. For one brief moment there was a balance, the number of lights on the ground reflected the number of stars in the sky, but the lights multiplied like bacteria, reducing the stars to a pale imitation. The lights that came on in the city extinguished the lights in the sky. The spotlights from the Sandia pueblo power bingo parlor were doing their spinning gambler's dance, annoying a lot of people and outshining the stars. Who would ever have thought the Sandias would be guilty of stealing the night? It could, from one perspective anyway, be considered sacrilegious.

When I got home my place at La Vista was dark. The red message light on the machine blinked on and off. I punched the Play button, and Terrance Lewellen's voice said "Call me." Before I did I turned on my lights and tried the R line again. I didn't get the same message. I didn't get any message. All I got was a ringing void, the buzzing black hole of the audio world.

"You get that buzz?" Terrance asked me when I reached him on his C phone.

"Yeah."

"Damn Wes Brown's hide," he said. "I went to see Colloquy this afternoon, and she was as sorry as a plucked chicken. Her feathers were all over the floor. She wouldn't even eat the granola I took her. Rick's getting ornery and making more noise about calling the police."

"What do you want to do?" I asked.

"Wait it out." The feral yellow at the center of Terrance's eyes was probably gleaming somewhere inside his dark, purring Jaguar. The backbeat I was hearing was the sound of the lonesome highway. Terrance would enjoy talking from his car phone; if he didn't like the way the conversation went he could always say he was going into a tunnel. We don't have tunnels in New Mexico, but that wouldn't be likely to stop him. "Brown's got us by the short hairs—for now," he said, "but I'll get mine before this is over."

I'd like to reserve a hole in the black volcanic rock of the malpais for people who make me wait. To me, waiting compares to lying in the hot sun watching the vultures circle overhead. The longer the wait, the more dangerous for the hostages, the more nerve-racking for me. When the Kid showed up with stuffed sopapillas from Tomas's on Sunday night, I told him they tasted like monkey chow. When Anna showed up with a new hairdo (narrow on the sides, high on the top) on Monday morning, I told her she looked like a clipped poodle. When Brink tried to tell me about his weekend with Nancy, I told him to buzz off. On Tuesday the man from the gas company blasted Rush Limbaugh from his car radio while he read our meter.

"Turn that right-wing asshole off or get out of my yard," I yelled out the window with the bluster of a pissed-off wind goddess.

"Jeez, what a bitch," he said, leaving the scene and driving down Lead with Rush Limbaugh still blasting his propaganda. It was a change from the usual booming basses.

The week's divorce was a woman named Roberta Dovalo from Ruidoso, a city whose name always gets mispronounced in New Mexico.

"I hear you do divorces," she said.

"That's right," I replied.

"Can't get me a lawyer in Ruidoso." She had a country girl's twang, but she got Ruidoso down.

"Why not?"

"They're all friends with my husband, Jimmie."

"You got any kids?"

"Twins," she said. "Jimmie's been cheatin' on me. I want to git him for every penny I can git." It had the sound of a country and western song. I envisioned Roberta on my mental screen, wearing cowgirl boots and a short red dress with a full skirt and silver tips on the collar.

"New Mexico is a community property state," I said. "Unless there's a prenuptial agreement, it all gets split right down the middle." People have been known in the heat of separation anxiety to take an ax and split everything (including the refrigerator) in two.

"Damn," she said.

"We should be able to get custody of the children and child support."

"That's good."

"Who's your husband's lawyer, do you know?"

"You ain't gonna tell him what I tell you, are you?" The nervousness in her voice made me wonder if she hadn't been doin' some cheatin' herself.

"Everything you tell me is in confidence," I said.

"That's good," she said.

"Can you get up here sometime so we can talk about it?"

She made an appointment for the following week, left her phone number and hung up.

Whenever I slept, Deborah and Perigee invaded my dreams. Monday, Tuesday and Wednesday I made a string of phone calls to the R line but there were no new messages, only the same black buzz. Wednesday night my dreams got tangled up. I dreamed about a red-haired parrot, a blue-feathered woman and a telephone that wouldn't answer. On Thursday morning Anna handed me a manila envelope as I came in the door.

"This was on the floor," she said. "Someone dropped it through the mail slot last night."

"Did you open it?" I asked.

She shook her head. "It's from the kidnapper. I have a feeling. Who else drops envelopes through the slot?"

I was conscious of the evidence-destroying nature of fingerprints, but I also had to read the message, so I took a letter opener and lifted the flap. I picked the envelope up gingerly by the corners and shook. A lock of hair and a feather fell onto the clean piece of computer paper I'd laid on Anna's desk. The feather was a match for my indigo plume. The hair was dyed red. Proof that the kidnapper had the hostages except that the feather could have come from Colloquy and the hair could belong to anybody who used Clairol. The message, which was on an unfolded piece of Xerox paper, read: "Offer accepted. Indigo dying without mate. No police. Put two hundred thousand in Deborah's BankWest account. Will pick up at ATM on Tramway or at Midnight Cowboy or Page One between eight and nine P.M. Friday. Thousand-dollar bills. Will deposit black-light instructions for rest of ransom and mates' return." The words had been clipped from a newspaper (most likely the *Journal*), taped to a piece of paper (I could see the corners of the tape) and xeroxed.

"Why'd he send a copy?" Anna asked.

"With all that cutting and pasting, the original had to be full of fingerprints. Also, a xeroxed copy would pick up less hair or anything else that could identify the perp." The Xerox, in fact, was antiseptically clean. The perp wasn't as dumb as Terrance had indicated.

I sent Anna out to buy some clear plastic folders. We put the letter in one, the hair and feather in another and taped them shut.

"If I have to put the ransom in all three of those machines, it'll cost me six hundred thousand," said Terrance when I reached him on his C phone. He had to be at home; I didn't hear the telltale whoosh of traffic or wind. He could be plopped in a leather armchair in his den with his legs on an ottoman, smoking a cigar and admiring his art collection. "I can't get that kind of money unless I sell the Lochovers."

"You'll only need four hundred of it for an hour. Don't you know a banker who'll stake you for that length of time?"

"I don't know anybody who'll do it without bleeding me dry. Of all the bankers in Albuquerque, we'll have to deal with Charlie Register at BankWest. Deborah *would* have to have her account with him."

"What's wrong with Charlie Register?"

"He's got a hankering for my Lochovers and a crush on my wife."

"Can the ATMs be programmed to make the transaction?" I asked him, since he knew more about the computer highway than I did.

"Sure. To arrange the ransom transfer, the bank could substitute thousand-dollar bills for the twenties in those three ATMs. Register's programmers can set it up so that no card but Deborah's can access the ATMs for that hour. As soon as the money comes out of one machine, the others can be programmed to shut down until the four hundred thousand goes back to the bank. Brown's only going to nail me once. Besides, my security men will be watching those machines and following Brown like hawks. If I don't get Perigee back alive and well, Brown'll be dead meat."

"And what happens if Deborah doesn't come back? Will you agree to call in the FBI then?" I asked.

"Only if I have to," he said.

"You do."

"Okay, okay."

"What's a black light?"

"A way of reading invisible ink."

"Do you think Brown has accomplices?"

"Naah. Brown's a loner. He's too screwed up to work with anyone else."

"Then why involve three machines? They're too far apart for Brown to get to all of them in one hour."

"He's so stupid he thinks that'll make it harder for me to track him."

Then we got to what I thought was the deep wrinkle in the fabric of this plan. "Why would Brown set up such an obvious way to make a money transfer?" I asked, thinking even as

I said it that the most obvious is often the hardest to see.

"Because when it comes to brains, he's down a quart," Terrance said.

Terrance, who was by no means a loner, asked me to go to Charlie Register's office with him. The office was in BankWest's Tramway branch in the high Heights and had a view that went into the last century. I had the feeling that a pair of high-powered binoculars would show Apaches galloping across the horizon with the cavalry hot on their tail. There was a thick gray carpet on Charlie Register's floor. His desk and credenza were made of teak and devoid of clutter. There wasn't a single sheet of paper or Post-it to mar the surface of his furniture. The only object in view was a polished petal-shaped bowl of Nambe ware on top of the credenza. It was a change from the usual collection of Indian rugs, pottery, snakes and coyotes that straddle the border between good taste and bad. The room was lit by ceiling fixtures and a long-necked halogen lamp that balanced as gracefully as a crane on its skinny leg. There was only one painting, and it took up half a wall. It was a painting I'd hang on my own wall if I had a hundred times more house and a thousand times more money. Close up it was an Impressionist's abstraction of feathery brush strokes and dabs of paint. From a few feet back, the brush strokes became ripples, twigs, branches, grass. Across the room the painting evolved into winter marsh colors and the reflecting ponds of the Bosque del Apache. It was subtle and exquisite. Not all New Mexico scenery is grandiose. There's a delicate, hidden side. As far as I was concerned, there was only one flaw in the painting—the artist, Albert Lochover, had scrawled his name in large letters and large ego across the corner.

Terrance, who could no more stop negotiating than an Amazon could stop imitating, walked up to the wall, sank his boots into the carpet and inspected the painting. "The later work is better," he pronounced.

Charlie Register looked at me and chuckled. Maybe the joke was that he too saw through Terrance, but that didn't necessarily mean that he saw what I saw. "Eat your heart out, Lewellen," Charlie said. "I wouldn't trade three of *your* late Lochovers for *my* early Bosque." He extended his hand to shake mine. Terrance hadn't been any better at man to woman introductions than he'd been at woman to woman. "I'm Charlie Register," he said.

"Neil Hamel," I replied, shaking the banker's smooth hand.

"Pleasure to meet you, ma'am."

"Mucho gusto."

Charlie Register's appearance was as subdued and elegant as the painting. His suit, shirt and tie were a careful blend of neutrals, very quiet, very expensive. His boots were a plain and polished brown. He was about fifty. His hair was silvery blond, his face friendly and ruddy. He was only a few inches taller than Terrance, but they were a critical few. He didn't need to compensate by any other type of expansion. Charlie Register didn't need to compensate for much. His manner was relaxed, western and jovial enough to make him a third- or fourth-generation New Mexican, but it was a manner, possibly even as big a front as Terrance's oil driller's bull.

"She's my lawyer." Terrance pulled out a cigar and lit up.

"No more Buddy Baxter?" Charlie asked.

"Not on this one," Terrance said.

Charlie winked at me. "Lewellen always did like doing business with women. How's your mother?" he asked Terrance.

"Pretty good," he said.

"To what do I owe the pleasure of this visit?" Charlie asked.

"Some So-Cal cowboy is trying to take advantage of me," Terrance said.

"Take advantage of *you*, Lewellen? I don't believe it." Charlie's eyes twinkled.

"He's holding my indigo macaw captive." Terrance told Charlie Register the story of the kidnapping and the negotiations, most of it anyway, and Charlie was quiet enough to listen. Terrance didn't tell Charlie how he came by the tape. Charlie didn't ask.

"Deborah's been kidnapped?" Charlie asked.

"Yeah," Terrance replied.

"Damn." Charlie leaned forward and placed the palms of his hands on the surface of his desk. "Don't you think you ought to be worrying about getting *her* back?"

Terrance shrugged. "The marriage was over."

"So what? Deborah's life is in danger. Why aren't you calling in the FBI?"

"That was my advice," I said.

"They'll screw it up," said Terrance. "Can you get your programmers to reprogram those three machines so Brown can take the money out?" He showed Charlie the feather and the lock of hair, and handed him the note with the addresses of the ATMs.

"Hell, Lewellen, two of those are our most active machines. I'd have to shut them down to my other customers, and that's not gonna make them happy."

"It's only for an hour," Terrance said.

"It's a prime hour. Everybody's getting their money for the weekend. In order for the kidnapper to take it out, you're gonna have to put it in. Where are you going to get that kind of money *if* I agree to do it?"

"I'm involved in a little company that's manufacturing a testosterone patch. If I have to, I'll sell some stock." If there was anything neither of these guys needed it was testosterone, even though they were into middle age and beyond. They exuded a buzz that was as old as mankind, maybe older, making me feel like a spectator at a mating contest or an athletic event. Like a couple of kids practicing slap shots, they were trying to beat each other and raise their own level at the same time, loving every minute of the competition. The one advantage big boys have over big girls in navigating the business world—their world—is that little boys learn how to win at sports, learn how to lose, learn how to compete. My big brother taught me those rules on the ice-covered Irish pond in Ithaca, New York, where we skated when we were growing up.

"You got six hundred thousand worth of testosterone stock to sell?" Charlie asked Terrance.

"Not right now I don't. The company's just getting off the ground." Terrance looked around for an ashtray and settled on an empty wastepaper basket.

"Well then, where's the money comin' from?"

"I can come up with four. I'm asking you to lend the rest."

"Thousand-dollar bills are still legal tender, but they're not being printed anymore. If I get them, I'm supposed to turn them over to the Federal Reserve."

"I know. You lend me two hundred, I'll come up with the thousand-dollar bills." Terrance didn't say where he'd get the bills, but the Indian gambling casinos we have in New Mexico were one possible source. If that didn't work, there was always Las Vegas. He peered down at the carpet, poked it with his boot and made an unsuccessful stab at humility.

There was a pause while they studied each other and Charlie considered how much of Terrance's hide he wanted or how badly he wanted Deborah to be rescued. It was a long pause. "How's the kidnapper going to access Deborah's account?" he asked finally.

"He's got her ATM card." Terrance shrugged. "He'll twist her arm till he gets the PIN."

"What do I get for collateral?"

"My word."

"Your word's not going to satisfy my shareholders."

"You only need the money for an hour, Charlie. Your guys can program the machines so that once the two is taken out of one machine, the others shut down."

"My systems analyst is a woman."

"She can do it then," Terrance replied.

"She's good, but I'm still taking a two hundred thousand risk."

"What risk?"

"Well, like I said, I do have my shareholders to consider. I'll need some collateral." Charlie seemed to enjoy tossing around the word shareholders, but my impression was that he ran BankWest exactly as he wanted to run it, by the seat of his pants.

"What are we talking?" asked Terrance.

"Your Lochovers." This was where they'd known the negotiations were heading, but to them the contest was more fun than the goal. "There's an empty space on my wall needs to be filled up."

"Looks good empty; sets off what you already have."

"No collateral, no deal."

"All right. I'll put up *Riverrun.*"

Charlie shook his head, and his hair was spun gold under the overhead light. "That's an inferior work."

"Bullshit. It's one of his best."

"It's not enough, Lewellen."

"What do you want?"

"What have you got?"

Terrance paused before he spoke. "*Riverrun, Gila Bend,* and *Santa Barbara Canyon.*"

Charlie thought before he answered. "Give me all of them," he said.

"That's highway robbery."

"Those are my terms," Charlie said. "Take 'em or leave 'em."

"All right," Terrance growled. "You get the paintings for one hour, the duration of the ATM transaction. Neil will write up a collateral agreement."

Charlie shook his head. "One month."

"What the hell for?"

"So I can look at them."

"Two weeks."

"If anything goes wrong, the bank keeps the paintings to cover my losses. We'll use your insurance appraisals to determine value." Knowing Terrance, the insurance appraisals were way inflated, but he didn't argue the point. The game was over; Register had won. "I want you to know I'm agreeing to this only because Deborah's in danger," Charlie said.

"Yeah," said Terrance. The starch had gone out of his shirt, but not for long; he was already looking for the next challenge. "Set it up so we can watch the transfer on your monitors, will you?"

"I'll do that."

"And while you're at it, why don't you take the Spanish off your ATM screens. This is America. Let those wets learn English."

"Spanish has been around these parts since 1540," Charlie said.

"The Indians were here before that. Why don't you put Indian on your screens too?"

"In some places we do."

"You'll get the papers drawn up by tomorrow morning?" Terrance asked me.

"Yeah," I said. "The bills used for the transfer should be xeroxed."

"Good idea," said Charlie.

"What for?" demanded Terrance.

"To record the serial numbers so they can be traced," I said.

"I'll get somebody on it," Charlie said.

5

I had other business that day, including a trip to family court, a place I dislike more than any other. The family court judge receives a lot of death threats, and it's easy to understand why. Anybody who has the power to take somebody's kids away is not going to be popular. My client, Tommy Denton, had already lost his son and was trying to get him back. The judge ordered tests and counseling. Nothing was concluded, everything was postponed; that's to be expected in family court. When we were done, I took Tommy to La Posada for a drink. It was happy hour, the band had a retro blues singer with the raspy voice of a Janis Joplin without the Southern Comfort. La Po is full of hand-carved beams and Old Mexico charm. Tommy had the blues; we stayed too long.

It was getting dark when we left the bar. Tommy had parked his pickup beside a yellow curb and had accumulated two parking tickets. A true New Mexican, he ripped the tickets into pieces and let the wind goddess carry them away. He climbed into his one-eyed Ford, thanked me for my help and offered me a ride to my Nissan. I declined; the car was only a few blocks away, and I felt like walking. A cowboy and a cowgirl passed me on their way to La Po. She wore a hat and a black dress with cut-out ovals for her shoulders. He wore a black hat and gloves with cuffs wide enough to convince me he was only a cowboy for the night. You see lots of one-night cowpokes around here. It was a change from daytime when the suits (male and female) walk around with cell phones on their ears.

A kid on a skateboard jumped the curb and let out a whoop. A police siren whined. The night had a raw and sensual edge. I wondered where the Kid was and what he was doing, but I put that thought out of my head because I had to get back to my office and prepare the agreement for Terrance Lewellen's collateral.

My car was only a few blocks closer than my office, but nobody in Albuquerque ever stops to think if the distance is worth the gas. Downtown street life is intense but narrow, and in a few blocks I was out of it, all alone on the empty sidewalk except for the homeless woman who'd made her ragged bed in an office building's vestibule. It looked snug if you didn't get too close and the wind was blowing the dumpster smell away. The homeless woman sat up, stuck out her hand and said excuse me in a loud voice. I slipped her a five and crossed the street, stepping one inch too close to the truck that was parked in front of the Nissan. "Back off," the truck squawked, "protected by the Viper."

"Shut up," I said, inserting my key in my lock. The only protection the Nissan had was that it was too shabby to steal. I drove it to Hamel and Harrison and pulled into the narrow driveway that abuts our building. A full-sized car would scrape its fenders against the wall; we've got the gouges in the stucco to prove it. As I passed the grated windows on the driveway side, I noticed that a light was on deep in my office.

It had been daylight when I left. Had Anna left the light on? I wondered for the brief instant before it went out.

Our parking lot is right behind the building, with spaces marked FOR OCCUPANTS ONLY. None of them were occupied, but I didn't park there. I kept going down the one-lane access road till I reached the lot behind Sanchez and Sanchez, our neighboring lawyers. I pulled in, turned off the engine, reached into my purse, found what I wanted, opened the car door, picked up the running shoes on the floor and put them on. I walked down the driveway as careful as a scout, keeping close to the shadows of the buildings, glad I wasn't in Anna's or Deborah's spike-heeled shoes. Something long, dark and feral slipped behind a garbage can and set a metal lid that was lying on the ground rattling. A police siren wailed from the direction of Central. It might have been prudent to call the police, but by the time they got here the intruder—if there was an intruder—could be long gone. I wanted to know who he or she was, and what that person was looking for. It's moments like this that make me wish Hamel and Harrison had an alarm system to respond to break-ins with strobe lights and barking dogs. The deadliest part of most robberies is walking in on a thief, but that's when the person being robbed is unprepared and the robber is a frightened teenager looking for cash and/or alcohol. You weren't likely to find any cash or alcohol at Hamel and Harrison, and I wasn't expecting to find a frightened teenager.

The only way to break into our office is through the back door; we have bars on the windows and front door. The bars are not impenetrable, but they'd take most of the night to get off. As I rounded the parking lot corner I could see that the back door had been jimmied open.

I might have waited for the intruder to come out, but I wasn't sure he or she was still in, and waiting has never been my MO. If I did it my way, I had surprise on my side and the possibility of discovering exactly what the intruder was after. The streetlights on Lead were bright enough to turn the edges of the parking lot dark and fluid. I submerged myself in the shadows as I circumnavigated the lot. When I reached the back stoop, I waited for a bass on wheels to cruise down Lead. Concealing my own noise in the beat, I carefully pushed the jimmied door open. As I stepped into the hallway I saw that the light in my office was on again. I know the places where the hallway floor squeaks and I avoided them, making my way slowly, timing each footstep to the beat of a passing car. I passed the confusion that was Brink's office, the bathroom that needed cleaning, and stood beside the doorway to my own mess. I took a deep breath, wondering if I was going to find a stranger or an acquaintance, a professional or an amateur, a cowboy or a yuppie, a man or a woman, a handgun or a semi-automatic. I clutched my weapon, extended my arm and stepped into the office.

"Don't move," I said, sinking into a crouch and giving the Punch a shake. Supposedly, its range is ten feet in still air. The air in my office was so still it was dead, and the space was only twelve feet wide. I had it covered.

The intruder was bent over my filing cabinet with a pocket light in hand, absorbed in deciphering the filing system. I could have saved him the trouble had he asked; there isn't one. While he looked up and slowly comprehended what was happening, I hit the light switch on the wall, blinked and took a good look around the office. The computer on my desk had been turned on. Apparently he had already made his way through the computer files, not an impossible task for a scientifically minded person, but he wouldn't have found anything there. He wouldn't find anything in my file cabinet either. Most of the evidence in the case he was investigating was oral: the tape Terrance Lewellen had made of the kidnapping, the microcassettes I had made of my conversations with the R line.

I'd left them in my desk drawer, unmarked, Terrance's on the left, mine on the right. That was my filing system. The only written evidence, other than my fee arrangement with Terrance Lewellen, was the note from the kidnapper, and that happened to be in my car along with a lock of hair and a parrot feather.

"Oh, shit," the intruder said. He was wearing jeans, a T-shirt and granny glasses. His name was Rick Olney. He didn't have the knee-jerk reaction of so many breakers and enterers. If he had a weapon, he wasn't going for it.

"What *is* that stuff?" he asked.

"Capsicum spray. You move and you'll be blind, vomiting, choking and gasping for breath. And that's just for starters. You're not packing, are you?"

"You mean do I have a weapon?"

"Yeah."

"No."

"Get up." I made him go over to the wall and lean against it with his arms extended and his forehead to the plaster. His glasses fell off as he put his face to the wall, and he made a motion to pick them up. "Leave them," I said. I picked up the glasses myself and put them on my desk. Aiming the red pepper spray at his head with one hand, I frisked him with the other, feeling him tremble under the touch of my free hand. Fear? I wondered. I'd never felt anybody tremble in fear. I'd never felt such a red blood cell rush of power either. It wasn't a feeling I wanted to get rid of, but it wasn't a feeling I'd want to remember. At the end of my search I discovered that he was unarmed, that he had nothing in his pockets that belonged to me, that he had a good body and that I could be just as excited by power and a good body as anyone else. I ordered him to sit down in a client chair.

He reached behind him and straightened his ponytail. "I'm really sorry about this," he said.

"You oughta be. Breaking and entering is a crime punishable by—"

"You're not going to file charges, are you?" He blinked his eyes, trying to bring me into focus. He had nice eyes without the glasses, brown and soft.

"Why not?"

"It would ruin my career."

"Looks to me like you're trying to ruin my career."

"There'd be no one left to run the lab if I went to jail." True enough. "I didn't take anything."

"Not for lack of trying."

"I'll pay you for the door. I promise. Don't tell Terrance you found me here."

"I have to tell Terrance; he's my client."

"Oh, God," he said. "I'll be in jail forever if he has anything to say about it."

I didn't think so. Terrance needed Rick Olney to manage the lab and take care of his parrot. "What were you looking for?" I asked.

"Anything that could explain Deborah's disappearance and tell me where she is. Terrance is responsible. I know it."

It wouldn't be the first time a husband had faked a kidnapping to get rid of an annoying wife. It was an idea I wouldn't have given voice to myself, but I didn't stop him from doing it.

"He's a power-hungry man. He hates Deborah, and he'll do anything to get out of the marriage. Anything. Especially if he thinks it'll save him money."

Anybody could fake evidence and clip the *Journal*, I knew, and Terrance's money could buy a digital voice changer just as fast as Wes Brown's.

"Where'd you get the feather?" he asked, pointing to the one in the glass on my desk.

"Terrance gave it to me."

"If you know where Deborah is or what he's done with her, tell me, please."

"I don't know where she is," I said. "And that's all I can tell you. Terrance is my client, and I am not at liberty to talk about his affairs with you or anyone else."

"Do you have to tell him I was here?"

"Yes. Now unless you have something pertinent to say, I want you out of here. I have work to do."

"Do you always work this late?" Some of his hair had fallen out of the ponytail and curled around his face. He brushed it away. I was close enough by now for our eyes to quickly meet and quickly dart away. I handed him back his glasses. Had the circumstances been different, we might have been friendly. We might even have flirted. He was only a few years younger than the Kid, but they were a critical few, and the Kid's background aged him, in my eyes anyway.

"Not always, but I had a drink with a client at La Posada, and there's a job I have to get done tonight so I came back here." If I hadn't, the back door would have been open all night, and who knows who we'd have found sleeping in our chairs in the morning.

"Was Deep Purple playing at La Po?" he asked me.

"The blues band?"

"Yeah."

"Yes."

"I like the blues. They have a lead singer who sounds just like Janis Joplin."

"She's grittier than Janis Joplin was," I said, thinking that Janis Joplin had been oil-town gritty.

"You were lucky to have lived through the sixties. The music was better then."

True enough. Some days I felt like I was walking around with a big six-o branded into my forehead. "Right. Tell me about Deborah," I said since he seemed to feel like chatting.

"What do you want to know?"

"How did she feel about Terrance?"

"She loved him, then she hated him, then she loved to hate him. It always was a difficult relationship."

"Does she have a big ego?"

The flash in his eyes made him look downright appealing. "And why shouldn't she?" he asked. "She's accomplished a lot."

"And Alice? Has she accomplished a lot?"

"No, not as much as Deborah anyway, but she's good with birds." Talking about Alice had brought a blush to his cheeks. He put the granny glasses back on.

"Go for it," I said.

"Excuse me?"

"Cut your hair, stop trying to be smarter than everyone else and go for it. Alice would notice."

"How do you know?"

"I'm a woman. Trust me. I know. And get rid of the glasses."

"These are John Lennon glasses."

"John Lennon could sing. Can you?"

"No."

"Then get rid of the glasses. Stuff the sixties. Find your own style and music." That was my advice for the evening. I like to give advice as much as anyone, but I had a collateral agreement to bang out. "Now get out of here; I have work to do."

"Thanks," he said.

"Por nada," I replied.

6

Terrance's comment on the break-in was, "I'll deal with him later." He got to Charlie's office before I did on Friday evening, and he'd kept his part of the bargain by delivering the Lochovers. *Gila Bend* was already hanging on the wall next to *The Bosque*. The other two were leaning in the corner. The paintings on the wall were perfectly matched in every way, like two strands of DNA, like a pair of Russian figure skaters, like Perigee and Colloquy. The early *Bosque* seemed even more beautiful with the late *Gila* at its side. They complemented each other in color and in spirit. *The Bosque* had the subdued reds and browns of winter. *Gila Bend* was autumn's old gold. And under the leaves of each, the blue water flowed. Up close both had a feathery attention to detail that from a distance became something else. After seeing these paintings together, I couldn't help thinking that separating them would be a crime.

Charlie stood under the ceiling fixture that highlighted the gold and silver in his hair. "They're a pair, aren't they?" he asked me.

"Yes."

"Take care of my paintings," Terrance said.

"Taking care of assets is my business," Charlie said.

When I walked in the men had been arguing about the use of security people to monitor the money drop. They resumed the argument. Terrance's plan, he said, was that his men would pick Wes Brown up at the ATM and tail him until Terrance got his property back.

"We do have a federal and a local police force with experience in these matters that your tax dollars are paying for," Charlie said.

"They'll screw it up." Terrance stuck to his guns. "My guys are good. They could follow Brown into the bathroom without being made."

"Where'd you get them?" Charlie asked.

"ABC."

"That place will hire anyone who'll pack a piece."

"Who do you use?"

"A-1."

"They'll hire anyone who'll work for minimum wage. You get what you pay for."

"Not always," said Charlie.

"I'm not going through with this without my men," Terrance said.

Charlie looked at his watch. "It's too late to change the plan now. Let's get on with it." He led us down the hall to BankWest's electronic surveillance room, where TV screens were mounted on the wall to monitor the ATMs.

I've never thought much about surveillance myself; when you've got nothing, you've got nothing to hide. Until the Circle K murder I believed ATM cameras came on when the customer accessed the machine. The Circle K case taught me that the camera is always on, and it records whatever happens to step in front of its eye.

We sat around the table in the windowless room that was command central and watched the monitors. It wasn't quite eight yet, but the cameras were already reporting back from the selected ATMs. Someone had left an ashtray on the table, a good thing; this could become a two-pack night. I lit up and watched the customers as they approached the cameras. Their faces widened as they got close, like curious fish. We might have been scientists observing them through a porthole. The customers were as silent as deep-sea dwellers too, but every now and then one of them mouthed an angry word because after eight the machines refused to take any card but Deborah Dumaine's.

"The kidnapper will go to the mall." Terrance spoke with his know-it-all executive authority. "They like to collect ransoms with lots of people around. Besides, it's right next to the Midnight Cowboy. He can always hang around there unnoticed until he's ready to collect the drop." Unless, of course, he was a good-looking cowboy; they never go unnoticed. I hadn't asked Terrance how good-looking the suspect was; when it came to Wes Brown, Terrance Lewellen had blinders on.

Our eyes turned toward Monitor Number 1, where the mall camera was recording and timing all that it saw. The door to Midnight Cowboy was visible in the background, but nobody happened to be going in or out. A woman who was wearing a squash blossom silver necklace walked up to the machine, inserted her card, punched in her PIN and blocked our view of the Midnight Cowboy door. She stepped up close and squinted, apparently trying to read the out of service notice. "I'll be damned," she mouthed and turned away.

I'd driven around that morning, scouted the various drop sites and made my choice. "He'll go to Tramway," I said. "It's more isolated." That ATM was tucked into a lonely corner of a supermarket parking lot in the foothills of the Sandias. "He'll have more time to collect the money without being noticed. How's he going to do that at the mall?"

"He'll create a diversion," Terrance said.

Alone? I wondered.

Our eyes turned toward the Tramway monitor. The camera was registering no customers at the moment, just a guy hanging around in the background. There was a blank, white warehouse wall behind him and beyond that, barely visible on the screen, the base of the Sandias. The only way he could have been more obvious was if he'd been wearing the turban of a Sikh security guard.

"No kidnapper's going to use that ATM with your security man in the background," I said. "You'd have to be down more than a quart—you'd have to be running on empty—to collect a drop with that guy there."

"You get what you pay for," Charlie said.

Terrance walked up close to the screen, took a good look, got on his cell phone and called his security.

"Get some cover, you asshole," he snapped.

The security guard obeyed Terrance's orders and stepped out of sight—of the camera anyway.

"Ever since Laura Simonson got held up at that machine, women won't use it," Charlie Register said. "We're thinking about shutting it down."

"How's she doing?" I asked.

"Not good. The robber knocked her to the ground and gave her a concussion." Another victim of Albuquerque crime. We see them nightly on the six o'clock news.

"My choice would be Page One," Charlie said. "That's a busy area; women like that machine."

"We're not looking for a woman," Terrance said. "We're looking for a man."

"Wherever you find a woman, you'll find a man," said Charlie.

Page One Bookstore is the Times Square of Albuquerque. If you hang out there long enough, sooner or later everybody you know in town will show up. As we watched the Page One monitor, a woman in a baseball cap, white leggings and running shoes came up to the machine, inserted her card and smiled for the camera. She tried it twice, not believing the machine had rejected her.

"Shit," she fish-mouthed, taking back her card.

My eyes turned back to Midnight Cowboy, where a guy in a fedora slouched up to the window, glanced at his reflection in the screen and straightened his hat brim. "What about him?" I asked.

"He's not Wes Brown," Terrance said.

"An accomplice?"

"Naah. Brown's a loner."

That ATM rejected the slouch as it had everyone else. "Screw you," fedora mouthed.

"Nice hat," I said.

"Good way to hide a bald spot," said Charlie.

"Um," said Terrance.

"This operation is costing me, Lewellen."

"Me too," said Terrance, eyeing his Lochovers.

Seeing the world through the ATM cyclops was entertaining for a while, but it was the same thing over and over; a face appeared at the screen, got rejected, went away. Fedora showed up again at Page One and got even more pissed than he had at Midnight Cowboy. I didn't blame him. Who'd want to spend their evening visiting ATMs? A lot of people went to Page One and Midnight Cowboy, only a few to Tramway, and all of them were male: a couple of skateboarders in turned-backward hats, a policeman in uniform, a cowboy. I'd never make it as a police officer or a cowboy myself; it's too hard to make the transition from slow boredom to quick terror.

Terrance grabbed my arm. "That's him," he said, pointing toward the Midnight Cowboy machine, where a cowboy was sauntering up to the screen. "Goddamn."

The cowboy looked at the ground as he walked, and his face was shadowed by a black hat, the kind of hat, the Apaches say, that fries your brains in the summer sun.

"How can you tell?" I asked. "All I see is the crown of the hat."

"I know his walk," Terrance said.

The suspect did have a distinctive, shuffling walk. Had there been any dust, he would have been kicking it. He wore a cowboy's wide-striped shirt (I could see a pack of cigarettes in the breast pocket), jeans that hadn't yet had the stiffness washed out of them, and a backpack. The clothes cowboys put on to come to town tend to be newer than other people's, giving them an untouched-by-civilization look. This cowboy walked up to the ATM, hitched up his pants, reached into his hip pocket and took out a card. He tipped his hat back, stared at the screen and gave us a good look.

The cowboy's hair was straight, thick and shoulder length. It could have been gray, it could have been blond. It was hard to tell on the black-and-white screen. His face turned as wide and white as a fish's belly as he closed in on the camera, but before it did I could see that he had the even features of a good-looking cowboy and the hangdog expression of a lonesome cowboy, a combination many women cannot resist. Wes Brown appeared nervous. He brushed his nose with a finger, straightened his hat, hitched up his pants and inserted the card into the machine. Deborah's PIN number—2473—came up instantly on the monitor Charlie had hooked up to tell him when Deborah's account was accessed.

"There goes your money, Lewellen," Charlie said.

Terrance made a fist and punched it into the palm of his

other hand. Kissing two hundred thousand dollars good-bye wasn't easy.

Wes Brown looked over his shoulder, then he keyed in the amount of two hundred dollars.

"He's missing three zeros," Terrance said. "I told you he was dumber than dirt."

"He's making a deposit," Charlie said. "Not a withdrawal."

"Maybe he's depositing the instructions *before* he takes the ransom," Terrance said.

Maybe, I thought.

"He has to key in some amount to make a deposit. Right?" he asked Charlie.

"True," Charlie replied.

Wes Brown took several bills and a deposit slip out of the backpack, put them into an envelope and deposited it. We couldn't read the bills from here. Maybe the deposit slip contained instructions for Deborah's and Perigee's return. Maybe not.

"Should I get someone over there to pick up the deposit?" Charlie asked.

"Wait a minute," said Terrance. "Let's see what he does next."

What Wes Brown did next was take his receipt and his ATM card and put them into his jeans pocket. He didn't ask for two hundred thousand dollars. He didn't ask for anything. He straightened his hat, shouldered the backpack, turned around and walked away. My eyes followed him into the door of Midnight Cowboy. Terrance got right on his C phone and told all his security men to go to the mall and tail him.

"Why's he walking away from the money?" Charlie asked.

"Your security man scared him off," I said.

"Then why did he deposit the instructions?"

"We don't know yet that he did."

"See that guy going into Midnight Cowboy?" Terrance asked.

"Yeah."

"He's mine. He's a professional. Something else scared Brown. He'll be back at the machine. He's not gonna walk away from two hundred thousand dollars."

"If you say so," Charlie said.

"He looks just like anybody else, right?" Terrance asked.

A man dressed in jeans and a cowboy hat was going into the bar just as Charlie had said, but he didn't look like a cowboy to me; his upper body was too well developed. This was a guy who pumped iron. His jeans were old and baggy, and he held a C phone in his hand.

"Cowboys don't carry cellular phones," Charlie said.

"Sure they do. Ranching is a business just like any other."

"Do you want me to send someone to pick up the deposit now?" Charlie asked.

"That'll scare him into the next county," Terrance replied.

While they argued the point, my attention was drawn to the Tramway monitor. Someone wearing a black cowboy hat identical to Wes Brown's, a long duster of the type cowboys wear in bad weather and gauntlets approached the ATM on Tramway. That cowboy, looking at the ground and hiding behind the hat, walked up to the machine, reached into the duster with the kind of quick and furtive gesture that produces a piece, pulled out a card, and inserted it.

"Look at your monitor, Charlie," I said. "Is a PIN number coming up on Tramway?"

"Yeah. Two-four-seven-three, and the machine is accepting it. He's keying in two hundred thousand."

"Goddamn," Terrance said, "look at that." The cowboy's face was still shadowed by the hat brim. The hair was hidden under the hat. The cowboy looked up into the camera, but all we saw was a mask made of feathers with holes for the mouth, nose and eyes. Some of the feathers were dark and bristly, others were soft and light. They could have come from parrots, they could have come from hawks, they could have come from sparrows. It was impossible to tell in the grainy black-and-white image of the surveillance camera. The mask had a frightening and primitive power. There was nothing behind it but the white wall, the darkening sky and the mountains where the coyotes yap all night.

Terrance was immediately on the phone, giving orders to his security men. "He's at Tramway. Tail him," he barked, but they had followed his previous instructions and left for Midnight Cowboy. Terrance turned apoplectic as the masked bandit collected the money, two hundred thousand-dollar bills, and put them into a money belt hidden beneath the duster. No doubt there was a pistol or a semiautomatic under there, too. Nobody walks around with two hundred thousand in cash and no protection. The machine did its duty and asked if the customer wanted another transaction. Feathered mask punched the No button, tipped the hat to the camera, turned around, bent over, slipped the mask under the duster and walked away, presumably to a vehicle that was out of camera range. The transfer had been made. Terrance had kept his part of the bargain. The question now was whether Wes Brown had kept the other part and left instructions for the return of Terrance's wife and bird. The answer was to be found in the deposit envelope. Feathered mask was not going to be tailed and, in fact, was long gone by the time Terrance's security men got back to Tramway. They never even discovered what kind of getaway vehicle had been driven—or flown.

Charlie got on *his* phone. "Now I'm getting someone to Midnight Cowboy to pick the deposit up," he said.

"You do that," answered Terrance, sinking into his chair. He'd lost his money and a suspect. The starch was going out of his shirt.

What do you expect from minimum wage security men? I was tempted to ask, but it hadn't been their fault. They'd only been following Terrance's orders.

"How many ATM cards did Deborah have?" I asked Charlie.

"We only issued one, but the magnetic stripe can be copied easily enough. Brown used the original, his accomplice used the copy, or vice versa. It doesn't really matter. They were both capable of putting money in and taking money out. Well," he said to Terrance, "I'd say your kidnapper had an accomplice after all."

Or a betrayer.

While we waited for the deposit envelope, Terrance burned up the airwaves talking to his security men, who had nothing better to do than go back to Midnight Cowboy and spy on Wes Brown. "He's picking up a waitress," Terrance said.

"What are your men going to do if he takes her home?" I asked.

"Follow him. Maybe he'll connect with the mask somewhere. I'm not letting Brown out of my sight until this is all over."

"It'll be hard to follow anybody to Door without being made," Charlie said. "No cover there."

The bank employee arrived eventually and handed Charlie the deposit envelope. "Thanks," Charlie said. He slit the envelope with a letter opener, put tape over the tips of his fingers and slid the deposit slip and money out. Terrance and I leaned over his shoulder to see. The money added up to two hundred dollars in twenty-dollar bills.

"Phew." Charlie wrinkled up his nose. "That money stinks."

It did have a moldy, earthy smell.

"I never heard of a kidnapper giving money back before," Terrance said.

"Beats me," said Charlie.

He examined the deposit slip. Brown had penciled in the amount, two hundred dollars, on one side. The other side was as blank as the wall behind the Tramway ATM. Terrance shined the black light on it; hand-printed letters rose to the surface with a yellow glow. "Send your lawyer Rte. 270, Mile Marker 62 Sunday night with two hundred thousand in hundred-dollar bills. No police, no phones, no security guards. Your valuables will be returned."

"Shit," I said.

"Hundred-dollar bills will be harder to carry, but easier to come by," Terrance said.

"Two-seventy is the road that will get you to Door," said Charlie.

"You'll do it, won't you?" Terrance asked me.

"I don't know," I responded. Acting as a ransom courier struck me as going above and beyond the call of duty.

"I'll double your fee," said Terrance.

"Um," I replied.

"Someone has to rescue Deborah," Charlie said. "Her life is in danger."

And Perigee, I knew, was dying without his mate. "Oh, all right," I said while asking myself why. For the money? For the love of adventure? For the sake of the woman and the bird? I'd already risked my life once for a bird, and I hadn't regretted it. "But only on one condition. I'm not going alone."

"No police or security guards," Terrance parroted the note.

"Not them. I'm taking a weapon, and I'm taking a friend." The person I intended to take was the Kid, the one friend I had whose taste for adventure was as keen as mine. The weapon was my LadySmith .38.

"Is this person reliable?" Terrance asked.

A lot more reliable than his security guards, I thought. "Yeah," I said. "And he knows all about birds."

"All right," Terrance said. "Do you have a cell phone?"

"No."

"Take mine."

"The note said no phones."

"Leave it in the car. I want to outfit you with a minicam so we'll have some evidence to use against Brown."

"What's a minicam?"

"A tiny video camera, about half the size of your thumb. Police departments hide them in their helmets. It'll work inside a cowboy hat."

"You want me to wear a cowboy hat at night?" I asked.

"It'll keep you from getting moonstruck," Charlie said.

7

The one addiction the Kid and I share is maps. We read them the way some people read legal thrillers. The places we haven't been are the unsolved mysteries. The Kid always keeps the two Mexicos, old and new, folded up in his glove compartment, and one Argentina in case he ever gets back. He folds his road maps carefully, keeping to the original creases as if to make sure that the roads and towns won't be mixed up when he opens them again. He brought his New Mexico map inside my apartment, spread it on the floor and located Door, a tiny circle at the far edge of Grant County with a dotted line (a dirt road, the kind of road that makes a car old before its time) leading to it from State Highway 270. Door was near the Gila National Forest, the first designated wilderness area in the U.S., land the Apaches once roamed. There are fewer people living in parts of the Gila now than there were when the Apaches and the cavalry were battling over it. The fact that a place merits a dot on the map means that somebody lived there once, not necessarily that anybody lives there now.

"There was a *mina* in that town," the Kid said.

"I know."

"Did you know that the New Mexico *loros* lived around there?"

"No."

"Not many people know that. They were illegals," he smiled. "They ate piñones. Sometimes you see them in Mexico now, but there are not many left."

"What do they look like?"

"They are this big." He held his hands about fifteen inches apart. "They are green with red here . . ." He tapped his shoulders. ". . . and here . . ." he tapped his forehead. "They call them thick-billed parrots in this country."

"What happened to them?" It was a question I should have known better than to ask.

"The *mineros* ate them."

"No."

"*Si.* They eat *guacamayos* in Mexico too. People there think they are good food. *Loros* are always together, they are *muy ruidoso* . . ."

Very noisy.

"They are easy to catch. The ones the *mineros* didn't eat were food for the *puercos.*"

The pigs. "That's disgusting."

"The *mineros* are gone now, but so are the birds. They kill everything in a place and then they leave. Crazy, no?"

"Yes."

"There is a man in Arizona now, trying to bring them back."

"Good," I said.

"Where is it exactly that we are going?"

"Mile marker sixty-two on Route Two-Seventy."

We found 270 on the map. I measured sixty-two miles in scale from the border. The Kid measured the distance in kilometers. We arrived at the same place, a few miles north of Door near an area marked Cotorra Canyon.

"*Cotorra* means parrot," he said.

"I thought *loro* meant parrot."

"It does, and it is more common than *cotorra*. *Cotorra* also means a . . . how you say it? . . . a woman who talks too much."

"A chatterbox?"

"I also hear it called Chatterbox Canyon."

"You know about that canyon?"

"Yes, but I never went there. It's a place the *narcotraficantes* go."

"Sixty-two miles from the border?"

He shrugged. "Why not? The police are more careful near the border. Look," he pointed to the map, "there is nobody around."

He was right. There wasn't another town for thirty or forty miles, and that town was an equally tiny dot. Door would be a good place to hide a woman or a bird or a couple hundred thousand dollars. "Why is it called Cotorra Canyon?" I asked.

"Maybe it is on the path the Indians used to trade parrots. The Indians here liked the red Mexican *guacamayos*."

"Maybe it's a place they are traded now. According to Terrance Lewellen, Wes Brown is a parrot smuggler."

"Maybe there is an *eco* there," the Kid said. "The voice of one woman is the voice of twenty."

"There's only one way to find out," I said.

We had calculated that Door would take us four hours, so we left at three-thirty to allow time to get lost and time to get ready. We brought along my aunt Joan's birding binoculars, which were worth more than my car. I was packing my Punch and my LadySmith .38. The Kid went unarmed. I knew he'd come, and I knew he'd come unarmed. His feeling is that if you can't take care of yourself without a gun, you won't be able to do it with one. We had a different attitude toward weapons, but the same love of adventure. Maybe the Kid and I weren't a perfect match in society's eyes, but there had to be some connection deep in the threads of our DNA. Also, this adventure would take place in former Apache country and, if all went as planned, we'd be coming back with a rare and beautiful bird.

Terrance had outfitted me with the minicam, two thousand hundred-dollar bills stuffed into a Patagonia backpack, and an off-white Stetson with a silver concho hatband. The one nonnegotiable demand I'd made was that I wouldn't wear a black hat. These days every would-be cowboy from Gallup to Nashville wears a black hat. The conchos made the Stetson the hat of a Santa Fe cowboy, but they provided good camouflage for the minicam. Terrance ran the wire from the cowboy hat through my hair (it blended right in), down my back to a fanny pack that carried the videotape. He showed me how to turn the camera on and off without being noticed. I had to keep the crown of the Stetson pulled down so that the minicam sat in the middle of my forehead like a third eye. Otherwise I'd be filming the stars in the sky. Any hat feels like a weight on my head, but the minicam was lighter than I'd expected. Terrance gave us a cage for Perigee, some of the parrot's favorite toys and an avian first-aid kit in case the bird needed help. He also gave us a plastic bag of granola for a treat.

"Take good care of my Perigee," he told us.

"Sure," the Kid said.

There's a saying along the border—*no pasa, no muera.* Don't cross and you won't die. The Kid had made enough border crossings to know what to expect at night in the desert—robbery and/or death. He'd been robbed and beaten, and he got tired of the fighting and fighting back. Everybody has a nonnegotiable point, although not everybody is unlucky enough to discover that; nonnegotiable points are danger points. On the Kid's last trip as an illegal, he reached his. Somewhere in the big lonely, he was held up at gunpoint. The guy demanded his gun. The Kid handed it over. He demanded his money. The Kid gave it to him. He demanded his watch, and the Kid said no. It wasn't a prized possession, it wasn't even valuable. It was just a watch, but the Kid had been pushed as far as he was willing to go on that particular night.

"You have my gun. You have my money. You can't have my watch," he said.

"Give it to me," the coyote insisted.

"No," the Kid said.

They stared each other down across the barrel of the coyote's gun. Maybe the Kid's fearlessness intimidated him. Maybe the coyote didn't think a watch was worth another illegal's life. He walked away and let the Kid keep the watch. He has worn it ever since; it is his invincible shield. It doesn't keep good time, but better than no time at all, which is what I wear. My never wearing a watch is also a shield; my defense against being a bill-by-the-minute lawyer. Possibly my empty wrist is as much of an illusion as the Kid's watch. You are what you are. What happens, happens.

The Kid's watch did get us out of Albuquerque at one-thirty and to Mile Marker 62 near eight. We went in his white pickup, which would provide better camouflage in Grant County than my yellow Nissan. We put the camper shell on and threw in some pillows and sleeping bags. The desert can be cold at night and dry any time. I hydrated well before I went to bed and was up all night peeing. We filled some plastic bottles with water and froze them. You stick the bottles between your legs to cool off, and when they defrost you drink the water. We brought along some chips and salsa and some

Snapple Ice Tea. The only Cuervo Gold on this trip was the José Cuervo bandanna tied, Apache style, around the Kid's head. I wore the cowboy hat with the minicam hidden beneath the conchos. A cowboy hat is good camouflage in Grant County too. A pickup in rural New Mexico without at least one Resistol in the cab raises suspicion. Sometimes you see as many as four or five. Men are more likely to wear hats than women, but seen in silhouette in the cab of a truck, who can tell whether the wearer is a man or a woman? Before I got in the Kid's truck, I arranged my hat in his industrial-sized side-view mirror. The brim tilted like wings.

"Looks good on you, Chiquita," the Kid said.

"Thanks," I replied.

The route we took was Route 60 through Magdalena, around the high bend where Robert James Waller had an out-of-body experience and immortalized it for millions of women, and up onto the vast Plains of San Agustin. We drove past the Very Large Array, the place where white satellite ears on tracks are moved around the high plain listening for a message—any message—from space. There's a bumper sticker seen often in New Mexico that says MAGIC HAPPENS, and a road sign that says GUSTY WINDS MAY EXIST. Does that mean the winds are allowed to exist, I always wonder, and if so who is it that's granting permission? That sign also makes me think that aliens may exist. There are people who brake for them. If aliens do exist and want to communicate, the Plains of San Agustin would be the place to do it.

The message I get from this space is that there's a different vibe where there are no people. There's a lot of nothing out here, more than any I've ever seen. Some people find emptiness terrifying. I find it exhilarating. On the Plains of San Agustin you can drive for sixty miles and see one truck and three or four ranches. It's peaceful, but it's not boring. Miles of nothing may be punctuated by a split second of lightning and fear. New Mexico can have more than twelve thousand dry lightning strikes in a day, and the area around Magdalena has the most active lightning field in the state. At any moment it can bolt from the clouds like the long, crooked finger of God or of fate. I'd driven this road before in summer; I knew the lightning is always there waiting and gathering its power. I knew the tricks the wide open plains play on your vision. We floated in a high blue universe. The blue sky and gray-blue mountains were real. The puddles on the road and the ponds in the fields were shimmering illusions.

It was a change to see Route 60 from the Kid's truck. I was higher. I didn't have to keep my eyes on the road. I could watch the purple cloud shadows and the dance of the golden fields. I had time to think about the two thousand hundred-dollar bills in Terrance's backpack. I wouldn't be human if I didn't wonder what I would do with the money. There was a lot of space in two hundred thousand dollars, room to buy a house, a business, several trips around the world or two Mercedes Benz convertibles. It could support you for the rest of your life if you lived cheaply or in the third world. I'd given money its due and moved on to my hat, which also gave me a different perspective, a cowgirl's perspective. The one pickup we passed had EAT BEEF and an American flag on its vanity plate. The driver gave us a neighborly wave; I waved back.

I remembered that I had a third eye and wondered if it was seeing what I was seeing. I'm not used to looking through the eye of a camera. For the sake of practice, I turned the minicam on the Kid, who, as usual, was driving with maximum speed and total concentration. The Kid is never a chatterbox. He knows the value of words; he has to think them twice, in his first language and then in his second. He doesn't talk much, and when he drives he doesn't talk at all. He sensed that I was looking at him, and he squirmed in his seat.

"Turn that thing off, Chiquita," he said.

"How'd you know I had it on?"

"By your expression," he said.

We turned south on 270, reached Mile Marker 62 by eight, pulled off the road and parked. Somewhere down here the mile markers would become kilometer markers, but it hadn't happened yet. The Kid concealed the pickup behind a boulder, hoisted the backpack, and locked up. The ground was hard and dry enough that you'd need to get close to see any tire tracks. Whoever had sent us here knew where to look, but the boulder would conceal the truck from a casual thief. The ground beyond the boulder was too sandy to drive any farther, and we didn't know where to drive anyway. There had been no instructions as to what to do once we reached Mile Marker 62. I'd been hoping it would become obvious; it didn't. No people or tracks were visible. The only sound was a couple of squabbling ravens. Maybe we were supposed to stand here and wait, but whoever had conceived that plan didn't know me or the Kid. Waiting wasn't our style. Still, we gave it a shot. Maybe the kidnapper had run into problems and was late, maybe the kidnapper was testing us, maybe the kidnapper was waiting for darkness. Hard as it was for us to wait in daylight, it would be borderline impossible after nightfall.

This was the desert, but it wasn't empty. Emptiness is another illusion of the road. The longer we stood here, the more we saw. Prickly pear cactus grew in a cluster of oval pods. Red fruit had sprouted from the pods and circled them like a string of two-inch hearts. The fruit is called *tuna* in Mexico, and it's sold in the market there. You need a pair of gloves to pick a prickly pear. If you cut into one with bare hands, you (and the fruit) will bleed.

Jimson weed bushes sprawled everywhere. The weed is also known as sacred datura, wild lily and trumpet lily. It's a member of the deadly nightshade family, with the ability to accumulate narcotics from the soil; it is believed that it can even absorb atomic wastes. It is hallucinogenic, and it is poisonous. In daytime it's a dumpster weed soaking up the earth's garbage, but at night it flowers with an otherworldly beauty. The flowers are six inches long, the white inside shading to lavender as the trumpets open up.

While I'd been thinking deadly nightshade thoughts the Kid had become an Apache tracker. He crisscrossed the shoulder of the road cutting for signs and found a triangular pile of stones that could have been put there yesterday or several hundred years ago. The sun was sinking, and the shadows of the cairn pointed toward a rock wall. The Kid followed the shadow, walked up to the wall and found a petroglyph that had been scratched into the rocks. A stick figure was holding a basket dripping water into a pair of wavy lines that had to symbolize a river or a stream. Petroglyphs are found everywhere there are rocks in New Mexico, and that's just about everywhere. Artist is the oldest profession in this state.

"He is giving directions to Cotorra Canyon," the Kid said.

"How do you know that?"

"I know that the canyon is over there, and when you follow the rock pictures in the desert you find water."

"Is there water in the canyon?"

"There was," he said. "The canyon was made by the water."

Talking about water made me thirsty, but the water was back in the car. "I need something to drink," I said.

"Put a pebble in your mouth. When the Apaches did that, they could go all day without water."

I found a pebble and took his advice.

"If you put a pebble in your shoe, you can make your walk look and sound different. Did you know that?" he asked.

"No," I said.

We followed the rock wall into an arroyo with a sandy

bottom that meandered in the direction of Cotorra Canyon. A butte had been formed by centuries of water seeking the lowest level. It wasn't a very high butte, a newcomer in geological time. A couple of coyotes loped along the top of it. Coyotes are the tricksters of the animal world, and in coyote country things aren't always what they seem. The Kid took my aunt Joan's binoculars and looked over the butte, beyond the coyotes and into the sky.

He pointed up. *"El buitre,"* he said.

He handed me the binoculars, but I didn't need them to see that to the east, above where Cotorra Canyon had to be, a black vulture was circling with a long prehistoric glide. It was barely bothering to beat its large wings, letting the thermals keep it up. You rarely see a vulture alone. If a vulture finds something to eat, it will be joined by more. Soon, a couple of them were circling like an airborne merry-go-round. But whatever was underneath wasn't merry. A vulture in the air meant that something on the ground was dying or dead. There's nothing like a vulture to remind you that we're not always at the top of the food chain.

The Kid untied his bandanna and wiped the sweat from his forehead. It was a hundred degrees in there and getting hotter by the minute. My gun was in its holster, my pepper spray hooked onto my belt. There's not a weapon made that can protect you from what is already dead, but a cigarette helps cushion the blow. I lit up.

"When I lived in Mexico, I knew a woman who went rafting on the Usumacinta River," I told the Kid. "The raft hit a rock and broke up. She swam to shore, but her leg was broken and she couldn't get any farther. She lay there for days while the vultures circled overhead, waiting for her to die." There could be a woman in Cotorra Canyon with just enough life left in her to keep the vultures aloft.

"El buitre is the sign of death," the Kid said, "but he is also

the sign of *purificacion*. He eats the bad meat and cleans the bones. Nothing can hurt *el buitre*. He can eat everything. The Indians believed in his power."

"How do you know that?" I asked.

"I listen." He looked at the cigarette in my hand. "You want someone to see that smoke, Chiquita?"

"Probably not," I said. I rubbed the cigarette out and buried the butt in the sand.

"*El buitre* will stay away if there is something dead and something alive," the Kid said. "When the *lorotraficantes* bring the parrots here from Mexico, they give them tequila to keep them quiet, they tape their mouths shut; they kill many of them. Smuggling is very brutal. Sometimes in Colombia they smuggle *cocaina* in dead babies. A woman carries the babies and says they are sleeping." He nodded toward Cotorra Canyon, where the vultures had taken a sudden dive, leaving the sky as bare as a picked-clean bone. "You sure you want to go in there? It could be *muy feo*."

Really ugly. It could be more ugly if we didn't go. The desert lizard crawled up my spine. Something lost its life in Cotorra Canyon while we stood in the arroyo.

We'd come across a tumble of rocks that had fallen from the butte. "I think we can get to the top here," the Kid said. "It's better not to walk into a canyon full of *lorotraficantes*. No?"

"Yes."

"We can see them from up there, but if we stay close to the ground they won't see us."

"Right," I said.

Before we climbed, he stopped to straighten the backpack, tighten his bandanna, and take a good look around. The sun was setting, and the sky behind us had turned the color at the center of a bud or a flame. A bird perched on a dead branch made a black silhouette against the rose-on-fire sky. The bird had the shape of a hawk, broad and hunched at the shoulders, narrow at the talons, an upside-down vase. It was the last chance for the diurnal hunters to get a meal before night fell.

"The sky is the color of *la encia del leopardo*," the Kid said.

The color of a leopard's gums, a line from his favorite Argentine writer. I'd heard it before, but this was the first time I knew what it meant.

"The moon will be coming up there." He pointed east.

"How do you know that?"

"Tonight it is *la luna llena* . . ."

The full moon.

". . . and *la luna llena* comes up across from where the sun goes down. When the moon enters Cotorra Canyon, it will be very light. Your camera will get good pictures from up there if it can see that far."

I hoped it would. My desire to enter a canyon filled with vultures had become very dim. Dextrous Horse Woman might have done it, but she was an Apache and she rode a horse. "It's not a very high butte," I said.

"Verdad. Lista?"

"Ready," I said.

"Vamos."

The rocks that had fallen from the top of the butte were so evenly spaced that they might been tossed there by a StairMaster. It was an easy climb, but rattlers like rocks at dusk, and we had to go slowly, watching and listening for the warning whirr. By the time we reached the top, the moon was rising exactly where the Kid had said it would. Puffs of clouds preceded it like the smoke from a signal fire. A lenticular hovered above the horizon, and the light reflected on its underbelly, turning it into a silver fish. The moon's aura was followed by a sliver, and then the rest of it slid slowly across the horizon. It was the biggest moon I'd ever seen, a perigee moon, a perfect circle, a hole in the sky, so full of light that I had the feeling I could see through it. The moon was bright enough and low enough to cast a long shadow, but when the nights are as clear as they are here, even the Milky Way will cast a shadow. We scuttled across the butte. It was flat and smooth, a faster and safer way to see into Cotorra Canyon, and possibly even Door, than wandering around the sandy arroyo.

When we reached the eastern end of the butte, we put our bellies to the ground (concealing our shadows beneath us), crawled up and peered over. I hoped our heads would look like rocks from the canyon—if anybody was looking up from the canyon. The vultures had gone wherever it is that vultures go at night and left a pile of bones behind. I glassed them quickly with Joan's binoculars and saw that they were the bones of a bird, not a woman. The vultures hadn't picked the carrion entirely clean. A pile of feathers remained that were a light and dark mix. Hawks, I thought, and the only predator a full-grown hawk has is man. Something had frightened the vultures away, and I didn't have to look far to find it. A man stood beside a prickly pear cactus wearing a black cowboy hat and smoking a cigarette. His name was Wes Brown. The moon's spotlight created a shadowy black and white scene in Cotorra Canyon like a night shoot or the view seen through an ATM surveillance camera. A couple of bats swooped by our heads.

"Is that him?" the Kid asked me.

"That's him," I whispered, turning on the minicam and laying the cowboy hat beside me with the camera facing forward. "I think those are hawk feathers. Why would someone kill a bunch of hawks?"

"Hawks kill *loros*," the Kid said. "He was protecting his contraband."

It was illegal, I knew, to kill a migratory bird. Crime one for Wes Brown.

It's widely believed that more crimes are committed under a full moon, but no obvious crime was taking place at the moment. Wes Brown tossed his cigarette to the ground, picked up a shovel and dug a hole. He appeared to be looking for something rather than burying something. There was a wooden crate on the ground next to him, and I could see through the binoculars that it was empty. The prickly pear appeared to be a marker. Brown dug down about a foot, found what he wanted—a plastic bag—and pulled it out. He opened the bag and took out several bills, but I couldn't make out the denomination.

"The smelly money," I said.

"What?" asked the Kid.

"The money he deposited in the bank had an earthy smell."

Brown put the bills in his pocket and buried the stash again, smoothing the ground carefully over the spot. He turned around and walked in our direction. We slid back from the edge of the butte. Brown must have hidden the shovel in a crevice in the wall, because when we looked over again it was gone. He went back to his bleeding-heart marker and lit another cigarette. I wanted that cigarette. Badly.

It might have been serendipity that brought us to this spot, but to me it had the feel of a master plan. We'd been sent to Mile Marker 62 and been diverted by the petroglyphs. The petroglyphs led to Cotorra Canyon whether we followed the steps or the arroyo. Brown was standing near the spot where the water had flowed. But he already had a pocket and a hole full of money. Bringing money to him was like pouring Perrier into the Rio Grande.

"Do you think he's waiting for us?" I asked the Kid.

"I don't think so, Chiquita," he said. *"Mira."*

He pointed toward the southeast, where a dotted line of

car lights was visible on a highway twenty or thirty miles away. It's possible to see that far where the nights are so open and clear. One car had left the line and was crossing the desert. Cotorra Canyon wasn't accessible by car from the arroyo, but it seemed to be from the southeast. We watched and waited while Wes Brown smoked his cigarette and the car's headlights approached. It was possible that he was waiting for someone to deliver Deborah to him, and he was going to give that person the money. It was possible that person was late and Brown still intended to meet us at Mile Marker 62. The car pulled up in front of him and turned off the headlights. Who needed them under *la luna llena*? All I could tell about the car was that it was a station wagon.

The Kid glassed it. "Ford," he said. "Pinto."

Two guys wearing the plastic cowboy hats of Mexican campesinos got out and walked over to Brown. Some conversation and hand gestures ensued. The conversation was a distant murmur from where we lay, but it was a murmur that had resonance like a mountain stream slapping on a hard rock bed. The guys walked around the side of the car. I hoped they'd open the door and Deborah Dumaine would climb out. I hoped she would be able to climb out.

"*Mulas,*" the Kid said.

People who get paid very little to carry something very valuable across the border. One of the men pushed a taillight aside, reached into a compartment hidden behind it and pulled something out. It was about a foot long, a few inches wide and tightly wrapped in a paper bag, a lot of dope or an average-sized bird. The man ripped off a piece of tape, opened the package and a parrot rolled out. Its wings didn't flap, its beak didn't open, its head flopped.

"*Tu madre,*" said the Kid.

It was *muy feo*, worse than that—*muchisimo feo*. The man swore and tossed the dead parrot to the ground. Wes Brown swore back, picked the parrot up and put it in a plastic bag, one meal the vultures wouldn't be getting. If the parrot wasn't dead already, the bag would have killed it.

"Why is he keeping it?" I asked the Kid.

"He can sell the feathers," he said.

The runner reached behind the taillight, pulled out and unwrapped another package, also a parrot, way feeble but still alive. Wes Brown looked it over. Apparently that bird was too maimed for him to care about, or it was the wrong kind of parrot. He held the head in one hand and the body in the other and twisted the neck until that bird's head flopped too. It was revolting to see something so big kill something so small, and for what? Money. It may have made Brown feel like a god, but it turned him into a despicable coward in my eyes. We couldn't hear the snap of the bird's neck, but I cringed and the Kid put his hand on my back.

Brown threw the dead bird away. The vultures would pick the bones clean tomorrow. Something else would get the meat and lick the brains out tonight. I looked away as the runner unrolled the next package, thinking of the vitality of Maxamilian and Colloquy, thinking of the flocks of thick-billeds that once filled the air, expecting another dead bird, but sound exited from this bag, a harsh sound that echoed around and around Cotorra Canyon, echo feeding on echo, until the squawk of one terrified bird became the cry of all endangered parrots. The men ignored the sound and continued their sickening business.

"*Uno,*" said the Kid.

The runner reached behind the taillight and pulled out more and more parrots, most of them dead. The Pinto resembled a car packed full of circus clowns—dead clowns. There could have been a pipeline under the taillight that ran all the way to the border and was jammed full of parrots: green parrots, yellow parrots, red parrots, blue parrots, their feathers mingling together in a parrot stew. When the runners were finished, they'd pulled out twenty tightly wrapped birds and sixteen of them were dead. The moonlight had robbed them of their color. The smugglers had robbed them of their freedom and their lives. Wes Brown taped the beaks of the live ones shut again and put them in the box. He put most of the dead ones in the plastic bag. He reached into his pocket and counted out some money. The amount provoked an argument, but eventually the runners took what Brown offered and drove away in the Pinto with the deadly hidden compartment.

"You know how they catch those parrots?" the Kid said.

"No."

"They cut down the trees they live in, and they fall to the ground. Many of them die. Many more die on the road. The guys who catch them get a couple of dollars each."

"And the runners? How much do they get?'

"Five hundred dollars maybe. Depends on how many live."

I didn't want to think about how much Brown would get for the live ones. A lot, but not as much as he could get for Perigee and Deborah Dumaine. He had come back for his shovel and started to bury the money he'd kept.

"*Vamos,* Chiquita," the Kid said. "Door is on the other side of the mesa. If we go now, we can get there before him. Maybe we will find the woman there."

"Maybe," I said.

8

We slid back from the edge until the depths of Cotorra Canyon weren't visible anymore. Assuming that if we couldn't see Wes Brown, he couldn't see us, we stood up and trotted across the butte. The Kid took the south side, I took the north, giving me the sandy arroyo, him the brush. Both of us were looking for any sign of Deborah and agreed to yip if we found anything. The Kid yipped first. He hadn't seen Deborah, but he had come across Door about half a mile back from Cotorra Canyon.

It was a pile of tumbled stones and broken beams in the desert moonlight, a twentieth-century ruin. What used to take hundreds of years to accomplish took, in the mining boom and bust years, ten. A lode was discovered; in New Mexico that could mean coal, silver, gold, turquoise, copper, uranium, potassium salts or pumice for stonewashing jeans. They've all been fuel for our extractive industries. A town sprang up near the mine complete with bars, hookers and con men. The lode got mined out, the miners left. There has been a constant ebb and flow of civilizations in Door's part of the world: warriors and misfits, soldiers and diggers. Had it been nearer a population center, artists and craftspeople would have moved in, set up shop and transformed it from a cheap rental to an expensive tourist trap.

Since it was a dot in the middle of Grant County, it was inhabited by rodents, reptiles and a parrot smuggler. When the miners moved out, the critters came back.

We stood at the edge of the butte and peered down into Door, which was also home to a sailboat in dry dock. The nearest places you'd want to sail a boat would be Elephant Butte or the Sea of Cortez. The sailboat sat in the spot where the plaza must have been. Its mast was erect, a beacon for something, but I couldn't say what. The name *El Vagabundo* was scrawled across the stern.

"*Que loco,*" the Kid said, shaking his head.

It was a touch of magical realism in the already surreal desert, and enough to make you wonder just what Door was the doorway to. *Vagabundo* was a wooden boat, made in the days before fiberglass became ubiquitous on the water. Woodies require a lot of maintenance, and this boat hadn't been getting any. It was scruffy and badly in need of paint, but it was shelter, which was more than you could say for the crumbling houses. The boat was about thirty feet long, the type of cruiser that can be picked up for several thousand dollars in the marinas along southern California and northern Mexico. I knew that because I did a tour of duty once along the Mexican coast. There's a dream many Californians have: to chuck everything on the mainland, buy a boat and spend their days cruising warm water. They call it "catching the rabbit" in honor of the racing greyhounds that manage to catch the mechanical rabbit and drop out of the race. Cruising is a cheap way to live, and there's always one way to make money if the savings run out. As to why anybody would put it in Door—possibly because the rules of civilization were as hard to enforce here as they were at sea.

A barbed-wire fence circled Door. The dirt road that lead to Route 270 was blocked by a chain-link gate and a couple of hand-lettered wooden signs that read NO TRESPASSING and KEEP OUT. A tired American-made pickup with an NRA bumper sticker was parked inside the perimeter of the fence, near a chicken-wire cage that was empty except for a couple of metal bowls and a branch for a perch.

The StairMaster hadn't provided steps for us on this side of the butte. There were no evenly spaced rocks, only soft earth that showed the gouges of erosion. We tried to descend slowly and carefully, but it couldn't be done. Our speed picked up, and we raced faster and faster as we descended. When we reached level ground, I ran several feet before I could stop. When I did, I looked behind us. If you didn't get too close, our path of descent resembled an erosion channel. The flat ground was hard enough that our footprints were scattered and faint. Wes Brown would be approaching from the other side of Door. Chances were he wouldn't notice the signs of our arrival. It never hurts to have surprise on your side, and he wouldn't be expecting us to show up here. Or would he?

The Kid lifted the top strand of barbed wire. I stepped through, turned around and held the wire for him. We approached the vagabond ship. Light flickered from behind curtained windows and peeked out of the top of the cabin. A shirt thrown over the rigging danced a jittery dance under the spell of the moon and the wind. In Door gusty winds did exist. The shirt's shadow partner followed, dancing backward on the deck in perfect sync. Everything had a partner tonight, and at this hour the shadows were longer than the originals. A ladder lead from the ground to the sailboat's deck.

"You want to go up?" the Kid asked me.

Did I want to be pushing the envelope or licking the

stamp? "You don't want to stop now, do you?" I asked him.

"No," he said, looking down at his watch.

"Anybody there?" I yelled, pointing the .38 with one hand and feeling the top of the Punch with the other. The only answer was the sound of the rigging rubbing against the mast.

"I go first," the Kid said.

"Why you?" I asked. "I've got the gun and the camera."

"I have more experience," he said.

"With what?"

"*Contrabandistas.*" I couldn't argue with that.

"Take the gun," I said.

The Kid climbed the ladder. I adjusted my cowboy hat, turned on the camera and followed. Our footsteps resounded as we crossed the deck, giving the impression that there was deep water under us. Seats had been built, with storage cabinets underneath, around the sides of the deck. The top of one of them was open, but there was nothing inside. The wooden slats that were the door to the cabin were gone. We looked down into the light, which had the tentative, wavering quality of candle flame. There weren't any power lines out here; I couldn't hear the hum of a generator. We could see most of the cabin's interior—but not all—from where we stood.

"Anybody there?" I called again. There was no response. If anybody was inside, he or she was gagged, dead or not talking.

The Kid stepped the three steps down into the cabin. I followed. A green parrot with red epaulets on its wings was perched in a corner. A black hood had been tied over its head, the falconers' method of keeping a bird quiet. The birds think it's nighttime, and they sleep at night. The parrot had the molted look of a stuffed bird that's been sitting alone for years on somebody's shelf. I knew it was alive, however, because it quivered when the Kid touched it.

"It's the bird the *mineros* ate," he said. "I see them sometimes in Mexico."

He put the gun down, picked the parrot up and began crooning to it softly in Spanish as he lifted the hood. The instant the hood came off, the screeching began, a sound as grating as claws on a blackboard. The Kid continued talking in Spanish, but he could barely be heard above the din. The parrot flapped its wings and pumped up the volume with each beat. The noise made my inner ears vibrate and my head hurt. The parrot was about fifteen inches long, had a red forehead and a large, black beak that could crack open a piñon and was itching to take a chunk out of the Kid.

"It's a *bronco*," he said.

"What's that?"

"A bird that will never be *domesticado*."

The parrot noise affected me the way a child screaming in a supermarket does; I wanted to forget whatever I'd come for and flee.

"Can you quiet it?" I asked the Kid.

"Momento," he said.

He put his hand over the bird's head in a sheltering motion and held it near his heart. The bird calmed down, and I investigated Wes Brown's quarters. The main cabin consisted of a tiny, messy kitchen, some bunks, the table and a chair where the Kid sat sideways, holding the parrot. A half-empty bottle of Jack Daniels and a couple of candles in clay candlesticks sat on the table. A ruana from Colombia was draped across a bunk. Papier-mâché demon masks from Mexico leaned against a counter, and the flickering light shadowed the eye and mouth holes and emphasized the meanness of the hooked nose. How much patience would it take to cover one of those masks with parrot and/or hawk feathers? I wondered.

The wind that rocked the boat had come a long distance, gathering power on its journey the way water does. The cabin was drafty, the boards creaked and the candle flames stretched and ebbed in the wind. Within the belly of the boat it was easy to imagine we were at sea. In my mind I'd left Grant County and was sailing the edge of a rich and dark continent, circling around the ancient Colombian city of Santa Marta; the new version that resembled Miami Beach; past the province of Guajira, where the Indians who've gotten rich on oil drilling wear loincloths and drive Cadillacs; into the harbor of Cartagena, the walled city, where a chain was once hooked across the harbor in a futile attempt to keep the pirates out. This cruiser had been a smuggler's boat, I had no doubt, and the coast of Colombia was where you'd go to pick up the most valuable loot. For some reason this smuggler had dropped out of that race. Had he lost his nerve? I wondered. Been broken? Busted?

The Kid cooed to the parrot. I picked up the gun in one hand, a candle in the other and walked past the head, ducking my hat as I went into the forward cabin, a triangular space that's usually used for a berth. The louvered door to the head swung behind me, causing the candle to flicker and flare and the shadows to advance and retreat. There was no berth in here, just a small desk built into the corner. The rest of the space was used for storage. I saw a bunch of duffle bags that might have contained sails. I also saw some scuffed and down-at-the-heels cowboy boots and a plastic bag full of red, green, yellow, brown and white feathers. Hawks and parrots. A backpack and a cowboy's bad-weather duster had been thrown across the duffel bags. The pockets of the duster were empty, as was the backpack. I didn't see a weapon, but I would have lifted it if I had. Wes Brown must have had a hunting rifle someplace, but not here.

A ledger lay open on the desk. The entries were a detailed record of parrot transfers. The record keeping was precise, right down to the name of the pet store in Albuquerque (Birds of Paradise) that the birds were delivered to. The handwriting was tidy. Maybe Brown was neater in his work than he was in his life. Maybe he had a partner. I was wondering if the mini-cam could record the entries in the dim light, considering ripping out a page, when the bird started squawking again. The half-open door to the head was hiding me from the cabin and the cabin from me. Then the bird stopped squawking suddenly, and my finger reached for the trigger of my gun.

"What are you doing in here?" I heard a man's angry voice say. The parrot had concealed the sound of his descent into the cabin—from me anyway. There was no way of knowing what the Kid had heard or seen. I was hearing Wes Brown's surly drawl.

"The parrot needs help," the Kid answered.

"It's not your parrot, *cholo.*"

"Now it is."

"Give it to me."

"No," the Kid said.

"Give me my bird."

"You heard me."

"This is a .45 I'm holding here. You see it?"

"Yeah."

"You want to get shot over a bird?"

"No tienes los cojones." You don't have the balls. You wouldn't need much Spanish to get the Kid's meaning. It was a nonnegotiable moment, and they take place in their own slow-motion time zone where every sensation is experienced with absolute and unforgettable clarity. The sailboat shifted on its mooring, and my heart skipped a beat. The cabin smelled of fear and people too close together. The candlelight flickered beyond the louvers. I felt the presence of a large, soft butterfly in the cabin. I felt it brush against me. My life with the Kid passed before me in an instant that seemed like a drop of water in an ocean of time. Give him the goddamn bird, I thought, give it to him. But my physical reaction was instinctive—no one was going to kill my man if my hands and feet

could prevent it. I was reaching for the door when Brown's weapon went off. I heard the floor splinter. I heard Brown swear—"Fuck." I didn't hear a sound from the Kid or the bird.

"Drop it," I yelled, pushing the door aside and pointing the .38 at Brown, who was looking at the hole he'd made in the floor. I could see the back of the Kid's head. His hair was electric. At the sound of my voice he turned around. His eyes had a wolf's feral glow. He was alive and alert, but there was no time to revel in that now. He'd put the black hood back over the parrot's head, and that's what had been keeping it quiet. I don't know what had kept *him* quiet. *Cojones* perhaps. That Wes Brown's gun was still aiming at the floor gave me a big advantage. That and the fact that the Kid and I began working together. I'd never really considered us a team before, but in danger we were in perfect sync.

The Kid didn't miss a beat. "Give me the gun," he said to Brown.

The eyes that looked out from under Brown's black hat wavered, the sign of a cowboy who couldn't commit. Deepwater smuggling takes split-second timing and hair-trigger acuity. I could see why he'd given it up. Stopping to weigh his options was—for Wes Brown—a big mistake. I kept the .38 pointed at his vital organs. The Kid grabbed his hand and knocked the .45 out. It hit the floor with a thud instead of an explosion, and the Kid picked it up while my cowboy hat recorded every motion.

"Why don't you take care of this bird?" the Kid asked.

"What the hell business is it of yours?" answered Wes Brown. "Who are you people, and what are you doing in my cabin?"

"My name is Neil Hamel," I said. "We're looking for Deborah Dumaine."

"Deborah Dumaine?" Brown pushed his hat back on his

head. "What would she be doing here?" He gave no sign that
he knew who I was or that he'd been expecting me.

"Why don't you tell me?"

"I haven't a clue." He did a lightweight's feigning dance,
shifting back and forth from one worn boot to the other. A
plastic bag full of hawk feathers and dead parrots lay on the
floor beside him. His eyes, seeking an escape route, circled the
room and latched onto the only woman present—me. He had
a pretty boy's way of fluttering his lashes. The lashes were
thick enough, and his eyes, a pale gray, were pretty enough. In
his boot heels he was about my height. His thick blond hair
fell to his shoulders. Good looks are the ruin of many men,
and he was good-looking from across a candlelit room, but up
close (and I had moved up close enough) his face had the
ruddy, burned-out look of someone who'd spent too much
time alone with the sun or the bottle. "I'm in trouble," his pale
eyes said. "Rescue me." A lot of women would have tried. A
lot of them had probably already failed.

I had expected Wes Brown's first step to be to demand the
money, then to negotiate the terms of the hostages' release. His
know-nothing reaction forced me to reconsider, and I came up
with some possibilities: One: He knew about the kidnapping
and had invited us here, but something had happened to Deborah and Perigee and he was stalling until he could produce
them—if he could ever produce them. Two: He knew nothing
about the kidnapping, and someone else had sent us here,
although Terrance's cassette was a major obstacle to that the-
ory. Three: He knew about the kidnapping, but he was pretending he didn't, setting it up for someone we wouldn't be
able to identify to collect the money. That other person should
have met us at Mile Marker 62 and might even be waiting
there now. That the voice on the cassette had been Brown's, I
had no doubt; I recognized the surly drawl. The digitally
altered voice on the R line could have been anyone's, but some-

one had written the script, and that had taken a certain amount of imagination and humor. I didn't see a lot of humor in Wes Brown, but I did see considerable fantasy. This was a person, after all, who lived in a ghost town in a wooden boat.

He continued his story, and he might—or might not—have been ratcheting up the fantasy level. "I haven't seen Deborah since she showed up here a couple of weeks ago." He shifted his weight, blinked and attempted to meet my eyes. "She came on to me." Maybe he was trying to appeal to some basic female instinct to outshine the competition. But if he thought Deborah's interest would make him irresistible to me, he was mistaken. And if he thought I believed what he was saying, he was also mistaken. Terrance had said he thought Deborah was too smart for Wes Brown, but Terrance's objectivity had been suspect, and smart women can be dumber than dirt when it comes to men. Still, I could see Brown coming a mile away, and I wanted to believe that Deborah would have too. As for Brown, I hadn't decided yet how smart I thought he was. He was a criminal; there was plenty of evidence of that. Criminals aren't known for their brain power, but the well-kept ledgers did show evidence of some kind of intelligence.

"Deborah came on to *you*?" I asked.

"Yeah," he shrugged. "I told her I wasn't interested." The message his eyes were sending was "But I could be interested in you." It's a sleazy guy who'll send that message five minutes after he threatens to kill your lover, although he didn't know the Kid was my lover. He did know he and I were Anglo and the Kid was not. I've gotten this look before from pale-eyes—you have more in common with me than him. I looked away, hoping my eyes remained noncommittal, because the message I was thinking was, Buzz off, parrot killer.

"How much time did Deborah spend here?" I asked, trying to keep my voice noncommittal.

"Couple of hours, I guess."

Long enough for . . . what? I wondered.

"Who are you people anyway? What's your game?" He looked from me to the Kid.

"I'm Terrance Lewellen's lawyer."

"That asshole's trying to blame his problems with Deborah on me?"

"Not exactly."

"And you, bird boy?" he said to the Kid. "Who are you?"

"*Cállate,*" said the Kid. Shut up. His head was cocked; he'd been ignoring us and listening intently to something else. He could be as still as a predator when he wanted to.

"What?" asked Wes Brown.

"*Oye.* Listen."

There was a sound coming from above us on the deck, a low, ferocious growl, the universal back-off threat. It could have been the sound of a mountain lion, a dog, a coyote. It might even have been, by the remotest of possibilities, a wolf.

"What the . . ." Wes Brown said.

The Kid was itching to get up on the deck, but he aimed the .45 at Brown and made him go first. I followed. The moon had risen a little higher while we'd been below. The deck had gotten a little brighter. The gusty wind had died down, and the shirt was resting after its ecstatic dance. There was no sign of a cat or a dog, but a big blue macaw was hanging upside down by its beak and swinging from the boom.

"Perigee!" I said.

"What the hell is going on here?" asked Wes Brown.

"Arwk," said the macaw, who appeared to be in magnificent condition and have every feather in place. The tail feathers were long and silky. The plumage on his breast and neck was a smooth, deep blue, becoming lighter and greener around the head. The Kid had a few nuts in his pocket and he offered them to the macaw, who climbed off the boom onto his shoulder and gobbled them up.

With the bandanna tied around his forehead, the parrot on his shoulder, the gun in his hand and the mast behind him, the Kid could have been a pirate. Too bad we didn't have a gangplank to walk Wes Brown on. The prospect of deep water might have convinced him to fess up.

"*Que guapo,*" the Kid clucked to the bird.

"Pretty boy," Perigee cackled. "Pretty boy, pretty boy, pretty boy." The rigging groaned as it rubbed against the mast.

"He couldn't have flown here, could he?" I asked the Kid.

"No. *Mira.* His wings are cut."

Perigee might well have been dangling up here the entire time we were talking to Brown. He cocked his head and looked at me as if he were trying to understand. The yellow circles around his bright eyes accented their intelligence and curiosity. "Pretty boy," he croaked, then, "Arwk."

"Did you bring him here with you?" I asked Brown.

"Me? You gotta be kidding. That's Lewellen's bird. I haven't a clue what it's doing here."

I looked over the deck and saw the faint prints of my running shoes and the Kid's leading from the butte. The only other footprints were the half-moon-shaped heels of a cowboy boot, put there by someone who came down hard on the heel. They were all exactly the same size, they all led to and from Wes Brown's truck to the cage or the path through the brush to Cottora Canyon. Perigee might have gotten here by magic if not on Wes Brown's shoulder.

The Kid was looking at the box of parrots Brown had put on the ground next to the cage. "I want to see something," he said. "Watch him." He nodded toward Brown and carried the macaw back to the boom.

Perigee gripped the boom with his beak and did a somersault, watching us with his bright eyes and flapping his large blue wings. He was a high-wire act, as playful and irresistible as a child, but I couldn't let myself get charmed; I had the devious and uncharming Wes Brown to think about. I wondered if he'd be any more forthcoming now that the Kid was on the ground and he was alone with me, an Anglo and a woman. Maybe if I played the eye game I'd get some answers. It had been a long time since I'd flirted to get what I wanted. I didn't know if I was still capable of it—if I'd ever been capable of it.

"The feds are hiring wets now?" Brown asked, looking at the Kid. A smuggler would suspect everyone of being a fed, but so would a kidnapper.

"He's not a wetback," I said.

"Is he a fed?"

"No."

"Then what are you two doing here?"

Meeting his eyes by moonlight was comparable to meeting them underwater; they lacked clarity. Still, I had to do it now if I was ever going to. The minicam couldn't do that for me. I swam into the fathoms, and I saw that Wes Brown was drowning. Water is a conductor, and the message it sent was that this man was full of confusion and pain. Misery leads to criminal activity, but was he miserable enough to commit a kidnapping? Smuggling is common, and bird smugglers are more likely to get a fine than a sentence. But kidnapping is the deep water of crime and it was possible that he'd gotten in over his head. It could be that something had gone way wrong, that Deborah Dumaine was dead and he couldn't see the way out. If Deborah was dead, there wasn't any way out, but the truth would cut him a better deal.

"You catch the rabbit?" I asked, trying to develop a rapport.

"I thought I had." He shrugged.

"What happened? You get caught?"

"Yeah."

"For drugs?"

"Right."

"Did you do time?"

"No. I plea-bargained and got a suspended sentence and a fine. They took everything I had but this." He kicked the cabin of the boat.

He'd been willing enough to tell me about the drug smuggling. Maybe because I was a woman and women existed only as insubstantial shadows to him. I attempted to move on to the next crime. "Tell me the truth about Deborah," I said, "it'll be a lot easier on you."

"Huh?" he said, branding himself indelibly as a So-Cal cowboy. A real cowboy would say ma'am.

"It could keep a bad situation from getting a whole lot worse."

"Right," he said with a short and bitter laugh.

"Tell me where she is."

"I told you I haven't a clue."

"Where's your partner?"

"What partner?"

"You'll be in big trouble if anything happens to Deborah."

"You got the wrong guy. I'm not responsible for Deborah Dumaine." He blinked his eyes and shifted his weight.

There were a number of options. The Kid and I could have beaten the truth out of him, but that was a felony. I could have bribed him, but the money belonged to Terrance Lewellen. I could have made a citizen's arrest, but that would conflict with my responsibilities to my client and there was no guarantee that Deborah would be better off if Wes Brown was removed from Door—if she was in Door. He could be her only source of food and water. It was a quagmire. I was ready to turn it over to the feds, but I couldn't do that either without consulting my client.

"Chiquita," the Kid called from the ground. "Come here. I want to show you something. *Watchate*," he pointed the .45 at

Brown, "stay where you are. Put your hands on the *mastil*." Brown swore out loud. Under his breath he called the Kid a fucking wet, but he followed orders.

I climbed down the ladder and circled the pickup, recording Brown's license plate number with the minicam. I looked into the cab of the truck, checked the glove compartment and under the seat and found no weapons hidden there. I walked over to the Kid and the cage. He showed me the parrots in the wooden box and I taped them too, making the feds' case for them. The parrots were a sad and sorry lot; they'd had a long, cruel journey.

"Those are yellow-headed *Amazonas* from Mexico," the Kid said. "But this one is a blue-fronted *Amazona* from Argentina. Beautiful, no?"

"Yes," I said.

"What do you want to do with him and the birds? You want to take them to Albuquerque?"

"No," I said. "That would be tampering with evidence. I want to call in the feds and let them do it, but I have to talk to my client first."

"Something could happen to these birds if we leave them here. That guy could hurt or kill them." He nodded toward Brown, who glared at us from the mast.

"He's more likely to sell them," I said. "I've got the name of his contact in Albuquerque. I'll call Terrance as soon as we get back to the pickup. Why don't we tie Brown up for a few hours anyway? If I can convince Terrance, we can call the feds and get them in here."

"Okay. Let's go. You want to take *Perigeo*. Right?"

"Right," I said.

"I want to take the thick-billed."

"Brown won't like it."

The Kid shrugged. There were times when a weapon was more effective than a watch.

We tied Brown to the mast with some knots the Kid had learned in his travels. A partner might well show up and untie him. Brown was a sailor; he'd know something about knots and might untie himself eventually. The rope was at best a temporary measure to get us over the butte and to the phone without Brown's interference. One of us might have stayed here and guarded him, but neither of us wanted to do it. There were too many unknowns out there in the desert, and no telling when and if help would come. No telling what my client's next direction would be, and I was obligated to follow my client's directions.

"Tell us where Deborah is and we might let you go," was my parting shot to Brown.

"I haven't a clue," was his parting answer.

The Kid put the parrots in the cage, took the tape off their beaks and gave them some food and water before we left. We began a tedious sideways trudge up the butte, slipping and sliding. Brown started yelling and swearing when we were about halfway up after it was too much trouble to go back down and beat the crap out of him.

"You wet bastard," he yelled at the Kid, followed by "cunt" for me.

"*A la verga,*" said the Kid.

"Prick," said I.

That's the kind of guy Brown was, a smuggler who'd turn on you whether you crossed him or whether you didn't.

9

Our shadows stretched west as we crossed the butte. My thoughts were on the treachery of some men and what I would say to my client when I reached him on his C phone. When the Apaches wanted to communicate, they lit a fire and fanned the flame. A warrior on another butte would see the puffs of smoke and pass the message on. The whole vast Apache territory could be alerted in a matter of minutes. It was almost as fast and a lot more interesting than a fax machine. Through their system of smoke signals, the Apaches were able to keep tabs on where the cavalry had been, how many there were and where they were going. For hundreds of years they stayed one step ahead. We're the air people, our thoughts ride the airwaves; the Apaches were people of earth and fire.

When we reached the north side of the butte, we climbed down the rock stairs very carefully and walked through the sandy white arroyo. Maybe we were a step ahead, maybe not. The C phone waited in the pickup for me to call my client.

While I did, the Kid attended to the parrots. Perigee squawked happily when he saw his toys. If he was having any return-to-the-cage anxieties, he didn't reveal them. He was not an anxious bird. The contrast between him and the thick-billed was pronounced. The thick-billed seemed scarred by something, the memory of the border crossing, maybe, or life with Wes Brown.

I called my client and listened to his phone go through the answering machine dance, ringing two, three, four, five times. Come on, Terrance, I thought. Answer the goddamn phone. It was hard to believe he could be sleeping in Albuquerque while I was in the desert negotiating the release of his wife and his bird with his two hundred thousand dollars. "Lewellen here," the machine came on. "You know what to do."

"Pick up the phone, Terrance," I said when the machine beeped. "It's Neil."

As I suspected, he was screening his calls, but who else was he expecting in the middle of the night? "You get the bird?" he asked me.

"Yeah. We found him on the deck of Wes Brown's boat."

"Yahoo. How's he look?"

"Wonderful. He's happy and healthy. He's in his cage now, playing with his toys. There's no sign of Deborah."

"Did you give Brown the money?"

"He didn't ask. He says he knows nothing about Deborah and he doesn't know how Perigee ended up on his deck."

"He's a liar. He won't take the money from you because you can identify him."

"We're not far from the border. Two hundred thousand dollars could take him somewhere and he'd never have to come back. It won't make any difference whether I can identify him or not once he gets to Mexico." Would the feds care enough to go looking for him? That could depend on how much he owed them.

"He'll want to come back. He likes it in Door; he's too screwed up to live anyplace else. His partner will show up with Deborah and take the money. Brown'll think there's no way of proving he was involved."

"There is a lot of circumstantial evidence."

"Did you get it on the minicam?

"Yeah."

"Good. The person who picks up the ransom will be someone you've never seen before. Mark my words."

"We came across Brown smuggling parrots. I think it's way past time to call in the feds."

"No."

"You don't know what kind of danger Deborah is in."

"She'll be in worse danger if they get involved. Believe me. They'll screw it up. And don't you do it yourself, either. Everything I told you I told you in confidence." Not if he told me over the cell phone. Anybody who tuned in could listen to the radio signals zinging between Door and Albuquerque. They couldn't hear my swear words riding the waves in English and in Spanish, but they were there too, if only in spirit. "Stay down there till morning, and if nothing happens come on back. Deborah could be in Albuquerque for all we know. If they contact me directly, I'll call you." He hung up.

He didn't go so far as to remind me of the lawyer's code of ethics; he didn't have to. One of the original purposes of that code had to have been to prevent lawyers from ratting on impossible clients.

"That's the last time I ever work for a corporate raider," I said to the Kid.

"What did he say?"

"He doesn't want me to call in the feds."

"Why not?"

"It's possible he came by the macaws illegally and is afraid he'll lose them. It's probable the kidnapping was taped ille-

gally. If he committed a crime, I can't reveal it." If Terrance
had committed a crime, the question was, how big a crime?

"You have to do what he says?"

"Yeah. He's my client. He wants us to stay here till morning and see if Brown's partner shows up."

"You think that will happen?"

"Who knows? Who knows if Brown has a partner? Who
knows if Brown is even involved?"

"You believed that guy when he said he knew nothing?"

"Did he look like an honest person to you?"

"No. He's a *lorotraficante*. He has the eyes of a liar."

"The evidence is not in his favor."

"If we wait, maybe the woman will come to us."

"Maybe."

I thought he'd be pissed about spending the remainder of
the night at Mile Marker 62, but he wasn't. He had too much
of an adrenaline buzz to want to get in the truck and drive the
six hours back to Albuquerque. He was having trouble just
standing still. A near-death experience activates all the senses—
for a while anyway. Then it wears off, and you either get the
shakes or collapse. I had a bit of a buzz myself, but mine came
from the feeling that I was being manipulated by a cosmic
puppeteer. There was tension in the strings. There was also
some unresolved business from the events in the boat.

"Why you not give Brown the parrot?" I asked the Kid,
lapsing into his English. Sometimes his English reflected me,
sometimes mine reflected him.

He shrugged. "I knew he wouldn't shoot."

"If you'd been wrong, you'd be dead now." My voice had a
sharp edge, and what was that reflecting? That I was pissed at
him for putting me through his death, if only for an instant?

"He's a *cobarde*."

"A coward with a temper. He has killed a lot of parrots
and hawks," I said.

"That's what a *cobarde* does—kills birds and animals."

"That's how people killers get their start."

"If I give him the parrot, maybe he shoot me anyway."

Maybe.

"You had your gun." He smiled. "I knew you would protect me."

"Brown fired before I could," I reminded him.

"*Verdad*, but it went into the floor. It's over. Forget it,
Chiquita. *Mira*." He pointed to the sky where a star had left its
constellation and taken a solitary dive, which happens often
enough in the summer skies. "Death is always there," he said.
"It can come like that." He snapped his fingers. "You can
never be ready, or you can always be ready."

"*No pasa, no muera,*" I said.

"I crossed the border a long time ago," he replied.

"I know." His hair was electric, the wolf glow was in his
eyes. We were in the Land of Enchantment; the night was
alive with sweetness and danger. The prickly pear cactus were
circled by a red heart string. The datura was releasing its scent
and its pollen. If moonlight had a fragrance, it would be the
scent of sacred datura. It's a magical plant that can rearrange
you or kill you. Its beauty was exquisite and abundant. We
were surrounded by hundreds, maybe thousands, of moon-
white flowers, a wedding party where every bud had become,
for one night only, a bride. I knew he was looking at me with
the thing I most dreaded—need—in his eyes, but I met them.
It was a need I had too—to say we were here and alive when
we could so easily have been vulture fodder.

"In the spring there are yellow flowers here that smell
exactly like chocolate," the Kid said.

"*Verdad?*"

"*Si.*"

"What does this smell like to you?" He picked a datura
flower and handed it to me. I ran my hand down the silky

trumpet to the place where the petal opened up. I stuck my nose into the pistil. It was, I thought, the most beautiful thing I had ever smelled. It was the odor of love in the face of death, its most pure and simple form. Love always exists in the face of death but we usually don't admit it.

"It smells like the moon," I said.

"Come with me," the Kid whispered.

"Okay," I responded. Yes, I was thinking. Yes, yes, yes.

We'd been brushed by the wings of death. I saw it as a very large butterfly, the size of a man or a woman. Its power was awesome, but its touch had been as light as a feather. It was terrifying; it was exhilarating. I wanted more than anything to lie down on the ground and make love.

We grabbed our equipment and a sleeping bag, walked into the desert and surrendered to the spell of the moon and the weed. It was so quiet I could hear the earth hum. The stars were bright enough to navigate from here to Tierra del Fuego. They were the color of diamonds: blue, yellow, red.

"*Mira,*" I said. "*Diamantes.*"

"*Magnifico,*" he replied.

The Kid took off the backpack. We spread out the sleeping bag and entwined like DNA strands that had found their perfect mate. When it was over, we separated and went to opposite sides of the sleeping bag. I thought I'd close my eyes for five minutes; we had a long drive ahead. The Kid sleeps like a stone. I don't sleep at all. We'd been careful. We'd locked the pickup, brought the weapons and the phone.

The sky was the gray that comes before dawn when I woke up. Minutes could have passed, or hours. The moon was setting. The birds were calling up the sun. I'd always wondered if the full moon looks as large going down as it does coming up. It doesn't. I rubbed my eyes. A cowboy was standing in front of me, and several feet behind the cowboy a white horse waited with its reins hanging down. The cowboy wore a duster, a black hat and a mask made out of feathers. The feathers were muted by the gray dawn, but I knew that in full daylight they'd have the brilliance of a rain forest. That they had come from parrots and hawks, I had no doubt. I was looking at two hands wearing gauntlets thick enough to grab a prickly pear and squeeze it tight. The right hand held a .45 and the left hand rubbed the fingers against the thumb in a gesture of universal greed. I reached over to wake the Kid, and the hand holding the .45 closed in on my forehead. One twitch and my skull would have exploded across the ground like an overripe melon.

"Who are . . . ? What do . . . ?" I started to ask, but the greed hand went to the mouth and made a *shhhhh* motion. I knew what the hands wanted, but I didn't want to give it up. We'd gotten back the parrot, but we didn't have the woman yet. The bargain hadn't been entirely kept. The hat with the minicam was lying on the ground. I'd turned ot off before making love. The camera wouldn't be getting the holdup on tape, but what did it matter? The identical image had already been recorded by the Tramway ATM. "Where's Deborah?" I mouthed, The head behind the feathered mask shook. The eyes were hidden inside the sockets.

Stuck between a .45 and a hard place, I handed over two thousand hundred-dollar bills. The cowboy shouldered the backpack, picked up the C phone and the weapons that were lying on the ground, got on the white horse and rode west, leaving not one word of instruction for the return of Deborah Dumaine.

I woke the Kid. "You're not going to believe this," I said, even though in this time and place almost anything was believable. By the time he was awake enough to comprehend what had happened, the pale horse and feathered rider had disappeared. Maybe it had been a dream, maybe a contact hallucination brought on by the proximity of too much jimson weed.

The trumpet lilies had shot their pollen and were beginning a sated, sensual droop. We heard horse hooves clomping down the not-so-distant highway.

"That's the sound of two hundred thousand dollars galloping away," I said. "The weapons and the phone are gone too."

"You hear anything about the woman?" he asked.

"Not a word."

"Why you not wake me up?"

Because I didn't have the *cojones*? "I would have gotten me a bullet in the head. You too."

"I told you that guy's a *cobarde*."

"I don't know that it was that guy, Kid. I couldn't see anybody's hands or face or eyes. All I saw was a mask, a pair of boots and a coat."

"Only a *cobarde* would hide himself like that. How big was he?"

"Brown's size, more or less."

"What hand did he use for the gun?"

"The right."

"What kind of gun?"

"A .45."

"That's him."

"We took his .45."

"He hid another one somewhere. Maybe he buried it with the money."

Maybe. "If that was him, then who wore the mask at the ATM?"

"His cousin," the Kid said. "I can't track the horse on the highway."

"I know." Paved roads were something Apaches didn't have to contend with.

He leaped up. "He didn't get the birds, did he? You hear them?" Parrots would probably be a better alarm system than a guard dog or the Viper.

"Not a squawk."

"*Bueno. Vamos.* Maybe we can catch him." The Kid pulled on his shoes and ran over to *his* white horse, the pickup, but it had been hobbled. The right rear tire had been slit and it was sinking into the dust. *"Mierda,"* he said.

The parrots were still there and glad to see him. He gave them water and food. I offered him the plastic bag of Terrance's special granola treat.

"What's that?" he asked.

"Granola."

"That's not food for a bird," he said, but Perigee gobbled it up.

While he changed the tire, I climbed the rock stairs and crossed the butte to see if there was any sign of Wes Brown. "I tell you he's not there," the Kid said, but I went anyway. The Kid was right; Brown had untied himself (or someone else had untied him) from the mast. It stood alone in the boat. The pickup truck with the NRA bumper sticker was also gone.

"Vanished," I said when I got back down.

The Kid shrugged. That didn't surprise him.

"What time is it?" I asked.

He looked at his watch, gave it a shake, looked again. The watch had stopped running. He saw it as a bad omen, an indication that someone's time had run out. The question was, whose?

When we reached Range around eight, I was wired tired. The strings that seemed to be controlling my movements were stretched taut. Range had the shimmering unreality of a movie set, as if the buildings were six-inch façades with nothing behind them but the beams that propped them up. I felt that if we came back a week later, the town would be dismantled. It was already hot enough to sweat through the Kid's bandanna and my shirt. The ice in the water jugs had long since melted.

We stopped at Bruno's Cafe for breakfast and to call Terrance Lewellen. Fortunately, Bruno's had food and depth. The *latilla* ceiling in the patio was made up of branches with the leaves still on. We found the one that offered the most shade and sat under it. A swivel-hipped waitress took our order. The patio walls had the smell of adobe. I leaned against mine. There's nothing that shelters as well as an adobe wall. The bathroom had vending machines pushing pink and blue New Mexicondoms, the huevos rancheros and chorizo were eye-opening hot, but by the time the food showed up I'd lost my appetite. While we'd waited I'd called Terrance from the pay phone outside, planning to tell him that I'd given up his money but hadn't gotten back his wife. Would he care? I wondered while the answering machine went through its five-ring dance.

"Come on, Terrance," I said after the beep. "Pick up the phone." But he didn't answer.

"What happened?" the Kid asked when I returned to the patio.

"Nothing. He didn't pick up."

"Maybe he had to go somewhere."

"Maybe."

I called again three hours later from the pay phone at the Kmart in Socorro. The machine answered after the second ring, indicating that Terrance had not taken the first message. This time it was, "Terrance, pick up the goddamn phone." Still no response.

"Our little lives are rounded by a beep," I told the Kid after I returned to my seat in the sweltering pickup.

"What?" he asked.

"Nothing," I replied.

I tried again at the McDonald's in Belen. This time it was, "Terrance, pick up the fucking phone."

There was no answer.

10

Terrance lived on Cristobal Road in a big house in the high Heights, not far from the wind goddess's canyon in distance but below the piñon and juniper line, which placed him in another life zone. It was noon by the time we got there. Not much grew under its own power on Terrance's property, and he hadn't done anything to change that. His yard didn't have xeriscaping. It had no scaping. Terrance wasn't a man to notice what grew around him. His house had a big view—too big for me. I like looking into forever when I'm on a hike, but I'd rather think of home as a nest, not an aerie. Too much of what you see from the Heights is blowing dust. Terrance had a trophy house in the style I call California modern, an architectural statement, but of what? It looked like a curved-wall house and a flat-wall house had gotten split up somewhere and slapped together on Cristobal Road.

A white Saturn was parked in the circular driveway. The black Jaguar was not in sight. The garage door was closed. PROTECTED BY ABC SECURITY decals were in the windows. The brown ABC logo had the charred look of a brand. The massive front door that must have been hand carved and imported from Colonial Mexico stood ajar. The Kid carried Perigee on his shoulder, and the bird seemed to recognize his surroundings. His eyes were bright, and he gurgled happily. Maybe he was anticipating a reunion with his mate. I pushed the front door all the way open, and we stepped into the hall. "Helloooo," the bird called into the long, empty corridor. I thought the sound of Perigee would bring my client running, but the only response we got was the red eye of the alarm system clicking on when it spotted us. The system tracked our path throughout the house but the alarm never sounded, or it had already sounded and rung until it ran out.

"You there, Terrance?" I yelled, but he didn't answer.

We began searching for my client. The rooms in Terrance's house were enormous, and there were plenty of them. On our right we saw a restaurant-sized stainless steel kitchen. The remains of breakfast—a glass, a mug, a bowl, a bottle of milk and a container of juice—were on the counter. Across the hall was a workout room with metal machines that resembled the skeletons of prehistoric animals. Maybe somebody rode them for exercise; I didn't believe it was Terrance Lewellen. We passed a study with a wall-to-wall entertainment center, a leather Eames chair and an ottoman. A classic red, black and white Navajo rug lay on the floor. The red light of an answering machine beeped three times. The end table was loaded with remotes. This, I figured, was where Terrance got *his* exercise.

The hall opened into a vast two-story living room. The beehive kiva fireplace was terraced with shelves for displaying a collector's art. Hopi kachinas danced in place on the God shelf. A large and valuable Indian pot sat in a trivet on the hearth, balanced at the angle of repose. Had it tipped one fraction of an inch farther it would have met the floor and shattered into worthless shards. Floor-to-ceiling windows faced west toward the long view, giving me the impression that if I had wings I could float from here to Mount Taylor. The window wall was the curved part of the house. The other walls were flat, and hanging on one of them was an Albert Lochover painting I hadn't seen yet, titled *Wild Flower* and consisting of purple sage and golden chamisa dancing in the wind. It was less muted than the others, marking it, I supposed, as very early or very late. The painting was large, the signature was bold, but the brush strokes were precise and delicate. The intimate feeling was appreciated in this grandiose room. I liked the brightness of *Wild Flower* myself, but I wasn't enough of an expert to know if that made it more or less valuable than the others. Had Terrance held on to it for sentimental reasons or to outfox Charlie Register? I was enough of a people expert to know that Terrance had lied to Charlie. He hadn't handed over all his Lochovers. This was one, apparently, that Charlie hadn't known about. White-on-white rectangles marked the homes of the Lochovers Charlie had known about.

An exquisite Navajo weaving made of subtle natural dyes hung on the wall next to the fireplace. I walked up close to find the line that leads out of the rug. I've heard different interpretations of this line: that it's a pathway to the gods, that the weaver puts it there as a mark of imperfection so as not to anger the gods by appearing to emulate them. Whatever the interpretation, the message is that the weavers are human, and the gods are not. I wondered if the rug would unravel if I pulled the string.

"The bird hears something," the Kid called. He and Perigee had wandered down a hallway on the far side of the living room.

I followed. Perigee's head was cocked as he looked toward the north side of the house.

I stopped to listen and heard the sound of a woman crying in the room at the end of the hall. "Deborah?" I called, but nobody answered. The bird gave a low growl; the woman continued crying.

The sound drew us down the long hallway to the master bedroom that had once been shared by Terrance and Deborah. Like the other rooms in this house, it was enormous. The eastern wall—all glass—faced the Sandias, the home of the wind goddess's mountain. It was gray rock today, shrouded in gray clouds, stern and indifferent to human fate. The wall on the north side held a king-sized bed with an elaborately carved headboard. A body was lying at one edge of the bed. It was not the body I'd been expecting to find. A woman knelt beside the bed, grieving the way a bird grieves at the loss of its mate. The body belonged to Terrance Lewellen. The woman was Sara Dumaine.

"Uh-oh," said the Kid.

"Shit," I said. "What happened?"

"He's dead," Sara sobbed. "Terry's dead."

"He can't be," I said. "I talked to him only a few hours ago."

"He is," Sara cried.

You're not supposed to touch a corpse, I know, but I couldn't believe Terrance was dead until I'd felt it myself. I put my hand to his wrist to feel for a pulse; there wasn't a flutter.

Perigee was terrified, angry or something else. It's hard to know the inner truth of a parrot's emotions; maybe he was only reacting to our reactions. The outer evidence was striking. All signs of calm and good nature vanished. His feathers fluffed up. His large wings flapped and fanned the air. His beak screeched a cacophony of abuse.

"I'll take him outside," the Kid said.

"Good," I replied.

"You okay here?" he asked me.

"For the moment."

"I will be outside if you need me."

"Thanks," I said. "What killed him?" I asked Sara.

"I don't know," she cried. "I got here a few minutes ago and I found him like this."

"Did you call the police?"

"Not yet."

"Do it," I said. "Now. There's a phone in the study." Terrance must have left his cell phone somewhere else; it wasn't here. I wanted Sara out of my way and out of the room. I needed a moment of peace and quiet to examine the scene and to think. Sara was stunned enough to obey my orders and give me my moment. Terrance was what people in the death business call DRT, dead right there. He lay flat on his back dressed in jeans, a short-sleeved shirt and his ostrich-hide cowboy boots. The top couple of buttons on his shirt were undone, exposing gray chest hair and a gold chain. His piece was awry, and his bare head had the startling whiteness of an underground slug. Going natural didn't make Terrance look distinguished. It made him look dead. There was no bullet hole, no mess, no blood, no sign of trauma. The only thing unusual was that his lips appeared swollen. Could Terrance have had a heart attack? I wondered. He was overweight and a type-A personality if ever I saw one. His heart could easily have the plugged arteries that would cause a coronary. But it was too easy and too convenient an explanation for me. With every sudden death, the medical examiner at least considers the possibility of homicide, and so did I. Terrance's right arm had fallen over the side of the bed and his bear claw paw was lying on the Berber carpet. There was a patch on his forearm. The testosterone it dripped wouldn't be doing him any good now. On his upper arm I saw a speck of blood. A hypodermic needle and a tiny empty vial sat on the bedside table. If this was a drug-induced death, I couldn't imagine what the drug had been, and I couldn't tell whether it had been administered by Terrance or someone else. Suicide was also a possibility a medical investigator would consider, but I didn't believe Terrance Lewellen was capable of it.

Sara returned. "They're on their way," she said.

"Good," I replied. "Did you see these?" I said, pointing to the vial and the hypodermic needle.

"Yes. They were on the floor beside his hand. I put them on the table."

"You picked up a hypodermic needle lying next to a dead man?" Whatever fingerprints had been on the needle and vial would now be covered with Sara Dumaine's. She had tampered with evidence, which was either very dumb or moderately smart, depending on who the bottom set of fingerprints belonged to.

Sara nodded her head yes.

"Do you know what is in the vial?"

"No," she said.

"How did you get in?" I asked her.

"I have a key."

"And the code to deactivate the alarm?"

Sara nodded yes, buried her face in her hands and began to cry again with deep, hacking sobs. I took a good look at her. She was dressed in her trademark white: white jeans, white beaded choker, white boots, white turncoat jacket. Her blond hair was tucked up under a white baseball cap that would have looked better on a younger woman, but the dollar sign tendrils hung down. When Malinche figures in pueblo Indian ceremonials, she is always a young girl dressed in white. I wanted to pull Sara's hands away from her face and look deep into her bluebonnet eyes. She was blonder than Deborah, younger than Deborah, and she wasn't going through menopause. She was a woman who'd look good on Terrance's arm; she was also Deborah's half-sister. Her grief struck me as excessive if that's all she was. Her presence here, her key and her knowledge of the alarm system, were beyond suspicious.

"Were you sleeping with Terrance?" I asked her.

The hands fell away and gave me my opportunity to look into her eyes. Sara had made herself up carefully at some point, but it was all for nothing now, because the makeup ran down her cheeks in rivulets of brown mascara and blue eye shadow. Her blue eyes, tinged with red, were terrified.

"Where is Deborah? Did you bring her back with you?" Her voice was a whisper.

"I didn't find her. I asked you if you were sleeping with Terrance."

She hesitated, but something—either the body in the bed or me—scared her into fessing up. "We were in love," she said.

Love, I thought. Almost as many crimes have been committed in the name of that as in the name of religion. I wasn't sure Terrance was capable of love; capable of trophy hunting maybe, but that's not love. There's a name for what people who sleep with their sister's husbands do, but I wouldn't call that love either. I'd call it betrayal, and about the worst betrayal a sister, even a half-sister, can commit. I don't have a sister myself, and somewhere down the road I realized that I didn't have any women friends who had sisters either. All my women friends are only children or have brothers. We've developed our own form of sisterhood, but it's not Sara and Deborah's form. Sisters and brothers learn to compete one way. Sisters and sisters learn another. Competition can bring out the best in you, or the worst. Sisters jab more, but they forgive more. A sister listens when a brother talks about basketball. Would a sister forgive her sibling for screwing her husband? I wouldn't; I knew that.

"Deborah was so wrapped up in her parrots," Sara said. "She traveled all the time. When she was here, she and Terry fought constantly. She was the smart and successful one. She got all the attention growing up. Nobody ever noticed me." Sara had entered victim mind, that place where everyone has been wounded and no one is responsible. She might get away with it in court, but it didn't wash with me.

"She was your sister," I said.

"My half-sister," Sara replied. "I had the time to give Terry the love he needed."

And Terrance had the money to give Sara all of what she needed, a match made of testosterone, envy and greed.

"Have you ever met Deborah?" Sara asked me.

"No."

"She was an only child and very spoiled until I came along. She's used to getting her way. This room is Deborah. She likes looking at mountains."

I heard the wail of the police siren as it pulled into the driveway. The fact that the Kid was a young, Hispanic male standing in a rich Anglo's driveway would make him a suspect even though the police were likely to be young and Hispanic themselves. Of course, if he were a real suspect he would have split long ago. Would the Kid remember what I'd said about not discussing the kidnapping? Most likely. He was not a chatterbox, and he had an innate distrust of law enforcement.

"Did Deborah know you were sleeping with Terrance?" I asked Sara.

Sara shook her blond curls no. "She would have said something, believe me. Don't tell her, please."

I'd have to find Deborah before I could tell her anything. Maybe Sara had just told me the truth. Maybe she was believing what she wanted to believe. I looked at Terrance. In death he appeared just as vulnerable as the rest of us. His corporate raider bluff was all gone. Without the cigar and the briefcase he seemed half dressed. Had he been enough of a shit to sleep with Deborah's sister and then fake Deborah's kidnapping to get her out of the way entirely? I wondered. Had Sara been in on it? In Texas they call that way of ending a relationship a Smith & Wesson divorce. They also say there that the worst thing that can happen to a man is to have an ex-wife with a mouth. A bullet is cheaper than a divorce lawyer. Could Terrance Lewellen have been working with Wes Brown? Did they fake how much they disliked each other, or did they dislike each other and work together anyway? Had Brown been the mastermind? Had he been the dupe? Where had *he* gone last night? That I would think such thoughts at a moment like this said something about me, something about my client. He was—like most clients—imperfect. And I—like most lawyers—have a soft spot for shits. My job, after all, is to defend them. I was pissed at Terrance for misleading me, pissed at him for dying, pissed at him for sleeping with Sara and also more than a little sad to see him go. I was downright depressed. On some level, I'd grown to like the guy. He was full of bull, but he'd been good to his bird. What made this even worse was that I felt, in a way I couldn't define, responsible. The hand behind the strings twitched, and I shivered.

The police and paramedics came down the hallway. I heard their equipment slapping against their hips. The paramedics went right to work on Terrance, but he was dead when they got there and he remained dead. There were two detectives: Rosalia Hernandez and John Snyder. John was tall, fair-haired and distant. Rosalia was stocky, tough and to the point. Her hair was brown with a coppery tinge and fell in curls around her shoulders. She did most of the questioning. It was one variation of good cop, bad cop, and it worked for them. As I had suspected, they'd brought the Kid in with them, but not the parrots. Rosalia asked the obvious questions about who Sara and I were and what we were doing in Terrance Lewellen's bedroom.

"I'm his sister-in-law," Sara said. "I got here about a half-hour ago and I found Terry like that."

"I'm his lawyer," I said, nodding toward Terrance. "I got here around fifteen minutes ago, and that's how I found my client. I'm *his* lawyer too." I indicated the Kid. If they intended to question him as a suspect, I intended to shield him—and me.

"That right?" Rosalia asked the Kid.

"Right," he said.

Rosalia was sharp enough to get to the heart of the matter. "Does the deceased have a wife?" she asked.

"Yeah," I said.

"Where is she?"

"I don't know."

"Do you?" she asked Sara.

"No," Sara said.

Rosalia rolled her eyes. She didn't believe us, but she let our stories stand while she and her partner made a visual inspection of the crime scene and recorded it with their video camera. The law of transference is that everyone who comes to a crime scene brings something, everyone who leaves takes something. The police aren't supposed to touch anything until the medical investigator shows up. It's a rule that's often ignored, but with the deceased's lawyer in the room they were careful to follow procedure. Their attention was drawn to the needle and the vial, as mine had been.

While they went about their video business, I thought about my obligation to my client. Anything Terrance had told me, he had told me in confidence. If he had committed a crime, I couldn't reveal it. If I had any evidence, I could not turn it over. If I knew that a major crime was about to be committed, I did have an obligation to disclose that, but it looked to me like the major crimes in this case had already been committed. If there were any more of them on the agenda, I didn't know what they'd be. There is a dead man's statute which says that communications from the deceased are hearsay and inadmissible, with the exception of a dying declaration. If there'd been one of those, Sara might have heard it, but not me. The trouble with this case was that the things I couldn't reveal— the kidnapping of Deborah Dumaine, the tape, Wes Brown's involvement, the handing over of the ransom, the person in the feathered mask—were all evidence that might help to locate my client's murderer, if he had been murdered. But my interpretation of the code of ethics was that attorney/client privilege obtains even after the client's death. The client's reputation and heirs had to be considered. Who were his heirs? I wondered. Did an about-to-be divorced wife qualify? His mother? Sara?

The natural course for a lawyer is to say as little as possible, and that's what I intended to do. I had decided, however, to tell the FWS about Wes Brown and turn over to them the tape I had of the smuggling operation. I wouldn't mind seeing Brown fall into the clutches of law enforcement. There wasn't anything on the tape that violated my agreement with Terrance Lewellen, incriminated him or ruined his reputation.

The medical investigator arrived, a brisk, gray-haired woman named Mae Capshaw. Medical investigators come from all walks of life in New Mexico, and my guess was that Mae was, or had been, a nurse. She was expected to touch and examine the victim and she did. If she discovered anything conclusive, she didn't reveal it. To determine the cause of death in a body as unmarked as Terrance's would require an autopsy, and it's standard procedure for an unwitnessed death. The autopsy would be done quickly, but toxicology, drug tests and stomach contents could take weeks. Mae's attention was drawn to the vial and the hypodermic just as everyone else's had been. She picked them up with gloved hands and dropped them in an evidence bag.

"What is it? Do you know?" I asked.

"Epinephrine, I'd say."

"What's that?"

"Adrenaline. It's used to counteract anaphylactic shock, a life-threatening allergic reaction."

"Why didn't it work?"

"Don't know yet."

Part of the medical investigator's role is to consider history and circumstances and to examine witnesses. "Did he have any known allergies?" she asked us.

"He was allergic to pollen," Sara said. "He went to Dr. Talbert for shots."

"He was allergic to parrots," I said.

"How about bee stings, antibiotics or food?"

"I don't know," Sara said.

"His breakfast food is in the kitchen," the Kid said. "He ate that cereal. What do you call it?"

"Granola," I said.

"I'll take a sample," said Mae.

"How long does an allergic reaction take to kill somebody?" I asked.

"Could be hours. Could be a few minutes," Mae said. "Did he have any other life-threatening medical conditions that anybody knows about? Was he seeing any other doctors?" She looked at me, then at Sara.

"No," said Sara.

"Not that I know of," I said.

"Did he have a nicotine addiction?" she asked, indicating the patch.

"Testosterone," I said.

"They're putting that in a patch now?" she asked.

"Right," I said.

She shook her head. "I don't have any further questions for the witnesses, do you?" she asked Hernandez and Snyder.

"Not now," said Hernandez, "but I could be bringing you in for questioning when I get the OMI report."

I gave the lawyer's standard response. "I have nothing to say. And neither does he." I indicated the Kid. That was his right and my obligation.

"We'll see about that," said Rosalia. "Take my card. You might want to get in touch with me."

I took a couple of them, but I had no intention of calling Detective Rosalia Hernandez myself.

Sara cried as the paramedics bagged and tagged Terrance and put him on a stretcher. The detectives were vacuuming for fibers and dusting for prints when we left the room.

"How'd you know about the granola?" I asked the Kid once we were back in the pickup with the birds.

"I saw it in the kitchen when I took *Perigeo* outside. I gave him some." The Kid looked out the window. He was embarrassed, and he had every right to be. This was a man, after all, who'd recently said granola was not fit food for a bird.

"What a soft touch," I said.

"*Perigeo* likes it. You think that granola stuff could kill somebody?"

"God knows," I said.

11

The next step was to return Perigee to the lab. As soon as we turned into UNM, he knew where we were headed. It meant back to the cage, but he didn't care; he was about to be reunited with his mate. The squawks and flaps, which had escalated once we turned the corner, became overwhelming when we opened the lab door. Colloquy heard Perigee coming, and she beat the bars of her cage. The perfectly matched pair were now separated by only the cage and the Kid's hands. I wished they didn't have clipped feathers, could meet in midair and fly off into the sunset together. Their regal size and royal racket were better adapted to high palm trees and cliffs than to a gray lab at UNM. The Kid and I made a half-hearted attempt to take off our shoes and put on the plastic booties, but the emotion of the reunion was too much.

"Oh, screw this," I said.

"Claro," said the Kid. He ran across the lab holding Perigee above him. The ruckus had jump-started all the other parrots into a barrage of sound.

Rick opened the door to the cage, and the Kid tossed Perigee in. The reunion was dramatic and touching. I was sorry that Deborah wasn't here and that Terrance wasn't alive to see it. I couldn't imagine two humans getting so worked up over being reunited, but we don't have brilliant blue feathers, beaks that can shear a nut in two or wings to fly us above the canopy. Compared to macaws, our lives are lacking in sound and color, and we don't necessarily mate for life. What we have is our big brain and the ability to build weapons and light a fire. That's why the indigos were on the inside looking out and we were on the outside looking in.

That they were not flying free in the Raso muted the joy of the reunion for the Kid and me, but Rick was thrilled to have the indigo back under his wing.

"This is fantastic," he said, grinning and gripping the bars of the cage.

Eventually the indigos settled down on their perch and Colloquy rubbed her neck against Perigee's. The Kid went into the lab to look at the other parrots while I talked to Rick. As often as I give advice, it's rare that anybody actually takes it. Rick had gotten a new look, the look that I'd recommended. The granny glasses were gone. He'd cut his hair short—too short for me—and too square along the neck. It was not a great cut, but it did bring out the highlights and some curl. His eyes were more accessible when they weren't magnified by the back-off-I'm-a-genius lenses. He looked younger, brighter, more determined. He looked like his own person instead of a pale imitation of someone else's thirty-year-old rebellion. His clothes were the same baggy T-shirt and jeans, but you couldn't expect one quick and clandestine encounter to cause a complete overhaul. "I like it," I said.

"Did you find Deborah?" he asked me.

"No."

"What happened to her?"

"I don't know."

"Where was Perigee?"

"On Wes Brown's boat in Door."

Like a lawyer at a deposition, he continued his line of questioning. "What were *you* doing in Door?"

"Somebody sent me there. Look, there's something I have to tell you. As soon as I got back to Albuquerque this morning, I took Perigee to Terrance's house and I found him lying on his bed—dead."

"Terrance is dead?" His hand went behind his neck, reaching for the ponytail that was no longer there. "What happened to him?"

"The OMI doesn't know yet. It could have been an allergic reaction."

"To what?"

"Nobody knows. The autopsy should tell one way or the other." I shifted into deposition mode myself, and my first question was, "What happens to the indigos now?" In captivity they have a human life span, which meant they might not outlive him but could easily outlive me. Some provision must have been made for their welfare. Four hundred thousand dollars would feed and house them nicely, I calculated.

"Terrance set up an endowment."

"Who administers it?"

"Deborah. They fought all the time, but Terrance knew she was the best person to take care of Colloquy and Perigee. She's terrific with birds."

"And if Deborah doesn't return? Who gets them then?"

Rick put his hands to his face in a reflexive move to straighten his absent glasses. Without the lenses his eyes were raw and full of ambition. Control of a rare pair of captive indigos would have to be a bright feather in his career cap. He looked away from me and peered down at his running shoes like he was searching for the source of the blush that was rising to the top of his forehead. "Me," he said.

"Forever?"

"Well, yeah. For as long as they live. You can't keep changing handlers. Parrots get attached to people, and they hate change."

"And who gets to run the lab?"

"I do."

"Does the endowment include money for the lab?"

"Yes. Terrance didn't support Deborah, but he supported the parrots."

It was comparable to achieving tenure at age twenty-five. As long as the indigos lived and the lab functioned, Rick would be set up. It was a good gig, a little too settled and secure for me, but people in their twenties think differently now than I did. Times are tough, jobs and job security are hard to come by.

"I'm good with birds. I've been taking care of the indigos since I was an undergraduate," he said.

"When they were still at Terrance's house?"

"Yeah. I have a doctorate in ornithology." He was the bright student again, the student who would always be the first one to raise his hand in class, the last one to get a date. The student routine might not impress Alice, but control of the Psittacine Research Facility should.

"Have you ever met Wes Brown?" I asked him. I was pushing at the edge of attorney/client privilege by bringing up Wes Brown, but the edge is the place where the interesting discoveries are made.

"He came in here a couple of times, trying to sell Deborah birds. She believed they were smuggled, and she'd never buy smuggled parrots. I don't know why she wasted her time talking to him. Smugglers are the rottenest garbage on the face of the planet. Do you have any idea how many smuggled birds die?"

"Yes," I said. "Brown's a good-looking guy. Deborah didn't have a great marriage. Maybe she found him attractive."

"Him?" His eyes turned big and incredulous.

"Do you know Sara Dumaine?" I continued.

"I've met her."

"Did she know Wes Brown? Were they ever here at the same time?"

"I think they were once. He likes to go to Santa Fe; he was asking her about it."

I remembered then that there was a phone call I wanted to make. "Could I use the phone in Deborah's office?" I asked him. "I have to make a call."

"Go ahead," he said.

He watched the indigos while I went into the office, where Deborah's essence lingered like a wild and pungent perfume. I looked again at her photographs—all in Kodachrome. Her scarlet hair, her glossy red lipstick and her purple dress seemed garish and overdone when seen through the haze of one near-death experience, one real death and no sleep that I could remember. She was a presence that could be stimulating if you felt good, annoying when you didn't. Deborah was a pedal-to-the-metal, full-throttle experience. Was she really a bitch? I wondered. Was she really a redhead? I stared at her picture until it appeared to speak. "Arwk," it said.

"Huh?" I replied.

Max waddled out from behind the frame. "Call my lawyer," he cackled.

"You scared me, Max."

"Nut," replied the bird.

I looked at the kachinas on the shelf and reread the quotations that said people are imperfect, and God is in the details. Being an imperfect person and a lawyer besides, I called home.

My machine rang three times, which meant there were no messages, so I hung up. I looked through the window into the lab. As Rick was still watching the indigos, I slid open the drawer he'd put the parrot feathers in on my last visit. It was empty. I opened a few more drawers just for the heck of it, but they didn't contain any feathers either. Deborah's calendar was on the desk, and I flipped through it. There were several appointments scrawled across the pages for last week, this week and the next. The writing was large, bold and in green ink. Max, who'd gotten agitated by my snooping, began to squawk and to scold.

"Okay, okay," I said.

In the lab the Kid was talking to Alice of the long blond hair and the long graceful body. They'd walked over to the Amazons' cage and she was showing him a piece of recording equipment. They were about the same age. He was tall, skinny and dark. She was tall, slender and blond. He'd been up most of the night, but any fool could see that they made a great-looking pair. A green-eyed monster the size of a fullback filled Deborah's office. The dark side of passion is jealousy, and jealousy is the worst emotion of all. Nothing can make a woman crazier.

Max had climbed up on top of Deborah's computer and bobbed his double-yellow head. Do parrots feel jealousy? I asked myself. Why not? They feel affection. Max studied me with his bright, curious eyes that seemed to be asking, What are you humans all about anyway?

"Damned if I know, Max," I said.

"Maxamilian," replied the bird.

Rick entered the office and saw in what direction I'd been looking.

"Is he your boyfriend?" he asked.

"You could say that."

"Alice and I are going out tonight." His eyes glowed with something other than intelligence and ambition.

"Good. Did you see her last night?"

"No. I was here with Max and the other parrots. Right, Max?"

"Arwk," Max said.

"Deborah has a lot of appointments." I pointed to the calendar lying open on the desk. "Have you been canceling them?"

"What else can I do?" he asked.

Maybe the Kid felt the heat of our eyes on his back. He turned around. I nodded in the direction of the door. "We have to go," I said to Rick. He didn't say good, but he might have been thinking it. "We found a thick-billed at Wes Brown's that we're taking to the FWS."

"Give it to Special Agent Violet Sommers. She's in charge of the parrot division. You'll let me know if you hear anything more about Terrance or Deborah?"

"Yeah," I said.

"So what were you and Alice looking at?" I asked the Kid when we were back in the pickup.

"She has a tape recorder, and they use it to talk to the parrots when they are not there. They say the same words over and over, and sometimes the parrot learns them. The indigos are very happy now they are together again, no?"

"Yes."

"But they would be more happy if they were in Brazil."

"I know."

"In Brazil they call the blue macaws *Ararapretas*, black macaws, because they look dark when the sun is behind them. *Loros* talk, and they are *muy amable* and people think they are pets, but in the wild they are fierce as a falcon or a *lobo*. They will fight to the death to protect their mate. What do you think would happen if you took *Perigeo* away now?"

"I think Colloquy would bite my finger off," I said.

"You're right," he replied.

While we negotiated the orange barrels of downtown on our way to the FWS office, I wondered why Rick had been so quick to raise the issue of calling in the police on my earlier visit, and so slow to do it now.

12

Our next stop was the U.S. Fish and Wildlife Service law enforcement office on Fourse Street. Parrot smuggling is a federal crime. So is dealing in endangered and protected species. Whether a species already extinct in the U.S. could be considered endangered was a question I couldn't answer. The thick-billeds weren't in trouble in New Mexico or Arizona; they were gone. I knew that the Lacey Act makes it unlawful for any person to import wildlife in violation of U.S. or foreign law and that Wes Brown's smuggling activities had to put him in violation of that act. For evidence I had the video in my fanny pack and the thick-billed parrot in the camper shell. I peered through the rear window at the thick-billed, which sat silently on its perch watching downtown Albuquerque go by.

"Do you think it's a male or a female?" I asked the Kid.

He shrugged. "You have to look inside to tell."

We turned into the FWS office, a nondescript government

building. Inside we confronted a gray-haired man at a metal desk who was acting as a receptionist and/or a guard. He eyed us and the bird with suspicion.

"I'd like to talk to Special Agent Violet Sommers," I said.

"Your name?"

"Neil Hamel. I'm an attorney." It goes against my basic instincts to seek out law enforcement. I was only doing it because the bird needed a home and Wes Brown needed federal attention.

The man at the desk picked up his phone and said, "A woman named Neil Hamel here to see you, Vi. She's a lawyer." He told us to wait in the reception area, where the government hadn't been wasting any of our taxpayer money on decoration. The furniture was metal, the walls institutional green, the artwork consisted of geodetic survey maps. I studied the maps while we waited for Special Agent Sommers. Door was a tiny dot, two hundred miles from Albuquerque, sixty-two miles from the border. Which direction had Wes Brown headed? I wondered. North or south? The Kid clucked to the bird, and I could see it was going to be difficult for him to give it up.

Special Agent Violet Sommers showed up in uniform: a short-sleeved shirt, matching long pants, sensible shoes, a wide belt and a holster at her hip. Considering the automatic weapons many smugglers would be packing, using her revolver would be like aiming a slingshot at Goliath. Vi's uniform was not designed for a woman's body. What would have been soft curves in something more forgiving was hard-packed cellulite under the law enforcement suit. But it was a body she seemed comfortable with, and her face was open and friendly. Her brown hair was cut in wash-and-wear layers. Her eyes were the color of violets in springtime. Either she'd been named for the color of her eyes or she'd chosen contacts to match her name. She wore a delicate ring of turquoise surrounded by diamonds. My guess was that Violet, when she went home, got out of the uniform and put on a dress.

She clapped her hands when she saw us and cried, "A thick-billed. Where did you get it?"

There was only one answer to that question—from a smuggler. "We found him on Wes Brown's boat in Door."

"Wes Brown, huh? Let's go talk in my office."

We followed her to her office, which was Spartan but had soft touches. She had a large metal desk. There were no Koda-chrome pictures of herself on the wall. Her photographs were of a towheaded boy and a golden retriever. She probably lived in the East Mountains and drove a four by four with a bumper sticker on the back that said MY CHILD IS AN HONOR STUDENT AT HIS MIDDLE SCHOOL. On her desk I saw a paw print of a wolf encased in plaster and a plaque in cross-stitch embroidery that read SCAT HAPPENS.

"Do you know Wes Brown?" I asked her.

"Actually, I've never had the pleasure." She brushed a stray curl away from her face. "Let's say I know of him."

At least *she* hadn't fallen under his rescue-me spell. Special Agent Vi Sommers seemed far too stable to be taken in by Wes Brown's maneuvers, but when it comes to women and men you never know.

"Wes Brown uses a number of aliases," she said. "He's been known at various times in his career as Charlie Brown, Eddie Green and Tom Jones."

"How original," said I.

"Isn't it? His activities are reported to be illegal whatever the names. How did you get my name?"

"From Rick Olney, Deborah Dumaine's lab assistant at UNM."

"Deborah talked to me about Brown."

"Do you know Deborah well?"

"Not really. We get together every now and then and talk birds."

"Do you know she's missing and is presumed kidnapped?" I wanted to ask. "Do you have any idea where she could be? Is she alive or dead?" But those questions had fallen into the quicksand of attorney/client privilege and gotten mired in the muck. The next question was, if she knew that much about Wes Brown, why hadn't she nailed him by now? But she answered that one before I had a chance to ask.

"I've been wanting to go after him, but it's been a matter of priorities and resources. Usually, when we catch one smuggler he rolls over on another to cut himself a deal. We catch a lot of them through snitches. No one has given us the goods on Brown yet."

I pulled out my video. "This is a tape of Brown purchasing parrots from Mexican smugglers in Cotorra Canyon."

"All right!" Vi said.

"I want to keep the original. Can you make me a copy?" I didn't have the equipment myself. I don't even have a VCR. That's how far off the information highway I am.

"Can do," she said. She left the office briefly, taking the tape, which I had labeled Cotorra Canyon, to be copied.

"How'd you get the video?" she asked when she came back.

"I filmed it." That was about as much as I was able to say.

"How did you find out about Wes Brown?"

"I can't answer that."

"Can you testify if the case goes to trial?"

"Probably not. I was in Door on business for a client. I may have to plead attorney/client privilege."

"How about you?" she asked the Kid.

"Sure," he said. "He's a bird killer. I'd like to see him go to prison for life for that."

Even with the evidence we had, Wes Brown wouldn't go to prison for life. He might not go to prison at all unless I could nail him for a different crime. The penalty for violating the Lacey Act could well be a fine that he'd pay with dirty money. Judges take crimes against property and people more seriously than crimes against wildlife. Of course, Wes Brown might have committed crimes against people too. If he'd killed my client and/or Deborah Dumaine, that could put him in prison for life.

Violet watched the sorry thick-billed pick at its feathers. "A lot of them come across the border like that," she said, "but often we can bring them around."

"What happens to the bird now?" the Kid asked.

"We've been turning the thick-billeds we get over to the Phoenix Zoo. The ones that are healthy go into the reintroduction effort. The thick-billeds that come from Mexico are tough and do much better than the ones that have been in captivity in this country. The ones that have been pets have forgotten how to act in the wild and the goshawks pick them off. Flocking is their only defense. It's hard for a goshawk to pick one out of the flock. Also, a flock has a lot of eyes, and they warn each other."

"Are goshawks endangered?"

"Level two sensitive."

"Brown's been killing them too. We saw a pile of dead hawks in Cotorra Canyon and found hawk feathers in the boat." I was going to get Brown for every offense I could.

"We'll look into it," Vi said.

"There is an up-close look at the other smuggled birds on that tape," I said. "There are three yellow-headed Amazons and one blue-fronted Amazon. Right?" I asked the Kid.

"Right," he said.

"I saw some of Brown's records while we were on the boat. He's been selling to the Birds of Paradise Pet Shop."

"Damn them," Vi said. "I can understand why some poor person south of the border would trap and sell a bird to feed a family. But nobody would be doing it if there weren't a market here, and that's what I don't understand—why someplace like Birds of Paradise would deal in illegal birds. Why people will either knowingly buy smuggled and endangered birds or try very hard not to know the birds have been smuggled. We have a long and porous border. If we can't keep people out, how are we going to keep out parrots? People will pay one hundred thousand dollars for a rare parrot, and that's what's driving them into extinction. The rare and endangered will always be procured by someone. What's extinct is gone forever. One thousand species of birds are threatened with extinction, and two-thirds of them are on the decline. Pretty depressing, isn't it? Then you've got people like Brown speeding the process along."

"Does captive breeding help?" I asked.

"The nature of the third world economy is that a wild bird there is always going to be cheaper than a hand-raised bird here. Breeding in the country of origin helps. So does involving the local population in the conservation effort. There have been some successes in that area."

"If you get an agent down to Door right away, you may be able to get Brown's records before he thinks to dispose of them."

"I'll do that."

"I'd check with the DEA too. I believe Brown was prosecuted for dealing drugs. He may be on probation." All that information would be on a government computer, but the computer wouldn't release it unless someone asked. The various branches of the federal government were not known for communicating with each other. I handed her my lawyer's card. "We have a strong interest in this case. Will you let us know what develops?"

"Of course," she said. "Thanks a lot for your help."

The guy from the front desk came into the office and handed Vi the tape and the copy. Vi gave me back my original. "I'm really grateful for this," she said.

"It's nothing," the Kid replied.

It's a lot, I thought.

The time had come to turn the thick-billed over, and the Kid was sad to see it go. Perigee was big and beautiful, but the Kid's heart was with the stray. *Mimar,* one of my favorite words in Spanish, means to pet, and that's what the Kid was doing to the parrot. The thick-billed was wary, but it did let him stroke its head.

"He'll be in good hands. Don't worry," Vi reassured him.

"Maintain, *lorito,*" the Kid said.

Before we left the FWS office I'd looked at the time on the wall: five-thirty. It had only been yesterday that we'd left for Door, but it seemed like a month. I'd used up all my adrenaline hours ago and was running on empty. I was so tired, downtown Albuquerque wavered like a poorly propped-up movie set. You know you're either tired or hallucinating when Albuquerque looks like anything but a cow town downtown. My office was only a few blocks away on Lead, but when the Kid asked me if I wanted to go there I said no, that I wanted to go home and mix up a batch of Jell-O shots but I knew I'd be asleep before they jelled. The near-death experience had made me want to make love. Real death made me want to pull the covers over my head. Alone in my own bed. When we got to La Vista the who-goes-where moment came up.

The Kid rubbed the palm of his hand against the steering wheel. Maybe he wanted to be alone too. "I think I will go home now, Chiquita," he said.

Out of the depths of my peripheral vision I had a glimpse of Alice of the long blond hair, but I considered that an

unworthy thought and banished it into the darkness from which it had come. "Okay. I'm really tired," I said.
"Me too," he replied.

I was too tired to eat or drink or even to smoke. I took a long, hot eucalyptus oil bath while burning a candle at the edge of the tub. I stared at the flame until I could reproduce its shape exactly with my eyes shut tight. That was the kind of focus I'd need to solve this case. The minute I hit the bed I fell asleep and dreamed of a flickering fire, a royal blue macaw, a red-headed woman and a dead white man. When I woke up after midnight, the wind was rubbing against the window like a giant disembodied feather. I considered turning on the TV but I knew what I'd find there—Ron Bell in a black leather jacket, Cliff Vole selling cell phones and the same thing I'd been seeing in my dreams—murder. What are the things people kill for? I asked myself. Love, hate, money, revenge, gold chains, running shoes. Wes Brown might have been collaborating with Terrance Lewellen. He might have killed Terrance to protect himself and keep the money. He'd proved he didn't have the *cojones* to kill someone face-to-face, but Terrance's death—if it was murder—had been murder by remote. There'd been no mess, no bloodshed, and quite possibly no confrontation. I wondered if the distance would lessen the killer's sense of guilt. It didn't change the fact that my client was dead, that I'd given up his money but hadn't gotten back his wife, that I'd tied up Wes Brown but not tight enough.

It was morning when I woke up again. I went to the window and paid my respects to the wind goddess, who was dove gray today, silhouetted against a sky of robin's egg blue. Something was burning in the Heights, and the black smoke rose as straight as a signal fire. The wind goddess didn't even bother to puff it away. Maybe she was still asleep. Maybe she was tired from a night spent rattling people's windows.

I was starving and went to the refrigerator, which was, as usual, a case of hope triumphing over shopping. I should have known there'd be nothing there but a cold burrito from Arriba Tacos left over since when? I had a cup of Red Zinger tea and a handful of blue corn chips and went to work.

Anna was at her desk, but Brink hadn't shown up yet. Anna's hair was approaching Lyle Lovett's pompadour in height and in slickness; the altitude looked better on her than it did on him. She'd added a few more inches by wearing her hooker's shoes. I didn't think the shoes were right for her, but I hadn't gotten around to telling her that yet.

"How'd it go?" she asked me.

"The good news is that we got the macaw back. He's with his mate now and in bliss."

"That's great."

"Yeah."

"So what's the bad?"

"Terrance Lewellen is dead."

"Yow! What happened to him?"

"I don't know," I admitted. "We took Perigee there first and found Terrance flat on his back in his bed. Dead. The medical examiner thinks it might have been an allergic reaction."

"To what?"

"Antibiotics, food or a bee sting."

"You think a bee sting could kill *him*?"

"It's possible," I said, but I didn't believe it either.

"He was tougher than a boot heel, but I kind of liked the guy. He brought me a rose one time when he was in here."

"Really?"

"Yeah. He had a soft side." For younger women he did. She stretched out a skinny leg and looked at her ankle-strapped foot.

"I don't know about those shoes, Anna," I said.

"What? They're not right for the office?"

That was a part of it, but not the whole story. "You go around looking like a hooker, everybody's going to be hitting on you. There's enough trouble out there without asking for more."

"I was at Nob Hill last night and some guy on a bike asked me for change. When I told him I didn't have any, he called me a fucking white bitch."

"What did you do?"

"Called him an asshole." She had *cojones*, I'll say that.

"He might have been carrying a weapon. Did you ever think of that? If they'll kill you for a gold chain, they'll do it for a swear word."

"You think he hit on me because of the shoes?"

"Who knows? He could hit on you for wearing combat boots, but if you'd had on running shoes you could have gotten away faster."

"Okay, I'll think about it."

"Any messages?"

"Roberta Dovalo called. She said she can't make the appointment tomorrow. She's thinking about gettin' back with her Jimmie." She imitated Roberta's cowgirl twang. She wasn't as good at it as the Amazons, but I got the message. "'Damned sorry about that, ma'am.'"

I wasn't *that* sorry. "Is that it?"

"One more. Charlie Register at BankWest."

That was no surprise. "Look up a couple of numbers for me, will you? ABC Security and Dr. Talbert. Talbert's an allergist."

"You got it."

I went into my office and crossed Roberta Dovalo off the calendar. It could be months before I heard from her again—if I ever heard from her again. The indigo feather made an arc in my cup. I took it out and ran my fingers down the barbs. Cowboy, Indian, hooker, soldier, scientist, bird. There's a costume for every actor (good or bad) in New Mexico. Something about the altitude or the air or the space here makes people want to dress up and act out. What would look ridiculous in some gray city looks normal in our movie-set scenery. I'd made the mistake of choosing one of the drab, brown bird roles myself—lawyer. Try as I did not to dress or act the part, it stuck to me like Velcro.

I called the other brown bird professional who had a role in this drama, Charlie Register.

"I hear that Lewellen died," he said.

"He did."

"What the hell happened to him?"

"I don't know yet. The OMI is investigating."

"Did you get Deborah back?"

"No."

"Where is she? Is she all right?"

"I don't know that either."

"Can we talk this afternoon?"

"How about tomorrow?" There were some other people I needed to talk to first.

"All right. Here? First thing in the morning?"

"I'll be there," I said.

Anna came in with the phone numbers I'd requested. The first one I called was Dr. Talbert. When I told the receptionist I was Terrance Lewellen's lawyer, she put me through immediately, indicating that Terrance's death had made the news.

Talbert got right to the point, which I should have expected from a doctor; they're too busy treating and billing patients to shoot the shit. "What happened to Lewellen?" he asked me. "The newspaper said he was found dead in his bed." There was plenty of drama in the subject matter, but his voice was as soothing as still water. I hadn't expected *that*. Usually, if there's anyone with a bigger ego and a louder voice than a lawyer, it's a doctor, and there's no love lost between the two professions in this age of malpractice suits.

"I found him yesterday morning," I said. "He was fully dressed. His arm was stretched over the side of the bed and his hand was lying on the floor. There was a small, empty vial and a hypodermic needle on the bedside table."

"Epinephrine," he said.

"Was that a medication he used?"

"Only if he was having a life-threatening allergic reaction. The effects of epinephrine are intense. It'll make the heart race like a runaway train. No one would take it unless he had to."

"What would have caused such an allergic reaction in Terrance?"

There was a pause while Dr. Talbert considered his options. Terrance's allergies probably fell into the area of doctor/patient confidentiality. I couldn't see any reason for that relationship to succeed the patient's death myself, but on the other hand, he didn't really know I was who I said I was or why I was asking. A patient of his had died, somebody might want to sue. "I'm not at liberty to talk about that," he said.

"I have reasons I can't go into for needing to know as soon as possible what killed Terrance," I said. "It appears to have been an unwitnessed death. At least, no witnesses have come forward yet. The OMI will be doing an autopsy, but a toxicology or a stomach contents could take weeks. The medical examiner has your name, and I assume someone will be getting in touch with you. If there is anything you could do to speed up the process, I'd appreciate it." I figured he'd want to know what happened just as badly as I did.

"I'll look into it," he replied.

"Thanks," I said.

Next I called ABC Security and asked to speak to the manager or the president or whoever it was that ran the place.

The voice I got belonged to Joe Brannigan. It had the slow-mo reaction time of someone who'd played football without a helmet for too long. "I'm Terrance Lewellen's lawyer," I said.

"Yeah," he replied.

"My client was found dead in his home, which was protected by one of your security systems."

"Yeah," he said again.

"He hired you to follow a person named Wes Brown who took some money out of the ATM at Midnight Rodeo last Friday."

"Is that right?" Joe said this time.

"Yeah, that's right," I said. "I saw it with my own eyes. Look, Terrance Lewellen was a good customer of ABC. I want to know what happened to him, and you're going to help me find out."

"Can you prove you're his lawyer?"

"Yup."

"Do it," he said, and hung up.

The only proof I had of my relationship with Terrance Lewellen was a lock of red hair, a long blue feather, a ransom note and a retainer agreement. I took the retainer agreement out to Anna and asked her to make a copy.

Brink had shown up and was hanging around her desk, looking more relaxed that he had been of late. Could he have gained weight since I last saw him? I wondered. When was that? Four days ago? Maybe he'd gotten so relaxed he'd stopped trying to hold his belly up and in. The belly contraction had been Brink's manifestation of up talk, an attempt to appear more positive and appealing. "How's it going with Nancy?" I asked him.

"Great," he said. "She's a good cook."

What did it take to be a cook, anyway? I wondered. The time to buy food and a cookbook and to follow directions. It helped to have someone to cook for. It helped to like to eat.

"What kind of law does she practice, anyway?" I asked him.

"Probate," he said.

That explained it. Probate was one of those niches in the legal profession where you don't have to be aggressive or quick. It's back-office work. It doesn't take you to Door and back and put you in life-threatening situations. You could come to work at nine, leave at five and take the time to plan for dinner. Half the conflict had gone out of that kind of law; the client was already dead.

13

That afternoon I went to ABC Security's office in a strip mall between the Valley and the Heights. If you ignore the background mountains, in mid-Albuquerque you could be anywhere in fast-food, string-of-mall U.S.A. There was one skinny and lonesome tree hanging over the mall's parking lot, but somebody had already parked under its six square inches of shade. I pulled up in front of ABC and left the Nissan to sizzle in the sun. I didn't bother placing a screen across my windshield; the sun never seems to be entering where the sunscreen is protecting. The storefront that housed ABC Security had a decal with the burnt edges of a brand in the corner of the window. They must have picked that name because A-1 and AA were already taken. ABC would put them in third place in the phone book. Did that mean they were a third-class outfit? Having nothing to protect, I don't know much about security systems myself, but I wouldn't have expected Terrance Lewellen to go third class. Maybe the tacky strip mall was—

like Terrance's infomercial salesman persona—a cover for a careful and subtle MO.

The interior of ABC was about ten degrees darker and fifteen degrees cooler than the exterior. I took off my shades and waited for my eyes to adjust. In the dimness, I saw a man standing next to a wall full of blinking but silent alarm systems. As he came into focus, I saw that he was short, broad and wearing a white shirt with the ABC brand on the pocket. His width came from muscle bulk, not fat. He had a flattop you could balance the phone book on. The person I saw fit the football player voice I'd heard. I could imagine him ramming his head into a line of padding and muscle.

"Are you Joe Brannigan?" I asked.

"You got it."

"I'm Neil Hamel, Terrance Lewellen's attorney."

"Right," he said. "Pisser that Terry's dead. He was a first-class client."

Over the phone his voice had a paramilitary terseness, but he turned nearly unctuous in person. The use of the diminutive "Terry" was a salesman's ploy. The alarm systems on the wall, I noticed, all had the prices on them.

"Here's my agreement with Terrance." I handed it over.

He flipped to the back and saw Terrance's careless and distinctive signature, which had the peaks and valleys of an EKG graph. One glance was enough to satisfy him. "So what's this all about?" he asked me.

"My client died under unusual circumstances."

"Like what?"

"I found him dead in his bed yesterday morning with barely a mark on him."

"Mighta been a heart attack."

"Mighta. The OMI is looking into it."

"Are the police gonna get involved?"

"That depends on what the autopsy turns up." I could be terse myself if need be.

"What is it you want to know?" His lips barely moved as he talked. His eyes focused on me without a blink.

"I presume his alarm was hooked up here."

"Yeah."

"Did it go off Sunday or Monday?"

"No."

"Was it on?"

"Probably. Terry paid for it; he'd want to use it. He'd put it on Home mode when he was in the house, on Away when he went out."

"Can you tell from here what mode it is in?"

"No. It signals here when the alarm has been activated and we send somebody over to check it out."

"Have you ever had to do that?"

"Nope. Sooner or later most clients set their systems off accidentally, but Terry never did."

"The red lights in the hallway trace an intruder whether the system is off or on?"

"Yeah. But it has to be on for the signal to sound here or the alarm to ring."

"Where did Wes Brown go the night your men tracked him?"

"He went home with a waitress from Midnight Cowboy."

"Do you have her name and address?"

"Yeah." He handed me a slip of paper. The woman's name was Katrina Cochran and her address was 150 Armenta Court NE, which would place her in the mid-Heights, not far from where I lived.

"Thanks," I said.

He nodded.

"When did Brown leave Cochran's place?" I asked him.

"In the morning."

"Did your men continue to follow him?"

"No. We had instructions from Terry to call off the trace."

That was what the ransom note had demanded—no security guards. "I have one more question."

"What's that?"

"Did ABC ever track Deborah Dumaine for Terrance?"

"That info's confidential," he replied.

"You can tell me about Wes Brown but not about Deborah?"

"What goes on between a man and his wife is nobody else's business. That's the way Terry would want it. I gotta respect that. You live alone?"

It seemed to me that that was my business. "No," I said, sticking to the KISS principle.

"You got an alarm system?" he asked.

"Yeah," I said. My alarm system used to be my .38. Now it was my key-ring Punch, plus the Kid whenever he happened to be at La Vista.

"What kind?"

"A-1." It was a lie, but he'd never know.

He scrunched his lips and shook his head, implying that A-1 was inferior merchandise, but if he thought he was going to sell me an alarm system, he was mistaken.

"Thanks for your help," I said. "I gotta go."

The shade had moved away from the car that had parked under it. The Sandias were a herd of resting elephants. The steering wheel in the Nissan was hot enough to make me wish I'd worn gloves.

Katrina Cochran lived in one of the mid-Heights developments that convince you there's no there here in Albuquerque. The houses had all been built around the same time. Mid-fifties, I'd say, when the Duke City first started to grow and suburban developments represented security. Now Albuquerque is sprawling all over the West Mesa and climbing the Sandias' foothills. Security is represented by gated communities, razor wire, alarm systems, killer dogs and semiautomatic weapons. The houses on Armenta Court were undistinguished frame stucco. An adobe house is warm in the winter and cool in the summer. It makes you feel sheltered, but a cheap frame stucco lets the wind goddess in through the windows and it rattles when an airplane flies overhead. An adobe house has a long life, and when its time is up sinks slowly back into the ground from where it came, but the houses on Armenta Court were not aging well. The neighborhood had begun to slide from middle class to lower middle class to below the poverty line. There were some tall trees on Armenta Court, some low bushes, a bunch of dogs and bikes.

I went in the early evening, before Katrina Cochran was likely to have left for her waitress job. The dog who met me at 150 was a small, champagne-colored mutt with a sharp and annoying bark. He circled my shoes and yapped at my ankles, making me want to drop-kick him across the yard. "*Cállate,*" I said.

The woman who came to the door did not strike me as a woman who would interest or be interested in Wes Brown. She looked neither rich, beautiful nor gullible, and she was bigger than Wes. Her brown eyes were close together and shrewd. She wore a shapeless body-concealing lavender dress, and she was smoking a cigarette.

"Hello?" she called, turning the greeting into a question.

"Hi," I replied.

"Quiet, Buster," she yelled, silencing the dog long enough for me to introduce myself.

"My name is Neil Hamel. I'd like to talk to Katrina?" I said, working in some up talk myself.

"She's taking a shower now, getting ready for work. Can you wait?"

"Okay."

"Come on in."

As she held the door open for me, the dog darted into the house, sending an area rug flying. He did a four-pawed slide across the living room with his claws scraping at the wooden floor and slammed into an armchair in the far corner. He yapped again and crawled behind the color TV, which featured Oprah.

"Shut up, Buster," the woman said. A cough lurked in her gravelly, smoker's voice.

"Shut up, Buster," growled another voice in a near-perfect imitation of the woman. The dog's antics had kept me from noticing a green and yellow parrot that perched in a cage in the corner. Buster whimpered, crawled behind the TV and shut up. He hadn't listened to the woman, but the bird cowed him into obedience. The bottom of the parrot's cage was littered with sunflower seeds, bird shit and feathers.

"Name's Ellen," the woman said.

"Is that your parrot?" I asked.

She shook her head. "Katrina's. She's my roommate."

What the hell, I thought, why not leap right in? Ellen looked like a sensible woman. "Did she get it from Wes Brown?"

"How'd you know that?"

"I know him."

Ellen hit the Mute button on the remote. Oprah mouthed silent words. With the TV muted I could hear the shower water running steadily in the background. "You know Wes?" Ellen was surprised. Could be I wasn't rich or beautiful enough to be of interest to him either.

"Yeah," I said.

"Don't get me started on him." She lit another cigarette, snapping the lid of her lighter shut and watching me with hungry hawk eyes.

"Why not?" I asked, lighting a butt of my own and establishing, maybe, a mutual addiction rapport.

"Their relationship—if you want to call it that—is a couple of sandwiches shy of a picnic. You know what I mean?"

"Not exactly."

"Brown has a zipper management problem. The number of women he's slept with in Albuquerque could fill the Pit. Katrina is the latest in a long string of women he's used. He comes up here every two weeks, sleeps with her, does his business, goes back to Door. She pretends he's working for her, fixing up the house, and gives him money when he needs it. Does this house look like it's been fixed?"

Not to me it didn't. "Does Katrina have that much to give?"

"She's a waitress." Ellen shrugged.

I'd seen Wes Brown's stash; I knew he wasn't broke. With the ransom money, he'd be rich. So why did he take money from Katrina? To stay in practice? "Does Katrina ever go to Door?"

"Rarely."

"Was she there last weekend?"

"Not that I know of."

The water stopped running and the pipes clanged as Katrina turned off the faucet. Ellen peered at me. "Why you askin' about Wes Brown? You're not a friend of his, are you?" She'd trusted me long enough to vent the top layer of her steam, but doubt was entering into her voice now that Katrina's appearance was imminent.

"I'm not a friend. I, um . . . ," I began winging it, not having thought this part through yet. "I'm a lawyer." I handed her my card. Usually, that shuts people up; nobody trusts a lawyer, even their own lawyer, but Ellen liked to talk and she did not like Wes Brown. "I'm investigating the death of a client that Brown knows."

"Is it a woman?"

"No."

She raised her eyebrows. "I didn't think Brown knew any-body *but* women."

"No male friends, huh?"

"None that I've ever heard of."

"So what is it that women like about the guy?" I asked. "He's not bad looking, but . . ."

"They think he's a cowboy. *He's* always on remote, but his body's available. You know what I mean?"

Actually, I did know. I also knew that particular combination has a fatal attraction for some women. It's a way of having a man in your life without the responsibility. Instead of acting out your own need for distance and independence, you pick a guy who'll do it for you. I knew what the outcome always was, too—too much of not enough. "What's the business he comes up here for?"

"All I know is he goes to the bank, then he goes to Midnight Cowboy, gets drunk and waits for Katrina to get off work."

"Does she work on Sundays?"

"No; it's her night off."

"Was he here Sunday night?"

"I guess. I was visiting my mother in Springer. He and Katrina were having breakfast when I got back Monday morning. Surprised me. Usually he's here on Saturday morning."

"What time did you get back?"

"Eleven."

The dog yapped and scooted across the floor. "Bad dog, Buster," the parrot hollered. Katrina stepped out of the bathroom. She'd gotten dressed in record time, but she hadn't had much to put on. She was wearing her Midnight Cowboy wait-ress uniform: a white miniskirt with gold stars on it, red cowboy boots, a blue vest, a white cowboy hat, a belt with a pair of holsters packing toy six-shooters. Her boots made her about the same height as Brown. I wondered which hand she used, the left or the right. Her knees had dimples and the skin under her upper arms was flabby. Her face was round, her eyes big and brown, her hair hung down her back as straight as an Apache's but without the body or the gloss. She was several years younger than me and Ellen, but still too old for the uniform. The attraction for Brown didn't appear to be money or beauty, so what was it? That she'd do his dirty work? That she'd provide a pillow?

"Hey, Buster," she said, reaching down to pet the scruffy dog. Her tiny skirt flipped up behind her. "Hi, Alex," she said to the bird. "Oh, hello," she said to me. "I didn't see you there." Her wide eyes gave no indication that she'd ever seen me before. Maybe she hadn't, or maybe she was a good actress. She *was* wearing a costume.

"What's your name again?" Ellen asked me.

"Neil Hamel," I said.

"Neil wants to talk to you about Wes."

"Oh?" said Katrina, shaking her head and flipping a lock of hair across her shoulder. The dog yapped again. "Shut up, Buster," she said. "What do you want to talk about?" There's a thin line between fear and hostility, and her eyes were walking it.

"I want to get in touch with Wes, and I was wondering if you know where he is."

"Why would I know that?"

"A friend of mine saw you together at Midnight Cowboy."

"Why do you want to get in touch with him?"

"I'm a lawyer."

"He works for me," she said, too quickly. "Around the house." I figured that was the cover story they'd worked out to explain where Brown's income came from. Maybe she thought I was an IRS lawyer, but Brown's tax problems weren't on my agenda yet.

"A client of mine died under mysterious circumstances," I said. "Wes had some dealings with the client. I was wondering if Wes had any information that could help with my investigation." It was bullshit; what I really wanted to know was if she'd been Brown, the loner's, assistant, the night I was in Door.

"What's your client's name?"

"Terrance Lewellen."

"Never heard of him."

"He's married to Deborah Dumaine."

"Never heard of her either." She did a little two-step and tugged at the rope under her chin that held her cowboy hat in place. Why the nervous gestures? I wondered. Because she was lying? Because she thought Deborah Dumaine was another of Wes's conquests? Both?

"Have you been in Door recently?" I asked her.

"No." She straightened her hat. "And I don't have to answer your questions."

"Not now, but you might somewhere down the road."

"Pull up your socks, Katrina," Ellen said. "Get rid of the guy. He doesn't give a damn about you. He doesn't give a damn about anybody."

"How long has it been since you got laid?" Katrina snapped at her roommate.

"Too long." Ellen sighed.

"You're jealous."

"Of *him*?"

"Of anyone. Look, I'm going to work. I'm not answering any more of your questions, and neither is she." She took her left hand off one six-shooter and pointed it at Ellen. "And I want you out of this house." She took her right hand off the other six-shooter and pointed it at me.

The dog barked. The bird squawked. Ellen zapped Oprah back on. "I'm going," I said. I knew Katrina would tell Brown that I'd been there, but I didn't care. That might even have been why I'd gone.

14

I stopped by Charlie Register's office on my way to work the following day. He'd hung *Santa Barbara Canyon* on the wall opposite *Gila Bend* and *The Bosque*. From a distance it was stream water sliding under leafy Aspens. Up close it was a collection of brush strokes, subtle and abstract, with Lochover's bold signature sprawled across the corner. The wall opposite Charlie's desk faced the long view, the wall behind him remained empty. Would he hang the last Lochover there, I wondered, or had he already hung it at home? The paintings were beautiful, but few rooms were big enough to hold them. Two were a balance; a third seemed excessive, a ménage à trois instead of a duo. To add a fourth would be a ménage à quatre and overkill. Charlie stood beneath the overhead light as he greeted me. His clothes were subtle, his hair was golden. The halogen lamp balanced on its stand like a long-legged crane watching for insects in the water.

"What happened to Lewellen?" he asked me. The question was full of emotional content, but Charlie's voice was calm.

"When I got back from Door, I found him dead in his bed," I said, trying to match his calmness. "A vial of epineph-rine and a hypodermic needle were on the table. Dr. Talbert, Terrance's allergist, told me it's a drug people take to counter-act allergic reactions. Did Terrance have any allergies that you know of?"

"No," Charlie said. The macho posturing that went on between those two might have kept Terrance from admitting any sign of weakness—like an allergy—to Charlie.

"Terrance wasn't alone when I got there," I said. "Sara Dumaine, Deborah's sister, was with him, weeping over the body. She said she found Terrance dead. She also said she and . . . Terry . . . were in love."

Charlie shook his head and the silver danced among the gold. "What the hell was wrong with him?"

"He'd been chemically sexed."

"Ma'am?"

"He wore a testosterone patch."

"What for?"

I shrugged; the answer seemed obvious to me.

"Deborah's a fine woman," Charlie continued. "You've got to be lower than a snake in wagon tracks to sleep with your wife's sister. If you ask me, Lewellen's only real loves were his mother and his parrots. You didn't find Deborah in Door?"

"No."

"Did you hand over the money?"

"Yes."

His eyebrows formed two quizzical and symmetrical arches. "May I ask to whom?"

"A person in a feathered mask with a finger on the trigger of a .45."

"Wes Brown?"

"I don't know," I admitted. "We talked to Brown, but he wouldn't confess to knowing anything about the kidnapping."

"You believe him?"

"I wouldn't say Wes Brown is an honest person." There was a place deep in the wagon ruts for him too. "I did get Perigee back."

"What happens to the birds now?"

"Terrance set up a trust for them. They'll be taken care of by Rick Olney at the lab."

"Did you get anything on the video?" Charlie asked.

"We caught Brown buying smuggled parrots in Cotorra Canyon, and I recorded that. I didn't get anything which would prove or disprove a kidnapping. I gave a copy of the video to the Fish and Wildlife Service. They're going after Brown for parrot smuggling."

Charlie leaned against his desk. "I always admired Deborah," he said. "She's loud, temperamental, and flashy, but she's very smart." It was the admiration a brown bird might have for a parrot, a banker for an actress, a lawyer for a con artist. Charlie was elegant, but he was monochromatic. "I'm going to be damned upset if she doesn't come back."

"I hear that Wes Brown comes up here every two weeks and puts money into his bank account," I said. "Can you tell me if his account is with BankWest and what he does with the money?" I wondered what kind of customer confidentiality Charlie Register was required to maintain. He might not be able to give me that information, but he would have to give it to the FWS or the FBI if they got a warrant.

"I'll look into it," he said. "By the way, my security people made some stills of the ATM transfers." He handed me a manila envelope with photographs inside, but I didn't open it yet; I already knew what Brown and the mask looked like.

"Thanks," I said. "What happens to the paintings now?" Legally, they belonged to Terrance's estate; I had the document to prove that. Other than Charlie Register, I was the only one who did.

"I assume they'll be left to Lewellen's mother." Did he assume or did he know? Charlie's poker face didn't give a clue. "It's my impression that he left everything to her, including," he said, "*Wild Flower*."

"You knew about *Wild Flower*?" I asked.

"Didn't you?"

"Not until I saw it hanging on the wall in Terrance's living room. Why didn't you make it a part of the collateral agreement if you knew?"

Charlie shrugged. "It's a late work and of inferior quality; I didn't want it." So much for my taste in art.

"Do you know Terrance's mother?" I asked.

"Yes. She banks with us."

"Where does she live?"

"At La Buena Vida retirement home."

Charlie Register had the sterling qualities a mother would appreciate. Did she know what the paintings were worth? I wondered. Would Charlie be able to talk her out of them? How badly did he want the Lochovers anyway? Badly enough to kill for? Charlie's hair gleamed beneath the overhead lamp. He had a gambler's heart, but a job that wouldn't let him gamble much. He seemed far too civilized to kill, although Terrance—if he had been murdered—had been murdered in a very civilized way. "There is a possibility that Terrance was murdered," I said, laying it on the table.

"How's that?" Charlie stepped out from under the overhead light and moved behind his desk.

"I don't know yet. The OMI is investigating."

Charlie picked up a pen and rolled it around in his fingers. "What are you going to do about the kidnapping?" he asked. "Are you going to the FBI or the police?"

"I can't; my duty to Terrance is the same in death as it was in life—to protect him. If the police question me, I'll have to take the privilege."

"Ma'am?"

"It would be an ethics violation to reveal anything Terrance told me."

"What's my duty?" he asked. "I don't think Deborah should be left to rot in the desert."

Neither did I, but I gave him a lawyer's advice. It was possible that Charlie had committed some illegal acts himself. For one thing, he hadn't been acting in the best interests of BankWest's customers when he set up the ATM transfer. "That's something you have to talk to your own lawyer about. Who is your lawyer?"

"Jed Martin."

I knew Jed. He came from the same good old boy network as Charlie and was known to be cagier than a coyote. I handed Charlie one of Detective Rosalia Hernandez's cards. "This is the number of the detective who'll be investigating Terrance's death," I said, "if there is an investigation."

"And the kidnapping?"

"That's a matter for the FBI."

He put the card in his desk drawer and waved his hand in an expansive gesture around the office. "Those Lochovers are damned beautiful, aren't they?"

"Yeah," I said.

On my way back to the office, I picked up some spicy chicken to go from Panda Express at the mall.

"Where'd that come from?" asked Anna when she saw the white box in my hand.

"Panda Express," I answered.

"I like their spicy chicken," she said.

"Me too." It had red peppers that could zing you out of a slump.

"Dr. Talbert's office called," Anna said. "They said to be there at three."

I took the pink slip and went into my office. Who was a doctor to be ordering a lawyer around, I thought, but I went anyway and I got there on time. Talbert wouldn't have called me if he hadn't gotten some information from the OMI. His ego or his curiosity had set that wheel in motion. Besides, miss an appointment with a physician and you're likely to get billed for your time. Should I have billed Roberta Dovalo for canceling? I wondered. Fat chance I'd ever collect a penny from her or that she'd ever get a divorce.

Dr. Talbert was situated lower in the Heights hierarchy than Charlie Register. The allergist's office was tucked away in a one-story brick building across from the mall. The only view from there was a taller medical building across the street. His waiting room was filled with sneezing children. Newcomers to the Duke City like to bring their vegetation from back home with them, which adds to our native pollens. The pollen count has gotten so high that Albuquerque is thinking about hiring plant police. It was keeping Dr. Talbert in business.

I sat down and watched his wall clock tick away ten minutes of my billable hour before he came out. He was medium sized with short brown hair. He wore a white lab coat and a wide, red tie with Mickey and Minnie Mouse on it. He had the bright eyes of an inquisitive animal. "Hi, Dr. Talbert," the children chirped. "Hi," he replied, calling each of them by name. "You're Attorney Hamel?" he asked me.

"Right."

"Let's go into the office."

I followed him down the hall to his office, where a video of the doctor himself was playing on a TV. "Beta-blockers," I heard the video say before he snapped it off.

"Sorry about that," he said. "The previous patient forgot to exit. I've made a video of some of the things I tell all my patients. It's cheaper for them to watch that than to pay for my time." He picked up a file from the counter and sat down on a stool with the file in his lap. He motioned for me to sit in a chair opposite him. His gaze never left my face while we talked. He kept his head cocked, and it seemed to be surrounded by invisible antennae that picked up clues I didn't even know I was sending. He could be sensing whatever I was allergic to, what I'd had for breakfast, whether I'd had sex last night. There was a low-level vibration buzzing around him like the hum of an insect's wings.

"I hope Terrance listened better to you than he did to me," he began.

"He did have his own way of doing things," I said.

"He would have been happy to treat his allergies with a cortisone shot every year, but I won't do that; steroids have harmful side effects. I tried to get him in here weekly for shots, but he wasn't good about it. He didn't have the patience. He came when he remembered or happened to be in the neighborhood."

"Do the shots work if you don't follow a regular schedule?"

"Not very well."

"What was Terrance allergic to?" If we'd come to the doctor/patient confidentiality zone here, he was willing to cross it.

"Pollens, grasses, weeds, when he first came to me."

"When was that?"

"About fifteen years ago, when he moved to Albuquerque. That was when he was married to his second wife, before he met Deborah. After I was treating him Terrance developed an allergy to parrots. That hurt him; he loved his birds. The best treatment for parrot allergies is avoidance. There are no parrot desensitizing injections. At first Terrance wouldn't listen, but eventually he got so bad he had to give up the birds."

"I saw him react to the parrots. He began to sneeze, and he

left the room. It didn't strike me as a reaction that would kill him."

"One thing I've learned in twenty years of practice is that allergies are not an exact science. In India they believe asthma can be cured by swallowing live sardines."

"That would cure me," I said.

"I don't believe it was Terrance's parrot allergy that killed him." Talbert paused while his antennae picked up the beat. Apparently, he didn't sense a malpractice suit in the air and he continued. "I talked to a colleague of mine, Dr. Hirsh at the OMI."

Why else would he have summoned me here?

"He told me that Terrance was wearing a patch on his arm that released testosterone?"

"That's right," I said.

"Where on earth did he get that?"

"He financed the company."

Dr. Talbert shook his head. "There are several ways Terrance could have died, all of them quick and relatively painless. Epinephrine is adrenaline. It's a jolt to the heart, and it is a remote possibility that a shot could induce a heart attack. It doesn't happen often, but it can happen. Sometimes with anaphylactic shock, the blood pressure drops low enough to bring on a heart attack. If the needle had been injected directly into an artery, that could kill him, but the needle mark was in his upper arm, and there aren't any arteries there. It's possible that the allergy attack was so severe the epinephrine couldn't revive him, which happens rarely, but it can happen. If the patient's potassium is low, after strenuous exercise, for example, or with laxative abuse, epinephrine may not work. Beta-blockers, taken for high blood pressure, will inhibit the effect of epinephrine, but Terrance's blood pressure wasn't that high and he had been warned often enough about beta-blockers."

"Could someone have slipped him some or done something to lower his potassium?" The strenuous exercise that was crossing my mind was sex.

"Possible, but that wasn't what killed him." He paused. His antennae quivered. I tried to stay as still as a lizard so as not to frighten him off. "It wasn't epinephrine in that vial," Talbert said. "That was the very first thing I asked Dr. Hirsh to check. Terrance has had allergic reactions before, and epinephrine always worked for him."

"What *was* in the vial?"

"Saline solution. Saline solution had been substituted for epinephrine. Both are clear fluids. The difference would not be apparent to the eye."

"Saline solution wouldn't kill him, would it?"

"No, but it wouldn't bring him out of anaphylactic shock, either."

"Is there any chance the pharmacy could have made a mistake?"

"Highly unlikely."

"Wouldn't Terrance have noticed if the vial had been tampered with?"

"That would depend on how carefully it had been done. I'm sure the police will check for fingerprints."

I was already expecting two sets. Who knew whether there would be any more.

"A person in anaphylactic shock is not going to be thinking or observing very carefully. The blood pressure drops precipitously, the tongue and lips swell, the bronchial passages close up, there is a strong sense of foreboding."

"That seems natural if a person can't breathe." I had a bad vision of Terrance gasping for air and clutching the vial. It may have been a quick and painless death, but it had to be beyond terrifying. And what had I been doing that morning? Making love in the desert and handing over his two hundred thousand dollars.

"What killed him was anaphylactic shock and the fact that he didn't have epinephrine to counteract it. I prescribed epinephrine and he was told to carry it with him at all times." Dr. Talbert tapped the file on his lap. *His* conscience was clear.

"What was it that put him into shock? Do you know?"

"An examination of his stomach contents should determine that. However, I believe it was peanuts. Ever since he was a small child Terrance had been highly allergic to peanuts. It's the one allergy he had that was life threatening. Peanuts were in the granola he ate for breakfast. The medical investigator took a sample."

They had the Kid to thank for that.

"There's a treatment some mothers use for children with a peanut allergy. I can't recommend it because it is not approved by the AMA, although it can be effective. The mother mixes a very small amount of peanut with water and feeds it to the child daily. It helps to establish and maintain a tolerance. Peanuts are a difficult food to avoid. There was a case of a woman in New England who was highly allergic. She ate chili in a restaurant and it killed her. You wouldn't think chili would kill anyone, would you?"

It might, I thought.

"A cook had put peanut butter in the chili to thicken it. I want you to know that I did not recommend this desensitizing technique to Terrance. He was using it long before he came to me." Talbert tapped the file, which, presumably, contained evidence to support his claim. "His mother started it when he was a small boy, and Deborah continued the treatment. He shouldn't have had such a violent reaction to the peanuts in the granola. There shouldn't have been any peanuts in his granola."

"What would happen if the treatment were discontinued?"

"He'd lose his tolerance, and his reaction could be severe."

"Did you know that he and Deborah had split up?"

His reaction was startled. This was one event that his antennae had not picked up. "No. I didn't." He paused for a moment while his mind sorted through the invisible stimuli. "That would explain it. Deborah would never have discontinued the treatment; she loved Terrance."

"That's not exactly what I've been hearing."

"I haven't seen her for a couple of years, but when she first married Terrance she used to come here with him. She loved him then, but who knows? Love is not an exact science. I hate to lose a patient," he said softly. He looked at the clock on the wall and sighed. "I have to go. I have a child with asthma to see."

"Thanks for you help," I said, but he wasn't listening. His attention had already shifted from the patient who was dead to the child who needed help.

I stopped at the Wild Oats natural foods store on my way back to the office. In the bulk bins they had raspberry granola, blueberry granola, maple syrup granola, honey-nut granola. They had a total of fifteen different types of granola. All the ingredients were labeled, and not one of them contained peanuts.

15

I worked late that evening and stopped at the lab on my way home to tell Rick how Terrance had died. The sun was sliding toward Gallup as I entered the university. When I stepped out of the Nissan, I heard the sound of a raucous party. I remembered from my UNM days that partying is what college students do best. I'd been pretty good at it once myself. Music was playing—loud. The first sound I pulled out of the cacophony was the beat, but it wasn't the nineties beat of grunge rock, or rap or Megadeth. It was the slow and raunchy retro rhythm of the blues. As I approached the lab I could see that the door was open a crack and hear that that was where the party sounds were coming from. The last time I'd pushed open an unlocked door I'd found a dead body, but that building had been as quiet as a vault and in this one a lively party was going on. Could Deborah have been returned? I wondered. Was she alive and well? Was this a celebration? Since the parrots ruled the lab, it occurred to me that this could be a party without a human present. It wouldn't take much to get the parrots to partying.

I pushed open the door and heard, "Start me talkin', babe, tell you everythin' I know," in the voice of a world-weary blues singer or an irascible Amazon parrot—or both. The radio was on loud; the rhythm section kept the beat. It happened to be blues night on KUNM, and parrots love the blues. Maxamilian was balanced on top of Deborah's computer, bobbing his head and belting out the lyrics. He watched the action through Deborah's window on the lab, showing me the back of his double-yellow head.

The other Amazons were on the lab table boogying and providing a disorderly backup chorus to Max. Colloquy and Perigee had been let out of their cage. They jerked and swayed on a manzanita perch. Their long blue tails shimmied, their necks stretched, their large heads bobbed in time, their eyes were bright and surrounded by yellow ovals. Rick Olney was dancing with the parrots. He snapped his fingers, swung his hips, shuffled his feet, and swiveled his pelvis, reaching deep into a collective and unconscious rhythm as instinctive in nature as a growl. He would have been surprised to see how rhythmically he could move once he forgot he was doing it. "Talkin' Babe" finished, and KUNM segued into another song.

"Round here," Maxamilian growled in the raspy voice of a Bo Diddley or a Muddy Waters, "round midnight. Make me feel so good, make me feel. . . ."

"All right," Rick Dances with Parrots shouted, leaping in the air.

"All right," the backup Amazons cackled.

My pheromone sensors went into overtime. I had a few in my eyes, a few in my ears, a number in my nose, and a whole lot just under the surface of my skin; they sensed enough testosterone zinging around here to create a baby, cause a war, commit a murder. Energy seeks its own level, and Rick's energy level said to me that he'd gained in power, succeeded at crime and/or gotten laid.

Max swiveled his head one hundred and eighty degrees, and I came into his line of vision. "Call my lawyer," he shrieked, laughing at his little joke. I made a *shhhh* motion with my finger to my lips, but it was too little too late and he wouldn't have listened anyway. Rick spun around and saw me standing in the doorway. He stopped moving as suddenly and awkwardly as a kid caught playing the game of statues. He was off balance, with his weight on one foot, his elbows in the air and his hips in the middle of a twist. I could have pushed him over with my little finger. A blush started from his toes and rose rapidly to the edge of his square haircut.

"Oh, shit," he said, finding his balance, straightening up and snapping off the radio.

"Midnight special, baby," growled Max.

"Be quiet, Max," Rick said.

"Quiet, Max," the bird echoed. "Be your pistol, too."

"I, um . . . it was um . . . it was Alice," Rick said, turning a deeper shade of rose.

So it *was* a celebration. I'd been right about that. "When?" I asked.

He looked around as if the walls had ears and those ears belonged to someone with money and authority, but no one with that profile was visible here. "A few hours ago."

"Was it all you expected?" I asked. In my own experience, it takes a while to get up to speed.

"Better," he sighed. "I'm in love."

I was reminded of the last time I'd heard the word "love," only a few days ago. "Sara Dumaine told me that she and . . . Terry . . . were in love," I said. I hadn't told him that before; I hadn't been sure it was any of his business.

"No!" Rick cried. If he'd been a parrot, his feathers would have been standing on end.

"Those were her words. She was at the house when I got there Monday, weeping over Terrance's body."

"Goddamn," Rick said. "It doesn't surprise me that Terrance was screwing around, but with Deborah's sister? No wonder Deborah had been in such a rotten mood."

"You think she knew?" Rick had let his guard down in love's afterglow. Trust a lawyer to step into the breach.

"She wouldn't have told me if she did, but something had been bothering her. I could see that."

"She *was* getting a divorce," I said, which, I knew as well as anyone, could ruin a mood.

"She's been divorced before," Rick said.

"That doesn't make it any easier."

"Deborah and I didn't talk about personal stuff much."

"Have you heard anything from her?"

He shook his head. "Not a word."

"If you're still thinking about calling in the police, I have the card of the detective who's investigating Terrance's death." Now that the OMI had discovered the saline solution, I was sure there would be an investigation. I handed Rick Detective Hernandez's card, which he stuffed into his jeans pocket without looking at it, but taking a hard look at his running shoes.

"I thought you told me it was an allergic reaction," he said. "Why would the police investigate that?"

"Someone substituted saline solution for the epinephrine that would have pulled him out of it, which makes it homicide."

"Really?" he replied.

"Really. Are you going to call Hernandez?"

"I'll think about it." He reached up to straighten the missing glasses. The rock and roller had vanished. The bright, stiff young scientist had returned.

My question was why he had to think about doing something today that he'd once been so eager to do. I wondered if the answer might be found in the file Terrance and his men had searched Deborah's office for. "I don't have a copy of Terrance's will," I said. "I wasn't his lawyer for that." And if Baxter, Johnson had handled it they weren't likely to tell me what it said. "Did Deborah have a copy?" It might contain information about the trust set up to provide for the parrots. It might tell me if Terrance had left anything (or everything) to Sara Dumaine. It might tell me whether Sara had a motive.

"I don't know where it is," he mumbled, but his skin color gave him away.

My next question was, "That tape that Alice showed my friend the other day, what was on it?"

"Parrot talk. It's a multiple-track tape that repeats phrases that Deborah wanted to teach them. Parrots learn by rote. With the tape, they could go on learning even when Deborah wasn't here."

"Can I listen?"

"It will get them worked up again." He looked at the wall clock. "It's bedtime."

The Amazons watched us with their pupils dilating and contracting, waiting for the next move. Colloquy preened Perigee. Max climbed up on the window ledge. "They don't look like they're ready to go to sleep to me," I said.

"I am." He turned around, walked into Deborah's office where God was in the details and Max was on the computer, and tried to coax Max into retiring for the night. There were a couple of keys hanging from a hook on the wall, and while Rick's back was to me I lifted one and put it in my pocket. If he wouldn't help me, I'd do it myself.

I followed him into the office, and subtle as a lawyer, asked, "What do you do with the feathers that fall on the floor of the cage?" I didn't want to admit that I'd been snooping through Deborah's office. Max knew. "Don't tell, Max"; I sent him an interspecies telepathic message.

"We give them to the Hopis to use in their ceremonials," he said.

"Do you have any left? I collect feathers." Not true. I don't collect anything.

He opened the drawer he'd put the feathers in before, only now it was empty. "No. We've given them all away," he said in the absentminded manner of someone who was a poor rememberer or a bad liar.

"Did Terrance come by the indigos legally?" I asked him.

"Actually, he did. He took them out of the country before Brazil signed an export ban. You wouldn't be able to do it legally now. Indigos were thought to be near extinction, but in nineteen seventy-eight a flock of about seventy was discovered in the Raso. The World Parrot Trust is taking steps to preserve them, and getting good cooperation from the local people. Deborah loved the Raso. In Brazil she was a queen. She got respect for being a linguist. Here, nobody's interested. Parrots can be difficult, but it's easier to get funding for studying them in America than for studying people. Time for bed, Max."

And time for me to go. "'Night, Max," I said.

"'Night, D," he replied.

"Deborah always put him to bed," Rick sighed. "That's when he misses her most."

16

The party was over. It was dark when I left the lab, and the parking lot was not lit. I stood outside the door for a minute to get my bearings. Lights came on in a vehicle in the lot, low beams at first and then highs. The bright lights spotlighted me standing in front of the Psittacine Research Facility doorway. I put my left hand up to shield my eyes. The vehicle backed out of the lot without dimming the beams, without revealing exactly what kind of vehicle it was. With my right hand I reached into the purse that was dangling from my shoulder. The most dangerous place for a woman is between her car (or her place of work or the store) and her home. The fact that this had been Deborah Dumaine's place of work, not mine, didn't lessen the danger factor. It might have escalated it. I found my key ring with the car keys and mini-Punch hanging from it, and I clutched it between my fingers while my eyes made the adjustment from too much light to too little. I walked to the Nissan, entered it without using my weapon and started the engine.

As I passed the parking lot near Central, two vehicles got into line behind me—one pair of headlights on high beams, one pair on low. I pulled onto Central heading east just as I would have if I were going home to La Vista. Both vehicles turned east behind me. When a clearing in the traffic opened up, I made a quick shift into the fast lane and spun a *U*. Nobody followed. I went a few blocks and made another *U*, turning me back east again. I hadn't been followed, but an imaginary parrot on my shoulder was squawking "Watchate."

I was heading for the ATM on Tramway; I wanted to take a few steps in the ransom collector's boots to see if that could give me an entrée to the kidnapper's mind. An electrical storm brewed over the Sandias. Lightning stabbed at the peaks and bolted laterally from cloud to cloud. Sunset was a recent memory, and the lightning was the rosy pink color of the reflected sunset, the color the Sandias turn when there's an afterglow, the color of Rick Olney's blush. *Sandia* means watermelon, and some say the mountains were named for the evenings they turn watermelon pink. Other people believe the mountains got their name because they have a watermelon's shape. In a place that has as long a recorded history as New Mexico, legends and place names get twisted in the wind of repeated tellings. The mountains farther north are called the Sangre de Cristos—the blood of Christ—but they turn the same pink color as the Sandias. If it's the color of blood, it's thin blood, blood that's been diluted by tears or rain.

I reached the solitary ATM on Tramway at the base of the mountains, the ATM where Laura Simonson had been mugged and where a masked person had claimed half of Deborah and Perigee's ransom money. The parking lot was empty, the warehouse was a blank, white wall. How anyone kept a wall that graffiti-free in Albuquerque was a mystery to me. I turned the Nissan around to see if anyone had followed. No one had. The road back to Tramway was deserted. I could have gone to the drive-in window, conducted my business from my car and made a quick getaway, but I parked, got out and walked into the building that housed the ATM just as feathered mask had done. Lights flashed in the western sky, beyond the curve of the horizon, too distant to see the shape of the bolts. Those lights also had a pinkish glow and seemed to be synchronized to the flashes over the Sandias, one flash echoing another. It could have been a reflection of the Sandia storm or another storm farther west, or it might have been its own storm system. I couldn't tell.

There's safety in numbers; there's safety in lookouts. The Apaches didn't have the numbers; they relied on awareness and lookouts. I didn't have the numbers either, only myself, but I was high enough to see anyone coming and would have had time to collect the money, get in the car and drive away. With my ATM card and keys in hand, I approached the screen, smiled for the camera and inserted my card in the slot. The screen prompted me to enter my PIN. I did it, I noticed, more by remembering the location of the PIN digits on the screen than by remembering the digits themselves. Deborah's PIN, I remembered, was 2473. I asked the ATM for one hundred dollars, and I got it in twenties. I put the money, my card and the receipt in my pocket. Having learned that punching in a PIN number is a rote action and that this was the most isolated ATM in Albuquerque, I left. I knew I'd been seen only by the eye of the camera, but I still felt that I was being pursued. Thunder rumbled. The storm was moving east, but the air remained charged with the electricity that produces revelations, hallucinations and squawking parrot mind.

I got in the Nissan and drove west on Montgomery. Fat rain drops hit my windshield and splattered in tiny, dusty explosions. I turned the wiper to intermittent, then moved it up a notch to slow. By the time I reached La Vista the wipers were running on fast and puddles were forming in the low places in the street. Soon runoff would be pulsing through the diversion channels like blood coursing through an unclogged artery. Ordinarily I park on the east side of La Vista in front of my apartment, in the space across from the dumpster that has my number on it, but the parrot on my shoulder squawked "Watchate," so I kept on going. It was possible that someone had anticipated my movements, come here and waited. It wasn't difficult to find out where I lived; my address was in the phone book. I noticed that La Bailarina, the homeless woman who lives in La Vista's parking lot, had parked her van beside the dumpster. My place was empty, which it isn't always when I come home at night. I left it that way and continued north.

My apartment is also accessible from the back side of the building, down a dingy hallway. I don't come in that way; it's dark, it's shabby, the parking spaces have somebody else's number on them. I circled the north wall of the building. As I drove down the west side, I saw a shadow under the dim overhead bulb in the hallway. As I got closer the shadow became a cowboy wearing a black hat and a long duster, standing under the stairway to the second floor. The cowboy didn't turn around to look as I drove to the south side of the building and parked in someone else's space. I walked back up the west side, keeping close to the wall. Lights were on on the second floor, but the windows on my floor, the first, were all dark. I didn't have a raincoat or hat; rain slid down my face. Weather doesn't mess around in New Mexico. When the sun shines, it sizzles. When it rains, it pours. Water dripped from the *canales* onto my head. I felt like I was taking a shower with my clothes on, but the running water did conceal the sound of my footsteps.

I flattened myself against the cracked stucco wall and stepped around the corner. The cowboy, who hadn't heard me coming, was leaning sideways against the wall and peering down the hallway, watching perhaps for headlights to pull into my parking space. Even in cowboy boots there'd be time to run down the hall and jump me as I crossed the danger zone for women and inserted my key in my lock. Would anybody have heard? Or reacted if they did? I wondered.

In boot heels, the cowboy was just about my height. Thick shoulder-length hair bridged the space between the hat and the duster. I held my key-ring Punch in my left hand, grabbed the hair and yanked it hard with the right at the same time that I rammed my knees into the back of the cowboy's. It occurred to me that I might end up holding a blond wig in my hand, and that when the cowboy turned around I'd see a feathered mask. The knees buckled. The head spun around. The hair was real. The down-at-the heels expression belonged to the So-Cal cowboy. I could tell by the smell of his breath and the ease with which his knees buckled that Wes Brown had been drinking. He stammered, trying to find a swear word to fit the occasion. The best he could do on such short notice was "cunt."

"You already called me that," I said. He hadn't had time to draw his weapon, but I doubted he'd have come here without one. "Hand over the piece," I told him.

He blinked. "What piece?"

"The one you're packing."

"If I don't?"

"I'll scream. I'll blow my whistle. I'll call the night watchman. I'll call my neighbor, who's a cop. I'll squirt red pepper into your lungs and your face. And if that doesn't work, I'll kick." Those are the self-defense tricks women are taught to rely on. Most of them were idle threats, but what did he know?

As the Kid said, Brown was lacking in the bravery department. He surrendered the gun, another .45. Brown had a gun for every occasion, but so far I'd seen only the same caliber. I made him precede me into my apartment and sit down on the sofa. His duster dripped onto the yellow shag carpeting. I sat down across from him with the .45 in my lap. He leaned his head against the wall, stretched out his legs and looked at me from under his lashes. He'd taken off his hat, revealing a bad case of hat head; his hair was flatter than Garth Brooks's.

"What's your game?" he asked in his surly drawl.

"Like I told you, I'm a lawyer."

"Yeah? Then why are you living here?"

"Beats living in dry dock," I said.

"You're the one who turned the FWS onto me, aren't you?" he asked.

The news that they'd already gotten to him was birdsong to my ears. "Yup," I said. "They arrested you?"

"Yeah. I had to post bond to get out."

He'd probably done it with the smelly money.

"Why have you got it in for me?" He poked the carpet with his scruffy boot. "What'd I ever do to you?"

"You're a parrot smuggler."

"What business is that of yours?"

"I like parrots."

"I had to find some way to pay back the IRS."

"How about getting a job?" I asked.

"In Door?" he blinked.

I could have suggested he leave Door, but what would be the point? Cause and effect were inoperative inside his Jack Daniels envelope. If I had my way he'd be trading Door for a prison cell and whatever abusive substances he could obtain in there. "Your girlfriend, Katrina, said . . . "

"She's not my girlfriend."

"What is she?"

"Someone I see when I come to Albuquerque." He shrugged. "That's all." He crossed one boot over the other and watched me from under the liar's lashes.

"Why do you come to Albuquerque? To deposit the money for the IRS?" I asked. Or to get laid? Or to sell parrots? I didn't ask. One offense at a time.

"I don't have to justify myself to you," he snapped in a tone of voice that suggested I was beneath contempt, which, when you think about it, wasn't all that different from the message his lashes had been sending. I let his answer pass. He would have to justify himself to the FWS, and anyhow, I had other means of getting my bank question answered. "Why'd you tell Katrina you wanted to get in touch with me?"

"I wanted to know where you went Sunday after you left Door."

"Like Katrina said, I was at her house."

"Actually *she* didn't say that, Ellen did." I was kind of curious to see what his reaction would be to Ellen. Even in his fantasy envelope he had to know she didn't like him.

"Ellen's jealous."

"Of what?" I asked.

"I met her before I met Katrina. She came on to me."

I'd heard that one before.

"So if I was at the house then? What business is it of yours?"

"Terrance Lewellen is my client. He died Monday morning."

"You can't be trying to blame that on me."

Why not? I thought.

"What killed him?" he asked, giving me another look that left the door open for seduction or misinterpretation. Terrance's death scared him. He'd been arrested for smuggling before and gotten out of that, but murder was a deep-water crime. I had a suspicion that if I responded to Wes Brown he'd back off, then tell some other woman that I'd come on to him. His fear of rejection could be so strong that he'd do it to you before you could do it to him. Maybe what he was really looking for was a woman who felt worse about being herself than he did about being himself. Although the come-on routine was an automatic response, I could see that he'd have no respect for anyone who said yes. A man with that poor a self-image is a coiled snake for an unwary foot, one reason I wear snake boots around my heart. Katrina probably felt that bad, I thought, but had Deborah? Or Sara?

"An allergic reaction killed Terrance," I said. "The OMI is investigating. Sara Dumaine found him dead in his house."

Sara's name produced—like a lot of things I'd said—a shrug.

"Did you know he and Sara were having an affair?" I asked.

He blinked. "How would I know that?"

"Did you know that Terrance had allergies?"

"No. I barely knew the guy."

"Where is Deborah?"

"I haven't a clue."

I had one more question. "How'd you know where I live?"

"Looked you up in the phone book."

That was enough to make me want to move out of La Vista in the morning and get an unlisted number. "I don't have anything more to say. Do you?"

"Yeah, I do." He leaned forward on the sofa, resting his forearms on his thighs. "Get the hell out of my life." His lips mouthed anger, but his eyes still begged "rescue me."

"Get out of my apartment," was my answer.

"Give me back my gun."

"No way."

"Cunt."

He drove off in his pickup, another loaded weapon cruising for targets on the highway.

After he left I went into the kitchen to see what time it was. Ten by the oven clock. Too early to go to sleep, and who could go to sleep after the evening I'd had? Adrenaline sends sleep out the window. I knew that from my own experience as an adrenaline queen. It was the Kid's night to play the accordion at El Lobo. I didn't want to interrupt him; I didn't want to go to El Lobo. It was a part of his world I didn't belong in. El Lobo was not a gentle place. Neither was the Psittacine Research Facility when you got right down to it, but I *was* thinking of going there. I took the lab key out of my pocket and twirled it around in my fingers. What I was considering might be called breaking and entering. Technically, I wouldn't be breaking since I had the key, I'd just be entering. If I got caught, I could always say my client had given me the key, that I was representing his best interests, that Rick Olney had been concealing vital information. Money talks even from the grave, and my client's money was running the lab. Besides, I'd already caught Rick Olney breaking into my place of work, so who was he to complain? I didn't intend to get caught, and I didn't intend to steal anything, only to listen and observe. I had a hunch about where the missing file was, and I wanted to hear what the parrot instruction tape had to say. There was always the possibility that the key I'd taken would not let me in, in which case I'd come home and forget about it.

I put Wes Brown's .45 in a drawer, intending to turn it over to Special Agent Violet Sommers. The only weapon of mine the feathered mask hadn't confiscated in the desert was the Punch on my key ring. I took it.

Before I left I called the lab. I didn't want to run into Rick Olney again; I figured I'd already gotten all the information I'd get out of him. The phone rang five times, then the answering machine picked up. I was more than a little spooked by the voice that answered, Deborah Dumaine's. Rick had not wanted to (or had not gotten around to) changing the tape.

Deborah seemed to be speaking from beyond the reach of the law or the curve of the earth. "The Psittacine Research Facility is closed," she said. "Office hours are from nine to five, Monday through Friday. Call back then." She didn't ask me to leave a message. I had no message to leave. I picked up a pair of gloves and a pair of headphones and I went out the door.

The rain had stopped, but the pavement was slick with black water. The stars were twinkling on one by one and the moon slipped out from under a silver-bellied cloud. Someone had stuck a note beneath my windshield wiper. "Park in your own space, goddamn it," it read.

I ripped the white paper in pieces and offered it to the wind goddess, but she wasn't taking. The scraps dropped into a puddle and sank.

There were no cars in the parking lot when I returned to the Psittacine Research Facility. The door was shut, the lab was silent, the lights were off. I put on my gloves and took the key from my pocket. The key slipped in like the lock was made of butter. The tumbler turned, the dead bolt slid open. I stepped inside and bolted the door behind me. The lab was pitch dark. The parrots, having squawked the sun to bed, seemed to be sound sleep. They were so quiet it was possible to imagine they'd flown the coop. Rick had gone home or to Alice's. I had a pocket flashlight, which I shined across the floor until I located the box of plastic booties. I managed to pull a pair on over my running shoes; I didn't want to be leaving New Balance glyphs all over the place. I also didn't want to waste my time taking running shoes on and off.

Following the flashlight's lead, I made my way across the lab to the room that housed the indigos. I lifted the light once to see what the birds were doing, and got a quick glimpse of two big macaws asleep, snuggled together on their perch. The one place in this lab an outsider would not be able to enter was this cage. The two scimitar beaks in there were capable of snapping a finger off, and one of the indigos, I knew, did not like strangers. If I were going to hide something valuable in this lab, I'd be tempted to put it inside the cage. If the macaws could keep Terrance out, they would have scared off any snooping security men. There was a tray underneath that collected the bird's droppings. I pulled the handle, slid the tray out and beamed my flashlight over the contents. Nothing but bird shit on the top sheet of a stack of white paper. Apparently the top paper was pulled off whenever the cage was cleaned. I ran my hand under the bottom sheet and felt only the flat bottom of the tray. I pulled the tray all the way out. There was a subfloor under it, covered by a plastic mat. One floor ought to be sufficient to catch the bird droppings. I shined my light quickly on the indigos again—still sleeping, still snuggling— stuck my arm through the bars and into the cage. I slid my gloved hand under the mat until it slipped into a depression, a compartment under the cage. Inside I found a box and a plastic envelope. I pulled them out and shined my light on them. The box had the familiar shape of a video, the envelope contained a manila file folder. "All right," I whispered.

I put the tray and papers back into place, took the envelope and video into the lab, sat down at the table and scanned them with my flashlight. The video was your basic black plastic model with a label that read "Property of Terrance Lewellen" in his EKG scrawl. The file contained the valuable papers of Deborah Dumaine, the first of which was her will. That document left everything to the parrot trust, but Deborah didn't have all that much to leave. Her prenuptial agreement (also in the file) said that she would take out of the marriage exactly what she'd brought in, which was close to nothing. Academics rarely get rich. I found letters to her attorney that said she was indeed trying to get out of her prenuptial agreement. The attorney had been encouraging her to pursue this path by whatever means were available, which is something I wouldn't have done. Different strokes for different lawyers.

Next I found the agreement, which stipulated, as Rick had said, that a trust fund had been established to care for the indigo macaws and the Amazons for the rest of their lives. The trust also provided money for the lab to continue its operations. Deborah was to manage the lab, and if she were unable to, Rick Olney would take her place. The lab's budget was attached and every expenditure was itemized, from the price of the birds' food to the size of the manager's income, which was even lower than mine. The budget was geared to the cost-of-living index and could be raised in times of inflation and lowered in times of deflation. Terrance continued to control the lab even from the grave, and he did it with a tight fist. Running the lab was a prestigious job in the bird world, but no one, including Rick Olney, would get rich doing it.

The last document was one of those do-it-yourself will forms that stated it was Terrance Lewellen's last will and testament and was dated July 15. Not one dime was left to Deborah Dumaine. Most of what Terrance had went to his mother, with the exception of two hundred and fifty thousand dollars earmarked for Sara. The will had been witnessed in the appropriate places and was signed with Terrance's uniquely sloppy signature. There was no evidence that Baxter, Johnson had been involved. Why not? I wondered. Because Buddy Baxter might have heard the testosterone talking and tried to change Terrance's mind?

I slid the file back in its plastic envelope and put on the headphones I'd brought. I plugged the male part into the cassette player and put the headphones over my ears so as not to disturb the sleeping parrots. I hit the Play button.

The first sound was the gentle but firm voice of Alice of the long blonde hair and the long graceful body.

"This is a . . . ?" she asked.

"Pen," replied a parrot.

"Good boy," she said, then, "pen?"

"Nut," screamed a bird who was probably Max, the brightest and loudest bird in the lab.

"Good boy," she said. Apparently she'd been testing him, showing him a nut and telling him it was a pen. This section of tape rambled on, with Alice showing the parrots an object, praising them if they identified it, correcting them if they were wrong. With his fascination for the newly beloved, Rick probably would have sat through this party dreamy-eyed, but I was soon bored. Why would he have had any objection to my listening to it?

I fast-forwarded to the next track and heard The Wicked Witch of the West cackle, "I'll get you, my pretty, and your little dog too."

"I'll get you, my pretty," echoed an Amazon, "and your little dog too."

The next voice belonged to Deborah in a cantankerous mood. "Terrance, you are *such* an asshole," she said.

"Terrance, you are *such* an asshole," an almost identical voice responded, but it wasn't hers, I knew, it was Maxamilian. Anger in, anger out. Parrots imitate sounds with emotional content. Deborah was using her emotions to get a reaction from Max, which didn't strike me as exactly scientific.

This track seemed to be aimed at encouraging the parrots to imitate, which came naturally enough. The next track tried for a response which wasn't as predictable.

"What's your name?" I heard Deborah ask.

"Maxamilian," her prize pupil answered.

"What's this?"

"Pen."

"Good boy," she said.

"Nut," he answered.

There was a pause, then I heard the tentative, querying

voice of Sara Dumaine. "Terry, sweetie," she cooed. "I love you so much."

"*Malinche,*" a parrot screeched, so loudly my ears hurt. That voice didn't sound like an imitation person; it sounded like a parrot, one of the parrots that was not a good talker. I snapped the cassette player off and yanked out the earphones; I'd heard what I wanted to know. Malinche was the Indian girl who had acted as an interpreter to Cortes and become his mistress. In Mexico a *malinche* is a traitor.

My inner clock told me that my time in the lab was up. I put the documents back in the file, put the file in the plastic envelope and returned it to the indigos' cage. One quick flash of my light told me that Perigee and Colloquy were still snuggled together on their perch. I pulled out the droppings tray, lifted the plastic mat and slid the file back into its niche. The video was coming with me. The mat buckled into a ridge, and I couldn't slide the tray back in place. I pulled the tray out, reached through the bars and was tugging at the mat, trying to smooth it, when a flapping, fluttering whirlwind descended to the floor of the cage and latched onto my gloved finger with a grip that could snap a Brazil nut in two.

"Ow," I yelled. It had to be Colloquy; Perigee knew me better and had better manners. He was awake now and beating his wings. Colloquy shook until my finger went as limp as a worm. "Goddamn it," I said. "Let go."

Perigee hissed "*Malinche.*" But I wasn't the traitor—not yet anyway. Perigee had gotten Colloquy's attention; she looked up at him, loosened her grip and dropped my finger, which I immediately yanked out of the cage. Blood was oozing through the glove. I pulled it off and sucked at my knuckle. I slammed the tray into place and rushed out of the lab, forgetting to remove the plastic booties, but remembering to bring the video and to lock the door behind me.

The booties came off in the car. The pain didn't kick in till I got home; the shock factor protected me that long. I let myself into La Vista, went into the bathroom, cleaned the wound, wrapped it sloppily in gauze with my left hand, had a shot of tequila and went to bed. I couldn't sleep—the finger throbbed to its own painful beat and lawyer thoughts dive-bombed me like mosquitoes—but I tucked my hand under the pillow and pretended I was out when the Kid let himself in around two. I knew I'd have to explain sooner or later, but I preferred later. He got into bed. When he leaned over to give me a kiss, I showed him the back of my head.

"What's that on your pillow, Chiquita?" he asked.

"Nothing," I replied, admitting that I was already awake.

"It looks like blood."

"I nicked my finger."

"What did you use? A machete?"

"It's nothing."

"Let me see." He tried to pull the hand out from under the pillow.

"Ow," I said.

"What is it?"

"I told you—nothing."

"Show me."

I pulled the hand out and showed him the gauze-wrapped wound. The only light in the room came from the mercury vapor lamps in the parking lot, but there was enough of that to see that blood had soaked through the gauze and stained the pillowcase and sheet. The Kid guessed the cause.

"A *loro*?"

"Right."

"Which one?"

"Colloquy."

He shook his head. "I told you she could take your finger off."

"Okay, so you told me."

"You put your hand in the cage?"

"Yeah."

"Why'd you do that?"

"There was something in there I wanted."

He had taken off the gauze and was examining the wound. The finger was swelling, but the cut still had the jagged shape of Colloquy's beak. "It looks bad," he said.

"It's not that bad."

"Was it worth it?"

"I'll know soon, but I think it was."

"You never stop, do you?" he asked.

He already knew the answer to that, so he got up and went into the bathroom for some antiseptic to clean the wound. It hurt like hell, but I didn't let it show. With two hands he could wrap the gauze a lot tighter and cleaner than I could with one. "You're lucky," he said. "It could be worse."

"Right," I replied.

"In the morning you go to the doctor."

That sounded like an order to me. "What for? You already cleaned it."

"I think it is broken."

"All right," I agreed, but the buzzing thoughts told me there were other things I had to attend to first. "Wes Brown was here earlier," I told him.

"Yeah?" the Kid replied. "What'd he want?" The pilot light that burns steadily on the range of male/female relationships flared behind his eyes. I know better than to fan that flame, so I didn't mention Brown's rescue-me manner or that he had been drunk.

"He heard I was looking for him," I said.

"Why were you looking for him?" The Kid knew Brown was trouble, and that it's better not to go looking for trouble. It comes after you often enough.

"I wanted to know where he was when Terrance died."

"You think that *cobarde* did that?" He didn't have a high opinion of Brown's abilities.

"Who knows? The FWS arrested him for smuggling parrots anyway."

"How'd he get out of prison?"

"Put up some smelly money."

The Kid shook his head. "That's all it takes?"

"That's it," I said.

17

Time is of the essence in law and in life. My instincts told me that while I could solve the crime if I waited, I might not catch the criminal. There was some bank account information that only Charlie Register could give me, but first I needed to find out whether I could trust Charlie Register, and that depended on how badly he wanted the Lochovers. The one person who might be able to tell me was Terrance's mother, Candace Lewellen. Before I went to work or the doctor, I stopped at La Buena Vida.

The receptionist in the main building had an Anne Richardson helmet of white hair. There was a bowl of hard candy on her desk, and she offered me a piece. Her ring finger wore a large, fake, yellow stone. Her nails were long and opalescent.

"Thanks anyway," I said. "I'm Terrance Lewellen's lawyer. I'd like to talk to his mother."

"I'll give her a call. What'd you say your name was?"

"Neil Hamel."

She. dialed Mrs. Lewellen's room. "Candace, honey," she said. "There's a lawyer here named Neil . . . Is that right? . . . Hamel."

"Right," I said.

"She wants to see you." She peered at me over the top of her glasses. "Candace says to go on up."

"What's her apartment number?" I asked.

"She don't have an apartment, honey. She's got a *casita*. Terrance provided good for his momma."

I'd been told to look for a good provider once, but the message didn't stick. Security has never been in my candy bowl.

"Pity about that poor boy," the receptionist said.

"Who?" I asked. If she meant my client, he'd been neither poor nor a boy.

"Terrance. The way he died." She rolled her eyes. What did she know about how Terrance had died?

"You mean the allergies?" I asked.

"That's right. His momma feels real bad that no one was givin' him the peanuts mixed with the water. She says that's what killed him. That nobody was doin' that for her boy."

It was a contributing factor, I knew, but not the whole story. "Terrance was a grown man. He could have done it for himself."

"That ain't the way a momma sees it, honey."

The receptionist would have kept me there all day, talking, if I'd let her. Seniors know all the little tricks for getting and holding your attention, and the ones with time on their hands are quite capable of wasting yours. "How do I get to Candace's *casita*?" I asked.

She gave me directions and offered me another piece of candy. "No thanks," I said.

Candace's doorbell played a tinkly tune, but her voice was a blast of dusty Texas wind. "Door's open. Come on in," she bellowed. I let myself into the living room of her *casita*, which, except for the Lochover overflowing one wall, was a study in birds and indifference. The furniture was beat up and beige. The color scheme was similar to Charlie Register's, but his look was carefully planned and this room had been thrown together. Birds were all over the wall in watercolors and oils, and all over the shelves in ceramics and wood. Her taste in birds ran to the small and the pretty. I saw a kestrel, but no eagles or peregrine falcons. I saw a parakeet, but not a single parrot.

I knew a girl named Candace when I was in grammar school who was more often called Candy Ass. If any boy had ever called Terrance's mother that, he'd only have done it once. She was small, but she was no candy ass. She was sitting in a large beige armchair. A wooden cane leaned against the arm of the chair. Her skin was weathered and her hair was tied in a bun. Her glasses had thick lenses and gold frames, but her eyes had Terrance's gray-green sparkle. She reminded me of a small, sharp nail. She held a cigar in her hand, but she hadn't lit it yet. A glass of something brown and medicinal (or recreational) sat on the end table. She took a sip.

"Excuse me if I don't get up." She pointed toward the cane.

"No problem." I sat myself down in a sofa that had the charm and comfort of a hunk of rental furniture.

"You care if I smoke?" she asked.

"Nope."

She lit up and was enveloped in a cloud of her own foul-smelling smoke. She puffed on her cigar with the same relish that her son had chewed on his. If God wasn't in the details, he might be in the genes. "You're a lawyer?" she asked me.

"Right."

"With Baxter, Johnson?"

"No," I said, lighting up my own smoking instrument. "With Hamel and Harrison."

"I thought Buddy Baxter was Terrance's lawyer." Her eyes narrowed from distrust—or smoke.

"Not for everything," I said.

"What did you do for my boy?"

"I can't discuss it. I'm sorry."

"Was whatever you were representing him for what got him killed?"

"It's possible," I said, which was as far as I was willing to go.

"A Detective Hernandez was here. You know her?"

"We've met."

"She said someone put saltwater into my boy's allergy medicine."

"I heard that."

She sipped at the brown stuff, put the glass down and gripped the arms of her chair. It was the first sign she gave of any emotion. "You know who did that?"

"No," I said, honestly enough, "I don't, but it occurred to me that the motive might be found in his will."

She shook her head and a couple of hairpins fell in her lap. "He left everything to me, and I didn't kill him."

"You sure you were the only heir?"

"Of course I'm sure. Who else was he gonna leave it to? He and Deborah were getting a divorce. He never had any kids." She narrowed her eyes. "You're not *her* lawyer, are you?"

"No."

"You positive?"

"I can produce a retainer agreement if you want proof that I was representing Terrance."

Candace studied me with her wary eyes. "You worried about getting paid? Is that why you're asking all these questions about the will?" Maybe I should have been, but that issue hadn't even occurred to me yet. That's how far I'd come from being a greedy lawyer. "You send me a bill showing me the work you've done, you'll get your fee."

"I'll do that," I said. "My feeling is that I am representing Terrance just as much now as I was when he was alive, and that I could do it better if I knew what was in his will." Actually, I did know what was in one will, but it appeared that it wasn't the only will.

She nodded. Something—our mutual addiction maybe, or our mutual pigheadedness—had led her to trust me. "What else do you want to know?"

"When the will leaving everything to you was drawn up, and who prepared it."

"Buddy Baxter prepared it years ago when Terrance married Deborah. He had an agreement with her that she wouldn't be gettin' anything, and he wanted it all down in writing. Terrance didn't want to think anybody would be marrying him for his money."

Maybe he'd softened with age. Maybe synthetic testosterone was gentler than the other variety. Maybe Sara and an affair scared him less than Deborah and a marriage.

"Do you get the Lochovers?" I asked.

"Right."

"What will happen to them now?"

"You ain't the only one who's been askin' about that." She looked at the painting on the wall. Candace may have had her own *casita* at La Buena Vida, but the rooms were small, and at this distance the painting was neither fine brush strokes nor leaves in fall or winter. It was a blur of paint. She lifted her glasses and squinted at the painting. "Damned if I know what everybody sees in those things. Terrance had them all over the house. They look like water to me." She sniffed. "I'm a desert rat, and I never did trust water. You don't know what's hiding in it."

Having grown up near the Irish Pond in Ithaca, New York, I knew: fish, snakes, turtles and frogs. All of them wriggle and swim, some of them bite. Desert critters bite too, but you can see them coming.

"Charlie Register's been here," she said.

"Oh?"

"You know him?"

"I do," I said.

"Charlie's a charmer."

"He can be."

"He told me he had an agreement with Terrance to keep those paintings for a month. You know anything about that?"

"I drew up the agreement."

"What was it? Some kind of bet?"

"Something like that."

"Boys will be boys," she said.

Not necessarily, I thought. Sometimes they even turn out to be men.

"Charlie offered to buy those paintings from me," she said.

"Did he?" I asked, easing forward on the lumpy sofa.

"You have any idea what they're worth?"

"An idea. What did he offer?"

"Three hundred thousand dollars for three paintings! You think they're worth that?"

She didn't believe it, but I did. Charlie had taken them as collateral for less. "I'd have them appraised before I'd sell them to anyone," I said, "but I suspect that's a pretty fair offer."

"I grew up poor on a dirt farm in West Texas," she said, looking into the distance. What I knew of West Texas was the smell of the cattle pens, and that the minute you cross the border into New Mexico you can start breathing fresh air again. "That was the depression. We walked five miles to school barefoot, and if we got an orange in our stocking at Christmas we were damn lucky. Terrance's daddy worked in the oil fields. He died in a drilling accident when Terrance was just a little boy. We never had nothin'. Terrance worked real hard to make some money. Now he's dead too, and it looks like somebody killed him. He took good care of his momma. He moved me here." She leaned forward and whispered. "To tell you the truth, I liked it better in Texas, but I never would tell Terrance that." She leaned back. "I been through a lot, and there's nothing worse than losing your boy." She clutched herself in the middle of the solar plexus. "It hurts real bad. Now I'm getting the houses and the art and all that stuff, and what the hell am I supposed to do with it?" She answered her own question. "I'm giving the paintings to the Dallas Fine Arts Museum, and after I die the rest of it goes to the Audubon Society of Texas."

Once a Texan, always a Texan. It was her choice, but it seemed a shame to me that the Lochovers would be leaving the state.

"You'll tell me if you find out who killed my boy?"

"I will."

She took a sip of the brown stuff, looked at her watch. "Now I have to start gettin' ready for the funeral."

"When is it?" I asked.

"Eleven-thirty at Rosario Cemetary. You comin'?"

"I'll be there," I said.

When a man dies in the heat, he gets buried in the heat. It suited Candace Lewellen's dirt farmer background to put Terrance in the ground beneath the blazing sun, but if it had been up to me I would have waited till nightfall. Candace didn't hold a church funeral for Terrance; she had a short and to the point service at the cemetery.

At eleven-thirty in the morning the only shadows around were under the mourners' cars and feet. If I listened hard I could hear the flowers on the coffin dry up and wilt. The rain that had fallen last night had evaporated or seeped deep into the underground aquifer. The ground was as hard and as dry as adobe brick. It must have taken a pickax to carve out Terrance's grave; a shovel would have been worthless against that soil. A grave site in the Heights struck me as a poor place to lay a body to rest. A back-to-the-earth burial is better suited to a softer place, a place with fungus and worms to keep the soil loose. Sometimes I think we ought to go with the fact that between the Rio Grande Valley and the timberline, New Mexico is desert, and put the bodies out on a ledge and let the coyotes and vultures pick the bones clean.

It was too hot to make polite conversation. It was too hot to make any conversation. Most of the mourners sat in their air-conditioned cars with the windows closed and the engines running, waiting for Candace Lewellen and the minister to show up. Once they did, everybody got out and walked to the grave site. Candace was the only one wearing black—a solitary raven on the barren landscape. She leaned on the minister with one arm and on her wooden cane with the other. Most of the mourners were wealthy businessmen in cowboy hats and bolo ties. Charlie Register was there. His boots were polished, his shirt and pants were white and beige, he wore a Resistol white hat. Candace nodded to me, said hello to the men, patted some of their arms and ignored Sara Dumaine. Except for her dark shades, Sara was all in white: a white dress, white moccasins, the choker made out of bone pipe and feathers, a white fringed bag hanging from her shoulder. Sara and I were the youngest women there, which wasn't all that young. I was there in a professional capacity. I didn't know about Sara's capacity, but her grief appeared genuine. Her shoulders shook as she bent over her white handkerchief and sobbed.

The minister said a few words. Candace leaned on her

cane. I heard the sound of a car engine running and turned around to look. Most of the cars here were larger or sleeker than Sara's white Saturn and my yellow Nissan. Many of them had tinted glass. If someone had remained inside, I couldn't tell which car or who it was. It seemed extravagant to keep a car running just so it would be cool when the driver got back into it, but it was a hot day, there were a lot of wealthy people here and nobody was likely to steal a car at a funeral even if it did have the keys in it.

The minister finished the service. I told Candace how sorry I was and squeezed her bony hand. "Who's the Indian?" she asked, squinting in the direction of Sara. "Is that Sara Dumaine?"

"Yes."

"Guess I should have known better than to expect Deborah to show up."

"Guess so," I said.

I said hello to Charlie Register, then stopped at the coffin to say adios to my client. *"Vaya con dios,"* I said. "You were a bad actor, but you're still my client, and I am giving your case my best shot."

Sara had her hand on the door of her white Saturn when I caught up with her. She dispensed with the greetings and got right to the point. "My life is a mess," she said. "I've lost Terry. I've lost my sister."

And whose fault was that? I wondered. "What will you do now?" I asked.

The dollar curls drooped beside her face. She raised her dark glasses to look at me. Her eyes were red and puffy. She hadn't bothered with eye makeup and no mascara ran down her cheeks. "I don't know," she whispered. She lowered her glasses and got into her car. Her windows, like mine, were clear, coated only by a fine layer of dust.

The first vehicle to pull away had the gray anonymity of a rental car and the dark tinted glass of a person who wanted to see without being seen. I hadn't noticed anybody getting into it, but I might have been distracted by my conversations with the living and the dead.

18

On my way to my office I stopped at Arriba Tacos and got a meat and potato sopapailla with green chile and an iced tea to go. That was my idea of brain food: vitamin B and potassium for sustenance, caffeine and chile for energy. Anna and Brink were still out to lunch when I got to Hamel and Harrison, which was all right with me. Time alone in the office is rare, and it's the best (if not the only) time to think. My first piece of business was the blinking red light on the answering machine. There was one message; Special Agent Vi Sommers asking me to call her. I took the microcassette out of the machine, brought it into my office, sat down and ate my power food. Then I called Vi.

"The video of Brown was superb," she said.

I like praise as much as anyone, but I had to give the credit to Terrance Lewellen's minicam. "I think that had more to do with the equipment than the operator," I said. I couldn't take any credit for the impeccable timing, either.

"We took a warrant out for Brown, sent a couple of agents down to Door and arrested him. We got his ledger, his bags of bird feathers and his goshawk bones."

"Way to go," I said.

"We found the yellow-headeds and the blue-fronted parrot at Birds of Paradise. They were preparing to put illegally obtained leg bands on them. We arrested the owner."

"*Bueno.*"

"Brown's out on bail. He paid in cash, and the bondsman complained about the smell. We found twenty thousand dollars buried in the hole in Cotorra Canyon"

"That's all?"

"That was it."

There were plenty of other places to bury money in Door. Brown might have hidden the ransom in one of them—if he'd hidden the ransom. "He came to see me last night. He was drunk."

"That figures. What'd he want?"

"To threaten me, I guess. Or maybe he just can't stay away from women and trouble, which are one and the same for him."

"Mr. Tough Guy, right?" She laughed.

"He had another .45 on him that I took. I'd like to turn it over to you."

"We would have confiscated whatever weapons were on the boat, but we didn't find any."

Both she knew and I knew that it wouldn't take long for a guy like Brown to come up with a new gun.

"Where's the .45?"

"At my apartment."

"Let me know when you'll be home. I'll send an agent over."

"Okay. Brown figured out I was the one who turned you onto him."

"You're identified only as a confidential informant in the warrant."

"It was pretty obvious; it was only last Sunday that I was down there."

"You were right about the DEA and IRS," Vi said. "He cut a deal with them for the drug smuggling and was paying off the back taxes in monthly payments."

That was one thing Brown hadn't lied about. "He told me he had to get into parrot smuggling to make the payments," I said.

"They've always got some excuse. The IRS will lose their payments, but we'll get him for violating the Lacey Act. If there's anything else you have on him, let us know. We might be able to help."

"I'll do that," I said.

"We turned the thick-billed over to the Phoenix Zoo's captive breeding program. It should do all right there. Maybe it'll even get turned loose some day. Your friend seemed pretty attached to it."

"He loves birds."

"Since the thick-billeds are endangered, we're not allowed to give them to private citizens, but we hold auctions periodically to find homes for the parrots we confiscate at the border. Brown's birds will be up for auction, but I'd like to offer one to you and your friend now. It's the best I can do in the way of a reward."

It was an offer as appealing and terrifying as a baby on the doorstep, and this was a baby that would never grow up. It could be a clever and amusing companion; it could also be a loud and jealous mate. I knew which illegal alien the Kid would want, too, the blue-fronted, the native Argentine parrot, the one he thought he'd heard calling him El Pibe back in Buenos Aires.

"Can I have some time to think about it?" I asked.

"Sure. No hurry. Well, thanks again."

"Glad to help," I said.

Anna had shown up while I was on the phone and waved to me from the doorway. She stepped out of my range of vision, did a double take, came back and pointed at the bandaged finger on my doodling hand. Not being able to draw could severely limit my ability to think, and this was not a day on which I could pull a no-brainer.

"What happened?" she mouthed.

"Tell you later," I mouthed back. Once I'd maneuvered my way out of the shower and into my clothes I'd forgotten all about the finger, but the minute she pointed at it, the pain started all over again. I looked down at the bandage, which was very neat and very white. Like a graffiti artist facing a blank wall, I had a powerful desire to put a tag on it.

When I got off the phone, Anna came back and plunked a cup of Red Zinger tea on my desk. She was celebrating youth, summer and a size six body by wearing a tiny black skirt and a tiny white top with a slice of black lace sticking out of the cleavage. I was wearing a boring lawyer's shirt buttoned far above my cleavage line. Anna had listened to my advice about the shoes anyway. Today she was wearing thick-soled black sneakers with her black ankle socks. It was an outfit that sent an approach/avoidance message: You can look at my underwear, but I'll run if I have to.

"It's just a cut finger," I said. "I can still make my own Red Zinger."

"Hey, I was only trying to help."

"You're right. Thanks."

"How'd you do it?"

"Do you really want to know?"

"Yeah."

"I put my hand into a parrot's cage."

"Yow! What for?"

"There was something I wanted inside."

"Did you get it?"

"Yup."

"What is it?"

"A video."

"Of what?"

"I don't know yet."

"Can I see?"

Why not? I thought. The video was as good a place to start my investigation as any, and Anna was sure to have something to say no matter what it contained. "Where's Brink?" I asked.

"Out to lunch."

"Okay," I said. "Let's go."

We took the black box into Brink's office where the VCR was. He bought one because he thought he'd use it to watch videotaped depositions, but there was a thick layer of dust on top. I closed the blinds, put in the tape, and we sat down to watch it.

The tape was in color and began with a woman walking slowly across a room. She was naked except for her white moccasins, the feathers in her hair and fringed pasties on her nipples. Cellulite quivered in her thighs, but she had a good body, slender and well proportioned. Her breasts were firm. Her legs were long. Her skin was pale, and her pubic hair was several shades darker than her blond curls. Anna and I were voyeurs at a private moment, but people who want to keep their moments private shouldn't videotape them. There's no telling whose hands the tape will fall into.

"Hey, that's the woman who came to the office with Terrance Lewellen," Anna said.

"Right."

"I thought she was his sister-in-law."

"She was."

The camera followed Sara to the king-sized bed in Terrance and Deborah's bedroom. I recognized the elaborately carved headboard. Terrance sat on the edge of the bed, naked too, except for a gold chain and the piece. His belly was white and furry. The testosterone patch had obviously been doing its work. Sara stood in front of him while he licked the pasties off.

"Yow," Anna said.

Terrance fell backward onto the bed and pulled Sara with him. A bronco with two backs rolled and bucked. Sara ended up eventually straddling Terrance, still wearing some of the feathers. It was exciting, it was ludicrous, it was embarrassing, it was infuriating, depending on one's point of view. The only detail that distinguished it from porn was that Terrance was overweight and not enormously endowed. Sara was actually better looking than most porn stars. It wasn't a turn-on—not to me anyway—although it must have been to Terrance when he watched it later. Why else would he have taped it? To further inflate his already overblown ego? As an advertisement for the patch? There was a certain fascination to the video that kept me from hitting the Eject button, and we stuck with it to the very end—a vigorous back-arching orgasm from Sara that seemed staged to me. Maybe she knew she was on camera, maybe she was earning her living.

"Overdone, don't you think?" I said.

Anna rolled her eyes. "Very."

Deborah must have seen this. What had she felt? I wondered. I knew what I'd have felt—rage at a sister for screwing my husband, fury at a husband for sleeping with my sister. It was about the worst betrayal two people could commit. It wouldn't matter whether a woman loved the husband anymore or didn't, she'd still be furious. Sex is territorial. That they'd done it in her bed made it even worse, and you could multiply the anger several times over by the fact that he'd taped it and then been stupid enough to leave the tape where it could be found.

Anna stood up, stretched and shook her curls into place. Some black lace peeked out from under her white blouse. "Kind of hard to go back to work after that," she said.

"Not *that* hard," I replied. I rewound the tape, hit the Eject button and took it out. I hadn't been aroused physically, but I had been stimulated mentally. I went back to my office, sat down at my desk, took the blue macaw feather from the cup and ran my finger down the barbules, smoothing them into place. The back side of the feather was silvery gray. The front was flat blue or shimmering indigo depending on how the light hit it. I thought about my client's death. If I looked at it from one perspective, I saw it one way. From another angle, I saw it differently. I badly wanted to pin it on Wes Brown, but knowing who you want to charge is never the best place to begin an investigation. The video I'd made was compelling evidence that Brown was a poacher and a scumbag, and Terrance's audiotape was compelling evidence that he had kidnapped Deborah in spite of all his denials. The camera doesn't lie, and you can't fool a tape recorder, I thought. Or can you?

I closed the door and got out the top of my own high-tech line of sound equipment, a thirty-dollar boom box from Price Club and a couple of blank cassettes. The boom box could run from an electrical outlet or six size D batteries. It had two decks that would play and record, and that was about it. I replayed the tape Terrance had made on his Marantz. It began with the beat of high-heeled shoes and ended with a cacophony of parrots. The shoes, I believed, were Deborah Dumaine's. The parrots, I knew, were the Psittacine Research Facility's. In between there was a conversation between a man and a woman. The voices were angry, and the words went like this:

"What are *you* doing in here?"

"What do you think? You're coming with . . ."

"No, I'm not."

"Yeah, you are."

"Stop it, you're hurting me. You can't take Perigee. Terrance will be livid."

"Fuck Terrance. Ouch. Goddamn it. He bit me."

"What did you expect?"

"Move it."

"I'm coming. Stop shoving me."

The voices belonged to Wes Brown and Deborah Dumaine. I'd heard enough of both of them by now to be sure of that. I played the tape again on deck one and recorded it on deck two. I stopped whenever Deborah spoke, fast-forwarded deck one to the next time Brown spoke and fast-forwarded deck two to leave some room for my own input. And then I made another tape doing the reverse, recording only Deborah's voice. I played back the tape with Deborah's voice first and heard:

"What are you doing in here?"

"No, I'm not."

"Stop it, you're hurting me. Terrance will be livid."

"What did you expect?"

"I'm coming. Stop shoving me."

If Terrance had faked the tape, he could have recorded a conversation he had had with Deborah, then taken out his voice, had Brown add his part later and copied the new tape. I ran my tape again, assuming that Deborah came upon Terrance unexpectedly, either in the lab or her apartment, and filling in words for Terrance Lewellen.

Deborah: "What are *you* doing in here?"

Terrance: "You're stealing valuable papers from me."

Deborah: "No, I'm not."

Terrance: "Give them back." (He grabs her arm.)

Deborah: "Stop it, you're hurting me."

Terrance: "You're causing a lot of trouble."

Deborah: "What did you expect?"

Terrance: "Let's get out of here."

Deborah: "I'm coming. Stop shoving me."

One problem with that scenario was, where had the "Terrance will be livid" line come from? It might have been something Deborah said in the lab or at home that Terrance's recording equipment had picked up. Starting at the place that said Terrance faked the tape, I let my thoughts wander down the highway. They didn't roam as freely as they might have if my finger hadn't hurt and I'd been able to scratch in the back roads with my doodling right hand. I tried using the left, but all I could make with that were scribbles.

I continued a little farther down the road, supposing that Terrance had hired Brown to either kidnap or kill Deborah and take Perigee along for authenticity. In this case Brown had to have had an associate. It could have been Katrina, or the *malinche*, Sara, or his cousin, or anyone else willing to wear a feathered mask, a cowboy hat and a duster. I'd turned over half the ransom to someone, come across Brown smuggling parrots and recorded it on Terrance's equipment. Maybe Brown was supposed to give some of the money back to Terrance, or he wanted more money, or Terrance knew too much about Brown's involvement, so Brown and/or his partner found a clever way to get rid of Terrance.

Next I played the tape that had only Wes Brown's words.

"What do you think? You're coming with . . ."

"Yeah, you are."

"Fuck Terrance. Ouch. Goddamn it. He bit me."

"Move it."

And then I began filling in the empty lines. Knowing Brown, I filled them in with a woman's voice, an angry woman's voice. But this time I played around with the order of Brown's words.

"Terrance thinks you're a scumbag of a smuggler."

"Fuck Terrance."

"Do you think Terrance cares that I came here?"

"What do you think?"

"Move it. You're coming with . . ." (Here I imagined him talking to a parrot and a parrot answering back.) "Yeah, you are. Ouch. Goddamn it. He bit me."

"What did you expect?"

The parrot in this scenario could be any parrot. It didn't really matter. Both Deborah and Brown's voices were real, but the roles they'd played could easily have been faked.

Next I played back the microcassettes I'd made of the voice on the R line in the handheld recorder I used for dictation.

"I'm so lonely without my mate. Bring me home soon, please."

"Max a million. I am verrrry valuable."

"Not enough. Double or nothing. Indigo dying without mate."

Just for the heck of it I called 12441 on the R line again. It hadn't taken long for them to assign the indigo's number to someone else. This time I got a woman speaking up talk with a southern drawl. "Oh, hi? It's really nice of you to call? I'm from Kentucky and a newcomer to Albuquerque and I . . . "

I'd heard enough of that and hung up. Terrance had said that anyone with a Scrunch could change a voice from deep male to high female, from Amazon parrot to indigo macaw. Of all the suspects, Wes Brown was the least likely to have a Scrunch or any high-tech equipment at all. The *r* rolled off the tongue in verrrry, which is a sound I've never been able to duplicate.

I had another microcassette to play, but I wasn't sure what—if anything—would be on it. That tape came from our ancient answering machine. The newer models erase every time you rewind, but on our machine the new messages record over the old ones, and if you've been out of town or had a busy day, some messages (or fragments thereof) can stay on the tape for weeks. I put the microcassette into my recorder, rewound and pushed the Play button. First I got Vi Sommers asking me to call her back. I'd already done that. Next was Stevie for Anna, with his bass booming in the background. Then Nancy for Brink. I couldn't hear any background noise, but I got the scent of cookies baking in the oven. Then came the Kid for me. "Pick up if you're there. If not, I'll hang." Didn't anybody ever get work-related calls here? After the Kid I heard someone trying to sell us legal forms and then, "Can't make the appointment 'cause I'm gettin' back with my Jimmie. Sure am sorry about that, ma'am," in the cowgirl twang of Roberta Dovalo. When I'd imagined a woman to go with that voice, I'd seen a red dress with a full skirt, silver tips on her blouse collar and cowgirl boots. I saw makeup that had been applied with a trowel, and hair as full and fake as Dolly Parton's. It's not unusual for a client to want to investigate a lawyer before hiring her. It usually isn't done over the phone. I called the number I had in Ruidoso, got the B & L Bake Shop and asked to speak to Roberta Dovalo.

"Nobody by that name here, ma'am," the person who answered said.

"Is this . . . " I repeated the number.

"You bet."

"Thanks," I replied as I hung up.

There were three women circling in this case's gyre. One of them had masqueraded as Roberta Dovalo and taken my measure. Had she done it for Terrance Lewellen, for Wes Brown or for herself? Was she working with or against a man?

I moved on to the physical evidence, the lock of dyed red hair and the feather. The feather was Colloquy's or Perigee's. The hair was Deborah's in color, but could have come from anybody's head. Then I reread the ransom note: "Indigo dying without mate. Put two hundred thousand in Deborah's Bank-West Account." The *Journal* had been clipped, taped and xeroxed, making the note impossible to trace. The hand-printed note on the back of the deposit slip (which might be traceable) remained with Charlie Register, unless he'd turned it over to the APD or the FBI, but if he had, I should have heard from them by now.

None of the evidence I'd examined so far was leading in the direction I wanted it to go. I took the videotape I'd labeled Cotorra Canyon into Brink's office. He'd returned from lunch and was peering into his computer. I had to clear my throat twice before he realized I'd entered the room.

"Oh, hi," he said, shifting his body to hide the computer screen from view as he hit the Escape button. His document went into a computer file, and the screen went blank.

"What were you working on?" I asked.

"Just a little will I'm doing for a client of Nancy's," he said.

"A client of Nancy's?" Who was his partner anyway?

"She's overworked now, and I'm not busy and . . . "

Doing Nancy's work on Hamel and Harrison's time verged on *malinche* behavior, but it did give me leverage to do what I wanted to do right now—look at my videotape. "I have a video I want to look at," I said. "Now."

"Okay."

Brink watched the video with me; he and Anna are always ready for a diversion. As I slipped my tape into the slot, I remembered how easy it had been to climb to the top of the butte, the rock stairs that seemed to have shown up exactly when and where we needed them. A man came on the screen, in black and white and at a distance, but clearly Wes Brown. He smoked a cigarette, waited and then exchanged a small amount of money for very valuable parrots, killing at least one of them in the process. The parrot transfer concluded, the video moved on to Wes Brown's boat. I should have straightened my hat for this one. There was the back of the Kid's head. There was a tippy image of Brown aiming his gun at the Kid.

Brink gasped.

The Kid knocked the gun out of Brown's hand.

"Whooo," exclaimed Brink.

The minicam zeroed in on Brown's face and I felt my own rage expand. It was a strong force, but I could control it.

The video was irrefutable evidence for the FWS and pretty much as I had seen it, except that the date and time showed up in the corner of this tape, which they hadn't on Terrance and Sara's. That information would be useful in court, but I hadn't put it there.

"Do the date and time usually show up on the videos?" I asked Brink, since he knew more about this subject than I did.

"Sometimes. Sometimes you have to program the camera to put it there," he replied. "Depends on the equipment."

I wondered if Brown always met the smugglers at the same time. It made sense; the desert was cool, dark and lonely at night. Did he meet them on the same day every week? Every two weeks? Every month? The tape finished, I rewound it and popped it out.

Leaving Brink to Nancy's will I went back to my office, where there was one more piece of physical evidence to consider, the still photographs of Wes Brown and the feathered mask at the ATMs outside Midnight Cowboy and on Tramway. Brown wore his black cowboy hat, a going-to-town striped shirt and a hangdog expression. I didn't have the videotape of this transaction, but Charlie Register at BankWest did. I ran through the transaction in my mind. Wes Brown had put Deborah Dumaine's ATM card (or a reasonable facsimile) in the slot, punched in her PIN number, deposited two hundred dollars into her account and left instructions in invisible ink on the back of a deposit slip. Whose deposit slip? I wondered. Everybody assumed it was Deborah's, but had anybody ever checked it out?

Deborah's PIN number and the number that put Brown into her account was 2473. I looked on my telephone dial to find the corresponding letters: ABC, GHI, PRS, DEF. Customers usually have the option of taking the PIN number the bank assigns them or choosing their own. People pick words or numbers that they find easy to remember. I had no idea what the numbers 2473 meant to Deborah or anybody else, but the word those letters spelled out (the only word they could spell out) was BIRD. With ten numbers to fill four digits, there are ten thousand possible combinations and there's bound to be duplication. Deborah would be the only person with her account number, but she might not be the only one with a PIN of 2473. The question, in this case, was who had gotten BIRD first? The person who would know was Charlie Register. I called and asked him.

"I was just getting ready to call you," he said.

I'll bet, I thought. "Does Wes Brown have his checking account with you?" I asked.

"Yes, ma'am."

"Do Deborah and Brown have the same PIN number?" I asked.

"They do. I looked it up; it's 2473."

"2473 means BIRD. Did you know that?"

"No, but it figures, doesn't it?"

"Yeah," I said, "it does. Who got it first?"

"Brown's had it for three years."

"And Deborah?"

"She got hers in July."

"Whose account number was on the deposit slip?"

"Brown's."

"But the money went into Deborah's account."

"Initially, yes. The deposit was made with an ATM card that had her account number on the mag strip. You may remember that we were preoccupied with the message on the back of the slip."

I remembered.

"It didn't have anybody's name on it, but we assumed it was Deborah's deposit slip until we took a closer look."

"Doesn't the name go on automatically?"

"It's the customer's option."

"How can the code be transferred from one mag strip to another?"

"You take a credit or ATM card that's been stolen or is out of date and erase the magnetic strip with a magnet. The raised numbers on the card are only there for the customer's information. The ATM doesn't read them. A nine-volt battery and a couple of wires can copy the information from one mag strip to another. Or you can buy a mag card reader that'll do it for you."

"So my Visa card could access Deborah Dumaine's account if I transferred her information to my mag strip."

"And you knew her PIN number."

"Right."

"Is there any money in Deborah's account now?"

"Five hundred dollars."

"Was Brown making regular cash deposits to his account?"

"Every two weeks."

"And writing checks to the IRS?"

"Every month. That's all he used the account for."

Brown was in a cash business, but he couldn't pay the IRS in smelly money. He had to launder it somewhere. No need to put his name, address and phone number on the checks and deposit slip for that. Besides, he didn't have a phone, didn't have a real address and had a name that shifted with the seasons.

"His last check bounced," Charlie Register said.

"Because his deposit went into Deborah's account."

"That's right."

"Have you talked to your attorney yet?"

"No, but I intend to."

Somebody had to call Detective Hernandez, and it couldn't be me. "I think you better put a flag on Deborah's account."

"Good idea."

"Will you call me immediately if there is any activity?"

"I will," he said.

I had one parting shot. "I hear Candace Lewellen is going to donate the Lochovers to the Dallas Fine Arts Museum."

"I know." He sighed. "I sure have enjoyed having them here."

I said adios to Charlie Register, he said good-bye to me, and we hung up our respective phones. I'd be willing to bet that he leaned back in his chair, beneath the lamp that turned his hair to silver and gold, and admired the Lochovers.

I took a moment to look at the kidnapping myself. There was a boldness and brilliance to that scheme that made it, in its own way, a work of art. I wished I could hang it on my wall and admire it. I wished I had a wall big enough to hang it on. The details had been sketched in carefully, but the overall effect was of water on the road, a shimmering illusion. It looked different up close than it did from a distance, which must have been the artist's intent. There was no bold signature scarring this work of art yet, as there was on the Lochovers, but there might be a line like the one that led out of the rug. It had, after all, been the work of an imperfect human being.

The whiteness of my bandaged finger flagged my eye and

brought me back to my office on Lead with the bars on the window, the diploma on the wall and the plants that needed watering. I'd forgotten the pain in my finger while I'd been working this out. The pain began to beat again. The bandage was still far too white. With my left hand I took a magic marker from my desk drawer and marked it with an X.

19

I figured that if Charlie's call came at all, it would come before morning. I lay in bed, waited and listened to the Kid's soft and regular breathing and the raspy, erratic rustle of the wind. It was a feline and feral presence howling in La Vista's hallway and rubbing its back against my window. I got up and paced the yellow shag carpet, keeping time to the wind's restless rhythm.

By four, tired enough to believe that God had not been in the details, I went back to bed, but it was the illusion of the hour—very late at night or very early in the morning. Nothing ever happens when you wait; I was back in bed and sound asleep when the phone rang. At first I thought it was the alarm. I reached over and punched it, but it rang again. The Kid groaned and pulled the pillow over his head. I picked up the phone and heard Charlie Register's cowboy-banker voice.

"Sorry to wake you, ma'am," he said. "I just got a call from my security folks, and there's something you'll be wantin' to see. Could you meet me at the bank? I'll be there in ten minutes."

"I'm on my way."

I thought about punching the Kid in the shoulder, but he was deep in the sleep zone and waking him would be a bitch. I knew he cared about the outcome of my case, but I was afraid this outcome wasn't going to be the one he cared about. I let him sleep, got up, threw on a pair of running shoes, jeans and a T-shirt, and drove to Charlie Register's office on Tramway. I didn't pass a single car on my way. I did pass several ATMs. None were in use.

Charlie was waiting at the bank entrance to let me in. He too had thrown on jeans, but his hung low on his hips and were held in place by a leather belt with a large silver buckle. He didn't yet have the middle-aged cowboy's belly-over-buckle silhouette, but he was working on it. He wore a white cotton shirt with a fine beige stripe. His blond and silver hair had been brushed into place. "Glad you could come," he said.

"Thanks for calling," I replied. "Someone accessed Deborah Dumaine's account?" Why else would he have called me so late at night and so early in the morning?

"That's right," he said.

"From what machine?" There were multiple possibilities: Tramway, the airport, the bus station, anywhere along the border.

"Tramway," he said.

I followed him down the hall and up the stairs to the video monitoring room. All the cameras were running. All but one looked at empty gray and white vestibules or car lanes. Charlie had gotten the tape from his security people, and he'd inserted it in the monitor on the table. The tape had been rewound and stopped at four-thirty, the minute the transaction began. The time and date were visible on the corner. I'd expected that, but was startled to see dots of color in the image.

"The color is a new technology we're experimenting with," Charlie said.

"Was it your decision to put it in that machine?"

"It was. You ready?"

"Go," I said.

Charlie started the tape. It was a moment like the one before sleep when reality shifts and images become surreal. I might have been entering someone else's brilliant and confusing dream. My dreams have been filled with soccer players and rock stars, no cowboys and never, even in the background, a banker. A cowboy wearing a duster and a black hat slouched up to the camera, and for a moment I could convince myself that it would end as it had begun, with Wes Brown's face on the tape. Then the cowboy took off the hat. The face widened and whitened like a fish belly as it approached the camera. The face was heavily made up. The lips around the teeth were bright red. The hair was full and scarlet. The eyes looked into the camera without a blink. It was the bold, technicolor face of Deborah Dumaine. She punched in her PIN—B I R D, and Charlie stopped the tape, giving us plenty of time to study her triumphant expression.

"Shit," I said.

"You were hoping for Wes Brown?" Charlie asked.

"Hoping."

"I didn't care who," he replied, "as long as it wasn't her."

"That's because you haven't met Wes Brown. Was it a deposit or a withdrawal?"

"Withdrawal."

"How much?"

"Four hundred dollars. That's the maximum we allow in a twenty-four-hour period."

"Did that close the account?"

"No. She has a hundred dollars left. I don't think she needs the money, do you?"

"Nope. I think she has four hundred thousand dollars somewhere in cash or traveler's checks or cruzeiros. I think she staged her own kidnapping, set up Wes Brown and collected her own ransom from this machine, and then from me by holding a .45 to my head." Because of the hour and the bizarre circumstances, I asked a question I might not have asked Charlie Register during the day. "Are you in love with her?"

"I love my wife," he sighed. "But I've always admired Deborah's spirit." There's a role a wild woman plays in a tame man's fantasies. What banker or lawyer hasn't considered chucking it all and running off to Brazil? And more than one of us has fantasized about bumping off a philandering spouse. People who act out what everyone else represses could be angling for a place on the God shelf. As *The Book of the Hopi* said, Deborah had traveled the Road of Life by her own free will and had exhausted her capacity for good and evil.

"She called my office to scope me out while pretending to be a client who wanted a divorce," I said. "She dropped off the ransom note and faked the Relationships line voice. Being married to Terrance, she must have learned a lot about high-tech equipment like the Scrunch. She sent me to Door at a time when she knew I'd come across Brown smuggling parrots, and she made it appear that he'd kidnapped her. Who's going to believe anything Wes Brown says?" My voice had turned into a whisper. Deborah's presence on the screen was so strong that I couldn't shake the feeling she was listening to us.

"You're sure Brown wasn't involved?" Charlie asked.

"I'm sure. Even Brown isn't fool enough to write a bad check to the IRS. I thought we were playing liar's poker, but Brown wasn't lying. He told me Deborah had been down there to see him, and I wanted to believe it was his ego talking. She must have gone between his trips to Albuquerque. She probably took his credit card and tried out the PIN. Either she found BIRD written down somewhere or she guessed. Then she opened up her own account, took the same PIN, transferred her mag strip to Brown's ATM card, went back to Door and put the card back before he came up here and used it again outside Midnight Cowboy on Friday night. She printed her message on the back of his deposit slip. It was in invisible ink; he never noticed."

Charlie cleared his throat. "Do you think that she . . . slept with him to accomplish all this?"

"I hope not. She had to have been hiding with Perigee in Door somewhere and put him on the deck of Brown's boat while the Kid and Brown and I were down below. The only footprints on the ground looked like Brown's; she was wearing his brand of boots. Deborah's on her way to Brazil."

"Are you sure?"

"Yeah. They're not known for enforcing their extradition treaties—if they have any extradition treaties. Rick Olney, her lab assistant, said she was treated like a queen there. Rick knew Deborah as well as anyone, and he suspected her of murdering Terrance. As soon as Terrance died and Perigee came back, he became evasive and stopped talking about calling in the police."

"Why did you suspect her?"

"She knew about Terrance and Sara; she had a tape of them making love. She'd been giving Terrance small doses of peanuts for his allergy. She knew how vulnerable he'd be without the treatment."

"I don't understand why she didn't leave sooner."

"She needed time to launder the money. Maybe she stopped to admire her work and watch her sister suffer. Did you notice the rental car with tinted glass and the engine running during the funeral?"

"Can't say that I did."

"I think it was Deborah, and I think she wanted Sara to

know who was responsible for Terrance's death. She came to the ATM to leave her signature on the plan."

Charlie started the videotape again. Deborah's frozen face broke into a smile. She counted her money, pulled down her cowboy hat, tipped it to the camera, took her card and receipt and walked away. I couldn't hear them, but I could see that she was wearing high-heeled shoes. Maybe she hadn't expected Charlie to put a flag on the account. Maybe he wouldn't have if I hadn't suggested it. Maybe she'd thought Charlie admired her enough to let her get away. It could also be that her own pride and ego had tripped her up. You never know what motivates a killer. There's often a level on which they want to get caught and be punished. Taking a life is in the realm of the gods, but the people who do it are all too human.

We might have been watching a Western in which you hope the Indians will get away, but you know they won't. Deborah had become Dextrous Horse Thief Woman and we were the cavalry. The cavalry always wins in the movies and, even in real life, they won eventually; they had superior numbers and equipment. In this case, Deborah had had the superior technical equipment. All I'd had was my intuition and brains. Deborah had challenged me to do my best, and I'd responded. What else would a lawyer do? But now Charlie and I had the opportunity to hit the Pause button and change the outcome, which was more power than two people ever ought to have. How long would it take for the wild bird to fly away? How long would we have to hesitate? In an hour or two, the first flight would be leaving ABQ for anywhere on the road to Rio.

"Have you told anyone about the kidnapping scheme yet?" I asked Charlie.

"Not yet," he said.

Sooner or later Detective Hernandez was likely to get a

warrant if Charlie didn't volunteer Deborah's tape. Even if she didn't know about the kidnapping, she'd want to take a look at Deborah's account; the first suspect in any homicide is always the victim's spouse. We only had to stretch the law for a few hours. Who knew Deborah was on the lam but Charlie and me?

I felt as if I was carrying two large objects, one in each hand. One was a bird, and one was a stone. The stone was the murder of Terrance Lewellen, the bird was Deborah's desire to go free. It's not in my nature to hesitate. It is my nature to root for the birds and the Indians. Terrance had done the unforgivable by sleeping with her sister. He'd made it even worse by videotaping the act and including Sara in his will. For a moment, the objects were in perfect balance, but even if I did nothing, one of them would fly away and the other would weigh me down.

I looked at Charlie and he looked at me. I saw question marks in his blue eyes. You wouldn't know it from inside BankWest's security room, but somewhere out there birds were calling up the dawn and the sun was responding with rosy-fingered feelers. The jets were fueling up at Albuquerque International. If we were going to stop Deborah, we had to do it right now. It must have been why Charlie had called me here, to distribute the weight. If we hesitated, we'd be sharing a deep and incriminating secret. I'd have to answer to him, he'd have to answer to me, and we'd both have to answer to ourselves. Charlie was a banker. I was a lawyer. Deborah was a wild and brilliant bird who was used to the cage but who longed to be free. I saw her for a moment, flapping her wings high above the canopy.

But the bottom line, the place where dreams and flight end, brought me back. There always is a bottom line in law and in life, and mine was that my client was dead. I could forget about being manipulated. I could deal with being held up at gunpoint. I could admire Deborah for her brilliance in setting up Brown, but I couldn't forget that my client had been murdered. That turned out to be the heavier object. I don't know what the bottom line was for Charlie; it might have been that he had security people working for him or that he owned BankWest. It might have been that he'd let me make the decision. It wasn't, as it turned out, that he loved Deborah Dumaine.

"You have to call Detective Hernandez," I said. I knew now that Terrance had not been involved in the crime of kidnapping, but I still considered it my obligation to protect his reputation by keeping my mouth shut.

Charlie sighed and reached for the phone. In this light the highlights in his hair were more gray than gold. "You're right," he said.

On the drive home the sun was a ball of flame searing the back of the wind goddess, and my finger hurt. I let myself into my apartment at La Vista and into my bedroom. The Kid was still asleep. I crawled into bed behind him, laid my cheek against the soft spot on the back of his neck and pretended it had been a dream.

Detective Hernandez caught Deborah at the airport. She was booked on the seven A.M. flight to Dallas and from there to Rio de Janeiro traveling under the passport and ID of a Joan Kite. Most of the ransom had been wired ahead to a bank in Rio. She was carrying ten thousand dollars in cash and travelers' checks in her money belt—all the money she could legally take out of the country without registering with the customs service. There wasn't a single serial number that could be traced. All the ransom money had been laundered. God had been in that detail. The fact that she'd been caught fleeing the country with a phony ID and a lot of money was incriminating, but Deputy DA Anthony Saia, who ended up being the prosecutor in the murder case, had a tough job ahead of him convincing a jury that she'd murdered her husband. The saline solution could have been bought anywhere by anyone, as could the peanuts. There was approximately a twenty-four-hour envelope from breakfast to breakfast when the peanut substitution could have been made, and a much bigger envelope for the saline substitution. Any one of the suspects could have gotten into Terrance's house. None of them had a twenty-four-hour alibi. The only fingerprints found on the vial were Terrance Lewellen's and Sara Dumaine's. Deborah's fingerprints and fibers were all over the house, but so were Sara's. The only thing the prosecutor had going for him was motive. Deborah had an abundance of that, but Sara stood to gain two hundred and fifty thousand dollars from Terrance's death if she filed the will. Even with invincible evidence, it's hard to get a murder conviction these days, and nearly impossible to convict a suspect on motive alone. It's one thing to solve a puzzle, another to get a conviction from a jury of one's peers. Runaway juries have gotten softhearted in the nineties.

There was evidence, however, that Deborah had staged her own kidnapping. Sara Dumaine knew some of the details. Charlie Register knew most of them, and he fessed up. The FBI wanted the tapes and the ransom note, and I eventually turned them over. By now I knew that the biggest offense my client had been guilty of was infidelity. I felt that my obligation was to protect that part of his reputation by putting the videotape back in the cage, which I did. When I asked myself and his mother what Terrance's best interest would be regarding the kidnapping, the answer was to prosecute Deborah for fraud and to get the money back for the estate. Again, motive was very clear. Opportunity was there, but means was hard to prove. Deborah had covered her tracks well; God had been in most of the details. The feathers for the mask could easily have come from the lab, but the mask itself was never found. The voice on the Relationships tape was so garbled, it couldn't be proved that it belonged to anyone. The correspondence with the Relationship line went to a post office box, and the bills were paid in cash. Wes Brown, however, was happy to turn over the faked ATM card and squeal about Deborah's visits to Door.

Deborah was convicted of bank fraud. The estate got most of the money back, and it went to the Psittacine Research Facility. The murder charges remained unprosecutable. The only will that was probated was the one that left everything to Candace Lewellen. Sara Dumaine never filed a claim, never collected a penny. Deborah may have been in that detail. Maybe Sara feared that the will would make her a suspect in Terrance's death. Maybe Deborah had hidden the only copy. Maybe Sara had cared more about Terrance than the money. My obligation was tricky. If the case ever went to trial, it would become even trickier. I hadn't drawn up the will; I wasn't supposed to know it existed, but I did. Terrance wanted Sara to get the money, but would he have wanted me to reveal my knowledge of the will if it could be used as evidence against Sara? In the end I did what a lawyer does best, kept my mouth shut. Wes Brown got the maximum sentence and the maximum fine, which he paid with smelly money. The thick-billed was sent to the Phoenix Zoo, where it waited for a flock to form that would be big enough to release it in the wild.

The day Deborah was arrested on the road to Rio, I called Vi Sommers to make arrangements for an agent to pick up Wes Brown's .45 and bring me the blue-fronted Amazon. I turned over the gun, had the agent put the parrot in a box in the back seat of the Nissan (I didn't want to do it myself and get bitten by another pissed-off bird) and drove to the Kid's shop on Fourth Street. Someone was going to turn this bronco into a pet, and it might as well be the Kid; he was good with birds. The coloring of the blue-fronted's feathers was exquisite, rain-forest green shading subtly to yellow, then sky blue on its forehead. When I stopped at the lights on my way to Fourth Street, I looked at the bird in the box and tried to determine its sex. It had been chopped out of its nest and taken from its family and flock, but its eyes were still bright and curious and its spirit hadn't been broken. It had to be tough to make it this far, and it had a kind of macho swagger as it stumbled across the box. "What are you, male or female?" I asked. The answer I got was a low growl. "Male," I said.

The Kid started smiling as soon as I walked in the door of the shop and climbed around the Honda he was working on to tell him about the parrot, and he didn't stop. When he's not talking or smiling, his face settles into a faraway expression punctuated by frown lines that are beyond his years. He went immediately to my car and picked up the bird. To my surprise, the parrot let him.

"It's the *loro* from Door," he said.

"That's right."

"How did you get it?"

"It's a gift to you from Vi Sommers for helping her catch Wes Brown."

"Thank you, Chiquita."

"*De nada.*"

He stroked the Amazon's head. "*Que guapa,*" he said.

"*Que guapo,*" I corrected him. "It's a male."

"Female." He shook his head.

"Why do you say that?"

"When I look in the eyes I see something fierce like I see in some women."

"He's got the walk of a macho man."

"Women can be macho." He laughed.

"Right," I said.

The next issue was what to name it. Like most people, we

had lists of names for future pets and offspring filed away in the backs of our brains. "Cacofonia" was always a possibility, but this bird had been unusually quiet.

"Mimosa," said the Kid, which was his variation on the verb mimar, to pet. A feminine name.

"Mauricio," I said. Masculine and the name of his favorite character in *Cien Años de Soledad*.

Someday one of us might have a DNA test done or have the bird surgically sexed to settle the issue. In the meantime we compromised on Mimo. It's masculine, but it means petting. It also means mime or buffoon, a good name for a parrot.

"It's your bird," I told the Kid. I didn't have the time or patience, and he could keep it in the shop, talk and sing to it all day. Music was, as always, blaring from his radio. They were a good match; Mimo was a survivor. So was the Kid.